To my friend,

Bob Church,

Best wishes,

Leo D. Stapleton

JAKES

Also by Leo Stapleton

Thirty Years on the Line

Commish

Fire and Water

JAKES

by

Leo D. Stapleton

dmc associates, inc.
Dover, NH

Copyright© 1994 by Leo D. Stapleton

Published by dmc associates, inc.
P.O. Box 1095 Dover, NH 03820

All rights reserved. No part of this work may be reproduced or transmitted in any form whatsoever, except for brief passages which may be used by a reviewer. Requests for permissions should be addressed to the publisher.

ISBN: 1-879848-07-4

Printed in the United States of America

Second Printing

DEDICATION

All Boston fire fighters are called *Jakes*. When I was appointed to the department over forty years ago, I asked my peers how the nickname originated. The most common reply was, "I dunno." Throughout my career I would occasionally pursue the answer without success. These ineffective research attempts terminated at my retirement testimonial when I asked a retired deputy fire chief, long noted for his historical knowledge of the department, and his thoughtful reply was, "Who cares?"

I do.

So, this book is named and dedicated to all Boston *Jakes*, past, present and future. May they be ever thus.

Leo D. Stapleton
South Boston, MA
May, 1994

JAKES

1

The elderly lady walked slowly down Bromfield Street, pausing at each store window to gaze at the variety of watches and jewels that were displayed in the small shops along her route. She had just exited the Park Street subway station where she had arrived on the MBTA train from the suburbs.

Most of her friends did their window shopping at the South Shore Plaza in Braintree or at the other giant malls in Quincy, Hanover or Kingston, but she still loved coming into Boston and going to Downtown Crossing. Something about the old, stately buildings lining the streets in the area, coupled with the excitement of being in the city, kept her coming back time after time.

She and all of those friends had fled the city in the great exodus of the post World War II days, and while she had to admit that Boston was not as safe or innocent as she remembered it from her childhood, it was still home to her.

Sure, you had to keep the strap of your pocketbook over your shoulder and hold the bag with arms crossed, squeezing it against your chest, but hey, her friend Marion had her car stolen last week at the supposedly high-class shopping center at Chestnut Hill in Newton, for crying out loud.

As she approached the intersection with Washington Street, she could hear the roar of truck motors. Turning the corner she was startled to see a number of fire engines in the vicinity of one of the six story buildings in the middle of the block that led to Winter Street. An enormous ladder was stretched up to the roof and several firemen were climbing up the steep elevation with a yellow hose over their shoulders and snaking down the ladder behind them.

She could also see smoke coming over the roof and drifting upward, so she crossed Washington Street and passed in front of Filene's to try to get a better view.

These poor firemen, she thought, they have such a dangerous job, particularly here in Boston. It seems there are bad fires all the time and whenever she sees one of them reported on the TV news, the camera always swings to a stretcher passing by with an injured fireman being taken to an ambulance.

Directly in front of her, on the sidewalk, another group of firemen were standing, looking up at their counterparts who were ascending with the hose.

Several paces forward of them, in the street, stood a man in a dirty white coat and hat who she knew must be the chief, because the others were all wearing dirty black coats and hats.

She approached a pleasant looking member of the group and asked what was going on.

"Oh it's serious, ma'am. There's a big fire up on the roof," he replied in a high-pitched voice.

"Really. Anyone get hurt?"

"Well, ma'am, we've had two fire fighters killed so far. Please say a prayer for them, they have big families."

"Oh, I will, I will," she exclaimed, "I'll go right down to St. Anthony's Shrine on Arch Street. This is terrible, terrible," she murmured as she made the Sign of the Cross and bowed her head.

Before passing by to get to the church, she felt she must express her grief to the chief, although he didn't appear to be too upset, he just kept glancing upward at his crew and talking, rather casually, she thought, under the circumstances, into the microphone he held in his hand.

"Er, pardon me, sir, I just wanted to let you know how dreadful I feel about the two men you've lost."

"What?"

"You know, the two men who have been killed."

"Where'd you hear that, m'am?"

"Why, from that nice fireman over there," she said, pointing at the group.

"Oh, o.k. ma'am. Well, let me tell you, that man is mistaken. I'll make sure he knows everyone is alright. But, thank you for your deep concern. It's just a misunderstanding."

"Thank God. He looks so distraught. Should I go back and tell him he's wrong?"

"No, that's alright ma'am. I'll make sure he knows it."

"Well thank you very much. I'm still going to go down to Arch Street and say a prayer for all of you."

"We sure need it, ma'am, and particularly that man who spoke to you. Thank you so much."

He turned to his aide, who was just preparing to mount the ladder truck to join the company going to the roof. "Wait a minute, Joe. First go over and tell the captain of Twenty-six to report to me."

The district chief up on the roof had already made a preliminary determination that the fire was confined to the roof penthouse over the stairway and could probably be handled by the engine company dragging the line up the stick and the ladder company members already on the roof. The deputy was just waiting prudently for confirmation of this evaluation before dismissing the other units at the scene.

"Yes, Deputy, 'ja want me, sir?"

"Yeah, Cap. Can't you handle that asshole, Ralphie?"

"Why, what did he do now?"

"Oh, the usual bullshit. He just told some old lady that a couple of us just got killed here."

"O.K. Deputy, I'll take care of it. Ya need anything else?"

"No, just keep that nitwit quiet, will ya? I know he's a great worker and all that shit you're gonna tell me, but so's a lot of other guys. He gets us in more trouble than he's worth. You oughta be able to shut him up."

"Well, o.k., sir, I will, I will. But, er, if you don't mind my saying so, you were his captain too, and you didn't seem to have any more luck than I do."

"Dismissed."

The object of this exchange was still yapping, this time to the other members of the company standing by, awaiting orders. He was giving them all kinds of advice on how they would make their attack if the fire extended. None of them were paying any attention to him, but instead were checking out the groups of young female office workers who had paused to watch the operation during their lunch hour.

When the district chief transmitted a report to the deputy that the fire was knocked down and two companies were all that were now required, the deputy released all of the other units from the scene and radioed the "All Out" to be sounded by the Fire Alarm office.

He put his fire gear into the backseat of the division sedan and got into the passenger's seat.

His aide entered from the other side and they edged their way through the throngs of shoppers that filled the streets and sidewalks. This part of downtown did not allow any motor vehicle traffic during store hours, except, of course, emergency equipment, such as themselves, and on a pleasant spring day, it was great to see the crowds enjoying themselves and Downtown Boston.

"You know, Joe, that Ralphie is really a pisser." He then related what had happened with the old woman.

"Yeah, I know it, Deputy, but he's a great worker."

"I knew you'd say that. You sound like his captain, for crissakes. It's the only thing that saves him, most of the time, but he still can be a pain in the ass."

As they cruised through the Downtown area, past City Hall and into Government Center, the deputy, Billy Simpson, continued thinking about Ralphie and he had to reluctantly admit that he didn't have any success in keeping him quiet, just as the current Captain of Engine 26 had said. He began telling Joe about the first time he had run into Ralphie, and while it was some twenty years ago, he still had no difficulty in bringing it to mind.

Billy had been a rookie fire fighter, temporarily assigned to a downtown ladder company, and it was during a spring season when there were hundreds of grass and brush fires occurring in the outlying districts of the city. These almost annual happenings were the result of dry weather and low humidity that combined to make certain sections of the city extremely hazardous. The fire fighters in those areas contended that when all the wonderful little children left their homes in the morning, their wonderful little mothers would give them their lunch boxes packed with two jelly sandwiches and a box of matches.

The fires would usually start just after school got out and as their numbers increased, the fire companies in such districts would all become engaged and several units would have to be pulled out from the more densely populated areas of the city to cover their firehouses and respond to additional fires.

It was rare to send out the downtown ladder companies but this particular year, there were so many fires in progress that Fire Alarm often had no choice.

As they approached the Roslindale, West Roxbury and Hyde Park district on their ladder truck, the in-towners could see a blue haze hanging over the entire area and they realized that they would be relieved out here by the night crew because it would take a long, long time to control all of the grass and brush that was burning.

Their instructions were to cover at the firehouse of Engine 30 and Ladder 25 on Center Street in West Roxbury and when they pulled up and swung the truck around to back into quarters, they could see that Engine 26 from Broadway, in the South End was filling the vehicle bay usually occupied by Engine 30. Engine 26 was known as a gypsy company because it was sent everywhere in the city as well as to all of the Mutual Aid fires in the surrounding cities and towns that adjoined Boston.

The way the response system is designed, some fire companies are known as "home guards" who seldom leave their districts, but other units from within the same area are used to respond to multiple alarms to provide the appropriate number of companies at the scene, while leaving at least some protection in the districts they are drawn from.

When the ladder truck was backed in and the rear wheels nudged against the wooden stop at the rear of the firehouse, Billy climbed out of the tiller seat and descended to the main floor.

Billy was quite pleased that he had been allowed to tiller the truck all the way out from downtown. He was permanently assigned to an engine company, but Captain Magna was trying to romance him into transferring over to the truck because he liked Billy and thought he'd make a good ladderman. Being tillerman was a prestigious assignment because he was also the roof man at a fire and if the guy doesn't get the roof open, the building could be lost. Billy still hadn't made up his mind but it had been exciting travelling all this distance on that elevated perch.

He and the other members of the company began climbing up the stairs to the second floor. They could hear a shrill voice berating someone and, since it sounded like an officer chewing out a fire fighter, nobody wanted to be observers. It sounded really serious, the type of confrontation that might have to be resolved "up the street," as Headquarters was often referred to, among many other, more derogatory nicknames.

The noise was coming from the kitchen at the end of a long hallway. Captain Magna shuffled along quietly, while the rest of the company remained huddled at the top of the stairs. When Magna arrived at the doorway, he cautiously peeked around the door jamb. They could see his shoulders relax and he waved them forward.

"It's just Ralphie, he must be senior man today." Senior man is a position on a company where, in the absence of an officer, due to vacation, injuries, fire college, death leave or other causes, the member designated is in charge of the company for the tour or tours of duty involved.

Theoretically, and according to the rule book, the senior man has all of the authority of a commissioned officer. In reality, most senior men, while they will receive orders from the officer in command at the scene of a fire, kind of suggest to the other members what the company is to do and make it appear as though it is almost a consensus or democratic approach to the duties, which is not what a regular officer does. The senior man knows that tomorrow, or next week, when the officer returns, he is back with the herd, so he doesn't want to rock the boat. After all, he may not be senior man the next time and no one wants a vendetta kind of deal.

No one, of course, except Ralphie. When Billy reached the kitchen doorway he could see this average size guy, with black, patent leather looking hair, standing in the middle of the kitchen table. Directly in front of him, seated on a long bench, were four other fire fighters.

The guy on the table was screaming as loud as he could and since his voice was almost like a woman's, his pitch was so high that some of the words would break off.

"I'm not gonna repeat this again. Pay attention, Manny, you shithead, or I'll run you right up the street. You too, Gigi. Whadda you fuckin' guys think, this is some kinda game?"

His arms were waving above his head and his face was contorted. "I'm in charge of this outfit and when I give you an order I want you to snap shit. If I was Captain Fleming not a fuckin' one of you would be in my company. This is Engine 26, not one of these hayseed outfits that couldn't handle a grassy that I could piss on. Now if any one of you doesn't shape up, I'll call my old pal, the chief of department, and get you railroaded the hell offa the company. You, Manny, I'll get sent to

Fifty-six in Eastie with all of your Eytie friends. And you Gigi, I'm so mad at you, you'll go to Brighton, out with all those do-gooders that you hate."

The reason Ralphie was senior man on this particular tour of duty was that Captain Fleming, a strong member of the Fire Fighters Union, was testifying at the State House on a bill that would insure that lung disease would be considered a job-related injury for fire fighters.

The tirade continued as Billy and the others got coffee from the huge urn located on the countertop near the sink. They sat at another table at the opposite end of the kitchen-mess hall, and Billy turned to Magna and said, "Hey, Cap, what the hell is goin' on?"

"Wait a minute, Bill, he ain't got to us yet."

Ralphie now turned to face the new arrivals and pointed his finger at them. "Lookit these stiffs. They're laddermen, can't you see? They don't belong in the same room with us hosemen. Keep away from them, they'll contaminate ya."

This was Billy's first view of Ralphie and he was a bit surprised that Captain Magna sat there and listened without defending his company. Come to think of it, neither did Herky, who frequently flexed his muscles over the most trivial slight against this premier downtown truck. What amazed him though was that the four guys on Twenty-six weren't paying any attention to their temporary leader and were drinking coffee and talking to each other. One of them was even reading a copy of *Playboy* with this unbearable din going on right over their heads.

"How's Elsie, Ralphie?" Captain Magna said during a pause, while the tyrant stopped to get his breath.

"Oh, great, Cap, thanks for askin'," Ralphie replied in a voice that had dropped to a normal level and was now conversational.

"She must be outta the hospital, right?"

"Yeah, howdja guess?"

"Because your hair is black again, you asshole. How else would I know? You're the only guy I ever see with red, green, gray and brown hair at the same time. Whenever your wife is away or sick you start lookin' your real age. Tell her I was askin' for her."

"O.K., Cap, I will."

Ralphie, completely subdued, dropped onto the bench opposite his crew, picked up his coffee and started reading the newspaper he had been standing on. The four guys he commanded didn't appear to notice that he had stopped or that he was sitting down. It was as if nothing had happened.

Billy looked quizzically at his captain. "You see, Bill, that's just Ralphie. He's always like that. He's one of about a thousand other characters you're gonna meet on this job. He absolutely loves this business and that scene you just witnessed is an act. I'll bet he jumped up on the table when he saw us coming and he's just doing his thing. Those guys with him are so used to him, they just pretend he's never there. That gets him even more outraged. But, to tell you the truth, they love him. He's as good a fireman as you'll see, he has great company pride, and that stuff about his wife is true. She has some kind of a debilitating disease that requires her to be hospitalized periodically, and I can tell you, he worries about her all the time. Good jake."

Soon after the discussion, the department telephone rang, and within seconds the member on house patrol duty down on the main floor pressed the two buttons that turned on all of the lights in the firehouse and set off the gong bell that indicated they were being dispatched to an alarm.

The members of both companies slid down the poles from the second floor and heard the message, "Both companies respond to the Gardner Street Dump."

Billy heard a loud groan as he climbed on to his assigned position on the side of the truck and looped his arm through one of the short ladders affixed to the side of the vehicle body. "What's the matter?" he asked Ted Francis, who jumped on beside him.

"It's the big dump, Bill. You ever been to one of these?"

"Naw."

"Well, they suck. The fire is usually so deep down in the garbage we'll never put it out. The place is loaded with rats and all kinds of bugs, too. Make sure you put your boots on and pull them up."

The blue haze they had seen on their way out to the district had now deepened dramatically into dense, black clouds which were hastening the darkness that was coming in the late afternoon. The smell of burning rubbish was also apparent as the two companies swung onto the VFW Parkway and sped down toward the street leading to the entrance to the enormous complex.

An aide to the district chief was waiting for them halfway down Gardner Street.

"Twenty-six, the chief wants you to drop two lines into your deck gun at a hydrant about a quarter of a mile inside. He's waitin' for ya. Cap, will ya take Ladder 8 right inside and help Twenty-six get set up?"

The smoke bit into their throats the closer the apparatus got to the designated location and it was obvious this would be a long duration operation. Sometimes the dump would burn for a couple of days until the argument between the city and the contractors about who would pay for the bulldozers and cranes that were vital to move the rubbish and get to the source of the deep-seated fires was settled.

In the meantime, fire companies would be at the scene day and night, playing heavy streams into the burning debris in what seemed a completely futile gesture. The smoke and smell would enter every home in a huge area of this Boston district and spread across the line into the city of Newton. The complaints from the citizens would keep the Fire Alarm switchboard lines constantly tied up and the Newton mayor would be doing his outraged act with the Boston leadership, demanding a more aggressive performance by the fire department. This usually ended up with the big city mayor saying something like, "Hey, Frank, knock off the shit. If you're so concerned, send your own fuckin' fire engines over there. Next time that hick town of yours has a big fire, put it out yourselves."

Ralphie conscientiously followed orders, made certain the equipment was positioned as best as possible under the circumstances and then ordered the hose lines to be filled with water under high pressure, so the huge stream could reach its maximum range and perhaps reduce the intense fire.

Several other companies were arriving at the scene and Twenty-six and Captain Manga's crews assisted them in getting into position, under the direction of the district chief.

It was now obvious all of the fire companies would be relieved at the fire by the oncoming night crews, but it was also clear that this wouldn't happen for several hours. The night shift wouldn't leave their firehouses until 1800 (6 P.M.) and since this would be in the middle of the rush hour downtown, the combination of the traffic and the several miles they would have to travel would result in long delays.

Yeah, but once they get here, we're outta here and they'll be good for the whole night. Meantime, keep as low as ya can, below the smoke if possible, don't wander off in the dark (one fire fighter had gotten burned years ago when he stepped on a pile of rubbish that had been undermined by the fires and both legs sank in up to his thighs) and keep ya boots up high.

The darker it got, the more rats could be heard squealing as the smoke chased them back towards the fire fighters. They use the same air people do and they were looking for the best spots—just like the jakes.

"Watch Ralphie, Bill," said Ted. "He's scared shitless of the rats. Lookit him, he's up on the deck gun and he won't come down."

It was true. The other engine companies had locked their heavy stream appliances into position and left them unattended so the members could keep low, but there was Ralphie on top of his apparatus, coughing and laying out flat, pretending he was directing the stream.

He eventually had to come down but he stood on the back step of the vehicle, which kept him a couple of feet off the ground.

"Hey, Ralphie," shouted Manny, "why doncha come down here with the rest of us swine?"

"I told you before, Manny, keep your mouth shut and obey orders. I'm in command."

"Yeah, and you're also fulla shit."

"You're lucky Captain Fleming ain't here, Manny. And oh yeah, why the hell ain't he? I'll tell ya why. Right now he's with all them union twerps we elected. I bet they're drinkin' up our dues in Friar Tuck's down near the State House. I'm gonna straighten him out when I see him. He left me here tryin' to run this show with the stupidest pricks on the job and all these bugs and stuff. It ain't right. I ain't gettin' paid for it."

He could see he was attracting a crowd from the other companies and this caused him to expand on his performance. He could also see that Manga was an interested observer, so he finally concluded with, "Cap, these assholes will never understand the tremendous pressure we officers are under, will they? Thank God you're here too, sir, I always admired you."

"Bless you, Ralph, I couldn't agree with you more."

Manny pulled Ralphie down into the road and two other members sat on him. "Ralphie, you're the worst ass kisser and stool pigeon we've got. And now, guess what?"

"What, what? Get off me Manny," he said in a panic-stricken voice.

"Naw, we're gonna stake you out in that pile of shit over there and let the rats eat your tongue out."

Deputy Simpson smiled as he continued his reminiscences. "I was his captain for a short while about ten years later, just like the present guy said, and he's right, I didn't have a hell of a lot of luck in keeping him quiet."

Billy had been newly promoted and was assigned to the replacement pool. This duty involved being rotated from one company to another to fill in for captains on lengthy absences until a permanent assignment was available.

Ralphie's long time leader, Captain Fleming, had become ill, ironically with the type of lung disease that he had fought so hard and successfully at the State House to have become a job-related injury for fire fighters, several years earlier. He was currently home recovering from a hospital stay and Billy was filling in for him.

The first morning, when he reported for duty at the huge old firehouse on Broadway, in the South End, after squaring away his gear, he went to the rear of the house where the kitchen was located to get coffee and meet the members of the three companies stationed in quarters.

He could hear Ralphie's voice long before he got to the rear and that was no surprise to him. Billy had been promoted from another company in the district and was well aware of how the show was run in this house.

Billy entered, went to the pantry, got a cup and filled it from the pot. He sat on one of the bench chairs and said hello to the other jakes at the table, most of whom he knew at least casually from being in the district.

Ralphie, at another table, pretending he didn't see Billy enter, casually walked over to the pay telephone, inserted a dime, and dialed a number.

"Hello, Cap, this is your best man Ralphie," he said in a tone that could be heard a block away. "Jeez, do I miss you, old pal. The house just ain't the same. I'm thinkin' of quitting," he sobbed. "They just sent in this real funny lookin' young guy to take your place. For cripessake, he's even wearin' your hat. He don't look that smart, either. Please get better quick before the company falls apart."

He slammed the receiver onto the hook, pulled out his handkerchief and wiped his eyes. He then walked down towards the coffee urn to refill his cup and threw his hands up in feigned surprise as he passed Billy.

"Oh, Captain Simpson. Congratulations on your promotion. Was I glad when I heard you were comin' here. I was so afraid they'd send one of those dummies from Division Two."

"Hey, Ralphie," said Billy.

"Yessir."

"Fuck you."

"Thank you, sir. I like an officer who speaks his mind."

Later as the house work progressed, Ralphie was doing his regular job of moving the dirt around with a push broom up on the second floor, which contained the various company officers' quarters. He knocked on Billy's door and entered to pick up the waste basket from under the desk. "You know, Cap, this is a wonderful job. I've been on twenty years now and I've learned a lot of things I never knew. You can develop some real skills as a jake."

"Like what?"

"Well, I started off cleaning the kitchen and then cleaning the pump and finally, Captain Fleming assigned me to Officers' Country because I'm his best man. Now, I am, without a doubt, the premier toilet cleaner on the department. And it's officers shithouses that I really shine at. It's a funny thing, and nothin' personal, sir, but it's been my experience that officers' toilets are more frequently used than fire fighters'. I'm not sure why that is except that Warren, my partner, says officers are more fulla shit than the men. Whaddya think, sir?"

"Fuck you, Ralphie."

"Thank you, sir. Does that mean I should continue my work?"

Later in the morning when Billy completed his paper work, he returned to the kitchen and as he entered, there was Ralphie, with a tall, white chef's hat on his head and a long, white apron hanging down over his chest and legs. His hands and part of his face were covered with powder.

"What the hell are you doin', Ralphie?"

"Why, Cappy, old pal, I'm makin' lunch. 'Cause I like ya, I'm bakin a coupla pies to welcome you aboard."

And he was. During the two months Billy spent in the house, he came to find out how irrepressible Ralphie was and how much he contributed to the morale of the company. Not only in the firehouse, but also at fires. He worked as hard or harder than anyone, always trying to beat the other companies at the scene to the fire, constantly talking and screaming, bragging about how much better Twenty-six was than everyone else. This was especially so when they responded to fires in the thirteen cities and towns that adjoined Boston and were part of the Mutual Aid System. Ralphie treated all of those department members like they were "lower than whale shit," as he frequently described them.

His partner, Warren, who had been teamed with him since they were appointed, was as quiet as Ralphie was loud. Warren could frequently be heard muttering, "Ralphie, you're an asshole. Shut up."

"I love you, Warren," was always Ralphie's rejoinder, followed by, "You're the only Protestant I ever met that I'd let become a Catholic. Whyncha switch over?"

"Lissen you nitwit, I've been watchin' you Catholics for all my time on the job and if I hafta become one of you thievin', drinkin', screwin' mackerel mongers to get to heaven, I ain't goin'."

Billy understood that both of these guys loved the job and were the type of men that insured the success of fire fighting operations. People came on the department for a variety of reasons, but many, like these two, had lived through the Great Depression and were so grateful to have any kind of work that no task was too difficult for them.

Once they learned there was a tremendous challenge associated with fire fighting and what enormous satisfaction was gained from succeeding in saving lives and property, you couldn't ask for more dedicated employees.

So, yeah, the other captain was right, Billy thought, I didn't have much luck in changing Ralphie. But who the hell would want to?

2

Billy sat at his desk in division quarters and opened the bulky manila envelope he had retrieved from his personal mailbox which was affixed to the wall behind him. The boxes of the other three deputies, his partners in the division, had similar envelopes sticking out of theirs.

It was early January and Billy knew, just as in previous years, the documents inside were General Orders that contained meritorious performances of duty of members during the year that just ended. This seemed like as good a night as any to read over the reports.

Next month the commissioner would have the Board of Merit hearing to determine which of those members who had been cited would be given awards at the Annual Ball that took place at the end of May. The Board of Merit consisted of the thirteen deputy fire chiefs in the Table of Organization.

Billy reviewed the information that listed the medals and other awards and what had to be evaluated for eligibility as a candidate. It's a funny business, he thought. Some years, there are many performances that are submitted and other years, very few. It's not very consistent. One thing that is consistent, though, is the determination of the Board not to cheapen any awards just to use them up. There have been several years when not all of the top three medals were awarded because the Board didn't feel the criteria had been met.

This doesn't mean, he thought, that the deputies wouldn't fight fiercely to get something for guys on their own shifts.

Far from it. Sometimes the discussions get kind of heated. But in the long run, it seems the right acts of bravery get the right awards.

"Beano" wouldn't be there this year because he got pensioned. He used to always be good for an argument and a laugh. He was only about five foot-two, and was constantly trying to prove how much better he was than all those taller jerks sitting around the conference room. He consistently had more General Orders submissions than any other group, division or deputy. Of course many of them were a little suspect and they were usually thrown out.

One year though, the Redhead, who was pretty good at raising Beano's blood pressure, said, "Joe, (Beano hated being called by his nickname) once again, you have more meritorious acts than anyone else."

"So what. My men deserve them. I got the best group on the job."

"Well, I've been doin' a lot of reading lately—you know, NFPA, *Fire Engineering, Fire Chiefs Magazine* and *Firehouse.*"

"Whaddya read all that stuff for? Those twerps don't know anything about the business."

"Oh, I don't know, Joe. They write up all kinds of strategy and tactics. They got Incident Command Systems, computers and a lot of nifty theories."

"Bullshit. Don't start on me Red, you're only tryin' to piss me off."

"No, Joe, no. Really. They got some world-beater chiefs from out west that know everything. There's a guy in Arizona who is so smart, he don't even get dirty. Unlike you Joe, he and his chiefs never hafta get outta their air conditioned cars at a fire. They just push a button on their computers and the fire goes out. After being enlightened by them, I've come to the conclusion that the reason your men are so brave is that you don't know what the fuck you're doin' and they have to keep endangering themselves to bail you out."

Beano jumped up, grabbed a jelly donut from the tray in the middle of the table and fired it across at the Redhead who had ducked down as soon as he finished speaking.

The commissioner, who was also chief of department and thus a member of the uniformed branch, shook his head wearily and said, "What ever happened to the dignity deputy fire chiefs are supposed to display as an example?" Red thought he caught a half wink from the boss as he concluded, "Red, you ought to be ashamed to make such an inference about one of my top men. Let's continue the review. The next case to be examined was submitted by," he glanced down at the list, "er, you, Joe. Ahem, I think that's your third this year."

Yeah, we'll miss Beano, mused Billy.

He glanced over the SOP that reviewed the procedure:

1. The Board of Merit shall meet once a year to investigate and consider any specially meritorious acts of members during the previous year.

They shall then submit an impartial report to the Commissioner, based on their investigation of cases submitted, for his consideration in determining what awards, if any, shall be made of medals, etc.

In view of the fact that the calling of a fire fighter is at all times surrounded with personal risk, it is essential that some greater degree of danger than this is necessary to entitle consideration by the Board of Merit, and therefore the following classifications are established to assist the Board in its deliberations:

(a) Medal: To entitle a member to a consideration in this class, the act performed should involve a degree of danger properly characterized as extreme personal risk.

(b) Roll of Merit: To entitle a member to consideration in this class, the act performed should involve a degree of danger properly characterized as great personal risk.

(c) Special or Other Commendation: To entitle a member to consideration in this class, the act performed should involve a degree of danger properly characterized as unusual personal risk, or an act of service of unusual merit outside of the ordinary performance of duty.

(d) Distinguished Service Award: A special scroll will be awarded to those members of the department who performed some act or service of unusual merit outside of their ordinary duties, which has brought outstanding recognition to the department.

2. Recognition shall be made publicly of all of the department members who have sacrificed their lives in the performance of their duties. A medal known as the "Medal of Valor" shall be presented to the next of kin. Eligibility of the award shall be recommended by the Board of Merit.

3. The "John E. Fitzgerald Medal" will be annually awarded to the member of the fire fighting force adjudged by the Fire Commissioner to have performed the Most Meritorious act within the previous year, provided such act has been accorded special mention and is, in the opinion of the Fire Commissioner, absolutely worthy of the award as well as relatively best entitled to it.

4. The "Walter Scott Medal" and the "Patrick J. Kennedy Medal" will be presented by the Fire Commissioner to the members of the fire fighting force who, in his judgement, have during the previous year distinguished themselves for valor in the performance of their duties as fire fighters; unless, in the opinion of the Fire Commissioner, there is no member entitled to receive such an award.

5. The names of members deemed by the Fire Commissioner to have acquitted themselves in a manner worthy of such recognition will be entered on the "Roll of Merit" together with a brief summary of the facts and circumstances in each case.

6. The "Award of Recognition" shall be presented to a member of the Uniformed Force who has performed a service or services that have resulted in improving the performance of the department at fires and/or contributed to the safety of members of the fire fighting force. This award will be presented only when it has been voted by the Board of Merit in any given year.

7. Members receiving a medal shall be granted four tours of duty off in addition to annual vacation. Members entered on the Roll of Merit, or receiving a Distinguished Service Award or Award of Recognition shall be granted two tours of duty off in addition to their annual vacation. Time off shall be given only for the year the award was received.

Yeah, all in all, it's a good system, thought Bill. He had looked at some of the awards given in other large cities and the lists of medals and commendations were enormous. Nobody got nothin' here for perfect attendance. Like the old Smith-Barney guy said on the add: They earn it. You couldn't say they did it for the dough, either. The actual medal winners had their salary increased by forty-eight cents a week (258 bucks a year) while the Roll of Merit and other guys got shit.

Only a couple of guys in the entire history of the department ever won two medals and boy, did they earn them.

The one medal that paid plenty was the Medal of Valor. Yeah, but you hadda get killed to get it. The widow of anyone winning it got the guy's salary and raises for the rest of her life, as long as she didn't remarry, and now the Feds gave her a hundred grand as a result of legislation that got passed by the IAFF.

Knowing that their families will be o.k. gives jakes a great feeling of security, but the average member would just as soon not be included in that list.

A list was on the wall in the office, of all those who had been killed over the years and Billy could count almost fifty in the time he'd been on the job. He knew quite a few of them, too. Some better than others. Yeah, and he'd been at a couple of fires where guys had been lost.

Of course the Vendome in '72 was the worst. Nine jakes went down—almost got him, too. But the one that always jumped into his mind uninvited—no one wanted to think about that stuff—was Trumbull Street, back in '64. Five jakes and one poor spark who was helping on the line. He could've been one of them, too.

Some of the survivors were the ones that got to him because after awhile, the dead seemed to slip into their own compartment in your mind and fade dimly.

One of the most tragic of the Trumbull survivors was the assistant chief in charge of fire prevention. During that period, guys with that rank, which no longer exists, were assigned to headquarters in Training, Personnel, Fire Prevention and other jobs that are now positions for deputy fire chiefs.

Those guys rotated responding to fourth alarms and, at the time of Trumbull Street, would assume command on arrival because the chief of department was out sick.

Just as this chief was pulling up on the major street adjacent to the location of the incident, the building collapsed, burying several jakes including those who died.

The dust, smoke and confusion at the instant that such a disaster occurs, along with the screams of those who are trapped, has an impact on anyone, no matter how experienced he is, but the chief began organizing a rescue effort immediately, commencing with instructions to conduct a roll call to determine who was missing. What he was unaware of for a brief period of time was that one of his sons, a member of Engine 3, was buried under the rubble and was killed instantly.

Billy was a lieutenant on an engine company and fortunately, was operating on the opposite side of the building away from the wall that fell and he and his crew joined in removing the debris, an operation that had to be done by hand.

A tough night and a tough incident for the department. The assistant chief was an extremely religious man who drew great strength from his equally god-fearing wife and their many other children.

Naturally, there was a massive funeral at the Cathedral of the Holy Cross within a week, with the cardinal, mayor, governor and numerous political figures in attendance, along with thousands of jakes who poured in from all over the state and from around the country.

The guy Billy and a host of other friends kept thinking about was Freddie, who was hospitalized and would be for awhile as a result of the fire. Freddie was the deputy who had been in charge of the fire when the collapse occurred. Several of the bricks from the tons that fell and buried so many members had struck his head, back and legs. None of his injuries were life-threatening or permanent, and everyone was glad to hear that. The few who had been able to sneak by the vigilant guards at the City Hospital, including Billy, tried to get into his room to cheer him up.

They were spotted at the doorway by the head nurse who was bearing down the corridor towards them with the bulk and determination of a battleship. "Deputy—Deputy," they called into the figure huddled on the bed because they knew they'd never make it inside against such formidable opposition.

Everyone called him Freddie while discussing him, but no one ever considered addressing him by anything but his rank.

He rolled over and raised up to see who was calling him. Those present would never forget the look of absolute despair and desolation they saw on his face as he placed his forearm across his forehead, closed his eyes and turned away without acknowledging them.

Anyone who worked with Freddie would never forget him, mused Billy, his hands clasped behind his head as he leaned back in his swivel chair, with eyes gazing at the ceiling. Yeah, even though he's been gone for several years now.

The department now has an excellent stress unit that includes a team that responds to tragedies such as those involving the deaths of fire fighters and/or children. The unit is extremely helpful in getting those members who are adversely affected from witnessing such events to be able to accept them as part of the realities of the job and part of the frailties of our existence that we have to live with.

This wasn't the case back in 1964.

Freddie had come on the department just before the Japs hit Pearl Harbor, and when they did, he and many other Americans enlisted in the armed forces and disappeared from civilian life for the next four years. When he returned, he plunged into his chosen career with a vengeance. The brief taste of the job he'd received before the war kept him thinking throughout those long months of combat around the world about what he wanted to do with his life.

He was already married, so he knew he was facing family responsibilities that had been set aside while he was away. But now it was time to get going and he knew he was lucky that he had a job waiting for him.

He quickly became known as someone special because, unlike many others who come on the job, he was able to grasp the intricacies of fire fighting strategy and tactics without any difficulty. Many members take several years to be able to understand not only the objectives of the fire attack but also the most practical way of reaching the goal. Some poor guys never get it at all, and if they become officers and chiefs, their superiors and subordinates acquire gray hair quite early in their careers from worrying about "what's he doin' now?"

But not Freddie. In addition to his obvious intelligence, he was a strong and determined worker who displayed little interest in his own safety at fires. Not reckless, just unconcerned.

At operations where it sometimes seems the task of advancing up a stairway or in onto a floor is virtually impossible because of the intensity of the smoke and heat, certain guys in the department and in the fire service have that intangible extra drive and determination that result in bringing fire company members to heights they didn't think were possible to achieve. The narrow, fragile line between success and failure in saving a life of a trapped occupant or saving or losing a building is determined more often than most people would ever realize by such people. Freddie could have been a national model for this role.

He also was blessed with a true photographic memory which proved to be the determining factor in his fairly rapid rise to leadership. The Massachusetts Civil Service system for fire departments is based on the purest form of impersonal head to head competition by written examination.

Back in the thirties, the written exams were followed by oral interviews before a civilian, politically appointed board that frequently resulted in some astounding upgrades (and downgrades) of the test scores of competitors. But, by the time Freddie started competing after the war, the scandals had been eliminated by the indictments that were a natural Massachusetts result of such excesses.

The material that had to be covered for the wide-ranging, fire related data that was used in the exams required most serious students to spend at least a year of intense study to be properly prepared. Freddie, with his exceptional skills, finished first on the list in every exam he took. There are five positions that are achieved by the examination route: fire fighter, fire lieutenant, fire captain, district (battalion) fire chief and the biggest prize of all, deputy fire chief or division commander. The job of fire commissioner-chief of department is a direct appointment by the Mayor of Boston. While the selection for the top job has been from the ranks of the deputy fire chiefs in recent years, anyone who doesn't think politics are involved in this selection process hasn't been paying attention to Boston politics, which were established in 1630 when the Pilgrims worked their way up north from their settlements around Plymouth Rock.

When members took exams, there was a sixty day wait for the results to be mailed by the Civil Service Department. As soon as the first applicant got his mark, the phone calls would begin and before nightfall a tentative list was in the hands of every serious candidate. The guys who routinely went up to just kill a nice Saturday, without having studied, knew they were going to flunk so they were in no rush to check their mail box.

Steve, who was Freddie's best friend, never was interested in studying. They had served as fire fighters on the same company in Roxbury and were as close as any two people could be.

When Freddie was preparing for the lieutenant's exam, he kept dragging Steve into the room and making him review past exams and answering questions, in spite of his lack of interest.

"Lissen, Freddie, I'm not interested. I'm single, happy and don't wanna be bothered."

"Shut up, you idiot, and pay attention. They're changing the work week hours from eighty-four to forty-eight next year and there's gonna be a bunch of promotions. This is never gonna happen again, so sit over there, open that book and keep quiet."

"Idiot" was Freddie's favorite word for people he really liked, and as time went on and his reputation grew, it became almost a badge of honor if he called you one. He called Steve one an awful lot.

Sure enough, with the change of hours, they made so many officers in the late forties that guys like Steve got swept in with the tide. It became known as the "Chinese Exclusion Act," because everyone who took the exam got made and since there were no Asians on the job at the time, it was a pretty good description.

Steve settled in at Engine 3 in the South End, a company he truly loved, where he established his own form of being a legend, without even knowing it.

Every two years, Freddie forced Steve to fill out an application for the captains' exam and would give him a bunch of literature to study. Steve would file for the test at Freddie's insistence, but they both understood it was a waste of time. Steve would say, "Freddie, unless they cut the hours down to twenty a week, there's no way I'll ever get a job. Whnya leave me alone?"

"Because, you idiot, you're my friend and I want to make somethin' outta you."

The first captains' exam Steve went to was the only one Freddie had to take with him, because he naturally topped the list and got promoted. Freddie was so good at it that when all those guys who took future exams with him for the higher ranks would assemble a list the day the marks arrived, the conversation would go, "Yeah, well Freddie's first, but who's second?"

Freddie tried to avoid sitting near Steve in the high school classroom the Civil Service Commission leased from the city for the exam.

The real serious students raced to get a desk that didn't have any holes in the top which could cause a pen puncture in the test paper; neatness counted, particularly in the report-letter that was always the opening portion of the test.

Steve didn't care. He just wanted to sit next to Freddie and harass him. He had already arranged with all the other non-student frauds in the room to go to lunch when they were done, so if the desk had "John Loves Mary" or the Gettysburg Address carved into it, it wouldn't make much difference in his test score.

The other frauds were mostly guys who had been forced to take the exam by their wives. When their failing marks arrived in two months time, they'd tell the spouses the whole process was a bag job and good guys like them didn't have a chance.

The main reason Freddie didn't want to be near Steve was that the monitors for the exam were Boston school teachers who were hired for the day. Those guys were strict. If they caught anyone talking they'd threaten to throw them out, and if you even glanced at a notepaper, you were gone and so was your chance for promotion for another two years.

"Freddie," Steve whispered.

"Shut up, you idiot."

"Freddie," he leaned over toward him.

"Shut up."

"Freddie, I got two of the questions."

"Leave me alone, will ya?"

"Freddie, lissen to me."

"Alright. What are they?"

"First is 'What are the hazards of a bloomer factory?'"

Freddie turned away, trying to suppress a grin, covering his mouth with his hand. The monitor glanced down their aisle with an irritated look on his face.

The teacher was called to the opposite side of the room by someone asking a question.

"Freddie," came the hiss. "Look at me. I'm tryin' to help ya. Wanna know the other one? It's a real good question from the old days."

"What is it, you idiot?"

"Give the complete nomenclature of a horse's fetlock."

Freddie burst out laughing and the teacher hurried over, uncertain who was responsible for the disturbance.

"If I hear one more sound from this side of the room, I'm cancelling the exam and reporting everyone of you to Civil Service."

Steve became a fixture for the next two decades at the biennial captains' exams, never passing of course, and with no one sitting close to him in the room. But he always said it was a nice social event that gave him a chance to see all of his friends on the job, go to lunch and have a few Wild Turkeys, his beverage of choice.

The people who were the happiest that Steve never scored big again were the members of the company who worked on his group. He became like a father to them all, and since he was an extremely skilled fire fighter, they felt he would not only protect them, but that he'd make sure they performed as well or better than any other company at the scene.

Billy, who only worked infrequently with Freddie during his own upward rise, spent a few months under his command while filling in for Captain Fleming at the Broadway firehouse. He came to understand that Freddie's daily routine didn't vary much unless there was a fire in progress. He visited several firehouses in his division on a rotating basis, always including the Broadway house first, then going over to Steve's location at Engine 3, near the Cathedral in the South End.

His main purpose in these stops along the way was strictly for entertainment. Ralphie wasn't the only character at the Broadway house, which was home to three fire companies and thus peopled by a larger number of members than the average two-company station.

The captain of the ladder company was an imposing figure who, while much older than the rest of the members, could be easily drawn into any argument and immediately assume the role of omniscient seer. His belief that no one could possibly know as much as he made him a ready foil for guys like the Hoss and his associates.

When the house work was completed every morning, which at best was just a halfhearted attempt at cleaning up the joint, the members would head for the kitchen-mess hall where Ralphie would be cooking breakfast and screaming orders at everyone. Of course, no one ever listened to him; it was just part of the overall din.

Since the Hoss was a vice-president of the International Association of Fire Fighters and had served as President of Boston Local 718 several times in the past, he would routinely bait his blusterous leader about some obscure issue that was included in the voluminous contract the union had with the city, and the argument would be on.

Freddie, whose objective was to remain in the corner at the back of the kitchen and enjoy the show, succeeded, at least most of the time, in not being drawn into the fray. During Billy's tenure in the house, Freddie would slide onto the bench beside him and just listen to the exchanges that were always conducted at fever pitch.

"I would have absolutely no hesitancy in filing a grievance up the street against you, Captain," said the Hoss. "These men are paid professional fire fighters and not, with all due respect, sir, servants to every whim of the officers. The contract explicitly forbids any personal services, isn't that right, Deputy?" he said as he turned towards Freddie. Freddie, with his photographic memory knew every comma in the contract but he waved the Hoss off, refusing to be part of what he knew was just a routine, get-the-captain-pissed-off effort.

"Lissen, you asshole," shouted the captain, rising up to his imposing six foot, four inch height, "all I told ya to do is wash the fuckin' windows. It's Wednesday, it's window day and you know it. What the fuck is personal services about that?" The Hoss could tell by his tone, though, the captain, who never knew one word of the contract, was a little uncertain of his legal standing on the issue.

"Well, it may sound a little too technical to you, sir, but there are two basic issues involved here."

"Like what?"

"The temperature sir, is eighty-one degrees Fahrenheit and no windows can be done above eighty. It's right on page seventy-two under 'additional conditions.' The other thing, though, and I really hate to mention this in front of the men, sir, is that I am quite certain you want your windows cleaned so you can get a better view of the hookers operating on the corner. A clear request for personal service, as any arbitrator would rule at the grievance procedure."

Freddie turned to Billy and said, and he really meant it, "You know, Cap, I'm the luckiest guy you'll ever meet. I've got the best job in the world and I get free entertainment from these characters every day I work."

The argument moved on to another subject, without any clear-cut verbal resolution, and the members started shuffling out of the kitchen to begin doing the windows, which the Hoss knew would happen anyway. The thrill was in the hunt, not the point of issue.

Freddie said goodbye to Billy and rose to move on to his next stop on the circus tour. The Hoss shouted, "Achtung" as he frequently did when the deputy was leaving, a reference to Freddie's German-Irish ancestors. As he did so many times in the past, he said, "Hoss, you're an idiot. Captain," he nodded to Ladder 17's leader, "I'll be a witness for you anytime when you prefer charges against him."

"Ya hear that, Hoss. You better watch your step. Me and the Deputy don't give a shit about the contract or any of those nitwits in Washington you suck up to all the time," a reference to the International's leadership. He viewed them all as bureaucratic political hacks who would never make it on any fire company he commanded.

Freddie's aide, Jim, didn't have to be told where they were going next, because the route never varied. Up Broadway to Shawmut Ave., left down to Waltham, left to go across Washington continuing on the divided portion of the street, past the huge Cathedral of the Holy Cross and onto the apron of Engine 3's quarters at the intersection of Harrison Avenue.

Jim preceded him into the house and it was obvious that no one was on watch on the main floor. The rules required that one member must constantly be in the patrol booth at the desk when the companies were in quarters, to answer the telephone, receive alarms, dispatch the companies to fires and be available for citizens who came into the house.

Freddie, realizing that Steve was up to something, knew he was required to appear furious at the violation, and stormed up the stairs, into Engine 3's officers' room. "Lieutenant," he started, but stopped as he saw Steve's bed lined with rolled up socks, folded shirts and underwear, all neatly arranged and spotless. He knew that Steve, the bachelor, always did his washing in quarters, but he had to ask anyway. "What the hell are you doing and where's the man on patrol?"

"Deputy, I'm so glad you could drop by, sir. Why I'm just doing the laundry for the priests over at the Cathedral. You know the nuns are on strike, some kind of a protest against the Cardinal and the role of women in the church and I want those poor fellas to look nice. Besides, they said I don't have to give in the collection next week."

"Yeah, well that's swell, but what about the man on patrol? Where the hell is he?"

"Oh, Deputy, sir, I didn't think you'd notice. Well, to tell you the truth, it's Spanky, and I hate to mention it, but he's drunk, sir, and I knew you wouldn't want the public coming in and getting the wrong impression of these wonderful men."

It was a setup of course, and Freddie would follow through with his expected role, but Jeez, what a choice. Of all the men in the firehouse or, for that matter, on the job, Spanky was the least likely candidate to be guilty of anything. As a matter of fact, he could very well have been one of those priests across the street and no one would have been surprised.

If Steve had named the Bug-Fucker or Razo the Rat or Bozo, the story could possibly have had some credence but not Spanky.

His innocence and his absolute dedication to the job were known throughout the department.

When he had first gotten married, guys used to question whether he would know what to do, to put it delicately, about his marital responsibilities. When one wag crudely asked him if his wife had "Anything in the oven," Spanky replied quite seriously, "We don't have an oven yet, we got a rotisserie.'

Freddie knew it was a normal procedure in the house to hang the latest centerfold of *Playboy* (after everyone was through with it, of course) lengthwise on Spanky's locker door just to see the shocked look on his face as he closed his eyes, tore it to shreds and said, "Jingos, I wish these guys would remember I don't like that stuff."

Freddie put his hands on his hips and said, "Lieutenant, are you expecting me to believe that Spanky's on the sauce? Try somethin' else, will ya?"

"Oh, it's terrible, Deputy. Ever since he got married, he started hitting the soup and it's a disgrace. His poor wife. She even got him to join A.A. and it lasted for awhile. But this morning, he was a disgrace, and when I asked him about A.A., he said now he's drinking under an assumed name."

The completely guiltless object of the discussion, knocked on the open door to the officers' room, stood at attention in his immaculate work clothes, with hat, tie and dress coat, saluted, and said, "Good morning, Deputy. Nice to see you, sir. Lieutenant, I brought that box of spare nozzle tips that you wanted up from the cellar. O.K. if I go back down on watch?"

"Yes, Spanky. Thanks a lot. Whyncha call Frannie and tell her I was askin' for her?"

That's the way it went. Always something with Steve. Each plan more elaborate than the last one.

Billy remembered talking to a fire fighter during his sojourn at Broadway who had transferred in town from out in Readville, from an engine company that was in an area so quiet the unit and its crew were the only occupants of the tiny firehouse. Coming to Broadway was like going to the moon, the differences in the work load and outlook were so dramatic.

He said after he had been on the job about six months, his previous captain lined them all up one morning and told them that the deputy was coming for the annual inspection of quarters in two weeks. The captain was obviously nervous about this royal event and laid out the cleaning plan in no uncertain terms.

When the rookie got home that night, he told his wife, a deputy was coming to inspect the house. "What's a deputy?" she asked. "I don't know but it must be somethin' pretty important 'cause my captain's scared stiff."

On the appointed day, the members were lined up in full uniform at 0930, awaiting the scheduled 1000 visit. The captain paced back and forth in front of them, checking ties, shirts, coats and shoes to make certain everyone looked good.

At 1030, a gleaming red sedan pulled up in front of the house. The imposing looking aide, himself immaculate, got out, went around to the passenger's door, opened it and stood at attention.

As the rookie related it to his wife that evening, "This little guy, all covered with gold, got out, accepted the Captain's elaborate salute, walked past us with a look of disdain on his face, glanced at the highly polished fire engine, went out, got back in the car and his aide drove him away."

"Well, what did he look like?"

"I don't know, I was so scared I never looked right at him. I was so afraid he'd ask me a question and I think I'd have fainted if he did. That gold really blinded me anyway. Before he came, I wasn't so sure a deputy was even a person, and believe me, I still wasn't after he left."

He said to Billy, "Now I come in down here, I see a deputy every day, everyone talks to him, nobody's scared of him, and he seems to be grinning all the time. Honest to God, one day he stuck up for the Hoss in an argument and the captain, for chrissake, said to him, 'Lissen Deputy, I am in charge of this house. You are just a guest and I can cancel your right to visit here with the snap of my fingers.'" He continued, "But you know, I never seen a guy that people love so much. They know he's the boss, without any question. And what a fireman he is! Everyone's got such faith in his judgement, they'd jump off the Prudential if he told them to."

Billy said, "Ever think of transferrin' back out to the woods?"

"No way, Cap. This is the fire department and I'll be here 'till I retire."

His reminiscences also made Billy think of the parade of civilian fire commissioners he had seen during the early years of his career. For the last fifteen years, the position was occupied by deputy chiefs who were elevated to the post by the mayor and then served with the title of both fire commissioner and chief of department. The arrangement worked well, or at least better than it had been.

Both jobs were in the City Charter with the fire commissioner charged with the responsibility of protecting the lives and property of the citizens from fire and other emergencies. The chief of department served as his executive assistant in charge of the uniformed force which varied in size from 1600 to 2200 over the years.

The appointed commissioner was always a civilian. The types that held the position varied from very intelligent guys who knew enough to get the best equipment possible for the department and then let the chief of department run the show, while basking in the limelight of publicity that accompanied the assignment, to those political hacks who arrived knowing they were much smarter than all of those Civil Service peons and determined to prove it every day.

The second type was usually put in when the particular mayor wanted to reorganize the department by reducing the number of companies and the number of members and then be just dumb enough to front for City Hall and tell the public how much more efficient the department was in spite of the puzzling increased losses from fire.

One of these winners was incensed following some supposed slight that occurred when he attempted to give orders to a new lieutenant who didn't recognize him at an auto fire. He directed the poor guy to use foam when the fire involved the back seat and when the lieutenant tried to explain that it wasn't necessary, the new leader stormed off, determined to let these people know who was in charge of the department.

He directed the chief of department to issue orders that commencing immediately, every firehouse in the city would have full uniform roll call for both the oncoming and offgoing shifts at 0800 and 1800 each day. Such lineups were to be supervised by the deputy fire chiefs of both fire fighting divisions who would visit various houses unannounced and put any violating captains or lieutenants in on charges.

Naturally, each deputy immediately called the chief of department, who had been quite forceful in his objections to this inane instruction. "Lissen," he'd reply, "he's pretty determined. Go along for awhile and I'll get to him. He's not the Rhodes scholar type, ya know. Have some patience."

It didn't take more than a couple of weeks for the diplomatic chief to get the decision reversed, but the interim period was memorable.

The new civilian would have no way of knowing, regardless of what the rule book said, that roll call was not as rigidly observed as he might expect, and to think a lofty deputy fire chief would ever participate in such activities was beyond the realm of possibilities, at least until this new directive.

Every house in the city operated on a man for man basis. When your relief arrived, you were gone. This common sense approach resulted in agreements between the parties that were most practical. If you were intown and wanted to beat the rush hour, your guy would come in at three in the afternoon and seven in the morning and you'd do the same when you relieved him.

Other guys, usually in other parts of the city, wanted to be "minute men" and relieve just as the clock struck the time the rule book required for the start of the shift. In general it worked out o.k. and since people were usually stationed on the same fire companies for years at a time, equitable arrangements were made to try to keep everyone happy. The officer in charge of a unit, once all of his crew were in for the shift, would assemble them to keep them informed of what the latest orders were from up the street, and anything else he wanted them to know. To consider lining them all up in uniform would be strange indeed.

Now, with the latest instructions, to keep everyone there from both shifts and in dress uniform was so absurd that no one could believe it. But, an unannounced visit from the deputy was no laughing matter so no one considered violating it and the Hoss and the union guys advised caution until common sense could return.

Of course, while a few martinet deputies enjoyed the feeling of power the latest instructions conveyed, the average guy had aides similar to Freddie's Jim, who would clearly overhear the deputy telling his partner in a loud voice where he was going this morning or this evening and a simple phone call alerted the targeted firehouse.

One visit to Broadway was enough for Freddie. He entered at the appointed hour and was pleased to see that both shifts were lined up in front of him. But as he inadvertently looked closer at them, he realized most of them hadn't put on their dress uniforms for years. The variety of shades of colors along with the ill-fitting trousers and sack coats he observed made him realize he was going to have great difficulty in maintaining his stern visage that he had been practicing on the way from his own quarters. One guy had on a pair of pants that had a suspicious looking blue stripe down the side of each leg, strikingly similar to the ones his brother wore on the Boston Police Department.

Billy was at one end of the line, resplendent in his brand new captain's suit, while the much older leader from the ladder truck was at the opposite end, red of face and practically bursting from the belt that was straining against the last hole in the leather that circled his ample waistline.

The three guys in the middle were the ones that got to him, however. There was Bunker, who would have been much taller if his legs weren't bowed so badly. Next to him was Bogue, whose knock-knees were such a contrast that all Freddie could think of was the letters O.K., which was a poor description for either of them in their ill-fitting garb. But the worst looking one was Ralphie who had on a winter overcoat and was covered with sweat in the August heat.

Not knowing what else to do but realizing he had to say something, he turned to the captain of the truck and said, "Captain, why is that man wearing that outfit? Where is his regular sack coat?"

The captain, who was startled by the questions, looked down the row and shouted, "Ralphie, take that goddamned coat off."

"Yessir," came the reply. He ceremoniously unbuttoned the silver buttons, shrugged the heavy, blue serge from his shoulders, and stood at attention. He was standing in an outfit that consisted of his dress hat, dickey type blue bib around his neck, black tie carefully knotted in place, black shoes, knee high black socks and a gleaming black belt around his waist. Otherwise, he was stark naked, with his legendary massive genitals exposed. He brought his right hand up in a salute that any Tommie from the British Army would have been proud of.

Freddie wished he had never asked the question and the best he could come up with was, "Captain, your men are a total disgrace. Have a complete report of this fiasco on my desk by noontime."

He raced out of the firehouse, into the car, faced away from the house and barely made it out of sight before doubling up with laughter.

Yeah, thought Billy, but it all ended with Trumbull Street. Billy recalled coming into the fire and being sent to the rear of the four story warehouse by the district chief with orders to run a line of hose into the stairway and attack the fire that had gained control and was showing from the second and third floor windows.

It wasn't very long after he and his crew had dragged the line into position and commenced plugging the powerful stream into the huge floor area that the order was given to back out and convert from an inside attack with a hand held line, to an outside attack with their heavy stream appliance.

He found out later that when Freddie arrived and consulted with the district chief they jointly determined that not only was the fire growing in intensity, but the hundred year old building didn't look very stable and it was prudent to get everyone out to safety.

At the front of the building, on the opposite side from where Billy and his crew were setting up, the companies that had gained entrance over hand raised ground ladders were backing out and descending to the narrow street.

Without warning the front wall came down and out and those who died instantly were on those ladders or directly below them.

The funeral was very sad and all of Freddie's friends were glad he hadn't been able to attend.

He was hospitalized for a few weeks and then sent home to recover. At first there was a steady stream of visitors coming to his house but his doctor and his wife finally stopped the flow.

Billy was one of the guys who got in but he came away even sadder than he had been at the funeral. Freddie had a theory that was incorrect but he was convinced was the cause of the deaths. After the wall came down, the remainder of the building was still somewhat intact and he believed if he hadn't ordered the members out, they would have survived in on the fire floors. This, of course, was nonsense, which his friends pointed out to him. Billy said the way the fire was taking off in his position, the best news he ever heard was the order to abandon the attack. It was his opinion a lot more guys would have been killed if Freddie hadn't made his decision when he did but he could see he wasn't listening.

Freddie's other concern was about his pal, Steve, who had been buried under the pile along with the rest of Three's crew. One of them had been killed, along with the poor spark who had been helping them on the line, and Steve had received several severe injuries to his head and legs.

His hospital stay was much longer but he would recover almost completely and eventually return to the company. He regained his spirits and was mentally his old self, although he was never completely the same physically. His legs gave him a lot of trouble and one of his shoulders had a constant ache. He thought about packing it in but when he mentioned it to his work crew, they held a meeting and came to him one night, with Spanky as the spokesman.

"Er, Lieutenant, we took a vote and the way it came out was like this. Excuse my language please, but I'm speaking for the company. We don't give a shit if you never touch a piece of hose or climb another ladder. Please don't leave us. We'll boost you in windows or throw you over fences if we hafta, but stay with us. This ain't never gonna be a good company if you leave, so you gotta stay."

Steve stayed.

Freddie too came back, but he never regained the same cheerful outlook that was his trademark. Billy got to know him much better during the next few years because of his own rise in the ranks and his admiration for him never wavered.

It was so ironic, though. Just five months before Trumbull Street, on May 22, 1964, Freddie had reached the zenith of his career when he directed the department at the Bellflower Street fire where twenty-nine wooden three deckers were damaged or destroyed in a conflagration that wiped out three streets and created its own wind that developed into a fire storm.

The magnificent way he had directed the fifty-five fire companies at the scene, combined with his tremendous command presence, had saved hundreds of similar buildings in this densely populated section of South Boston.

He was interviewed by national newspapers and magazines and visited by interested fire chiefs from around the country and even from overseas as a result of this outstanding achievement. He was startled by all of the attention.

He had such a natural knowledge of fire fighting and such confidence in his abilities to solve the most complex situations at a fire scene that he thought they were making too big a deal of it. "Isn't that what I got hired for?" was his most frequent rejoinder.

After Trumbull Street, while he didn't lose his evaluation abilities, he never really regained the same confidence in his aptitude to command.

Everyone else did though. The chief of department frequently asked him to fill in for him in his absences and he directed the department at many serious incidents. During the riots of '67 and '68 he was assigned as the Civil Disturbance Director and did a superb job of designing response systems to adjust to the changing society.

But Billy could see it wasn't the same. He didn't visit firehouses like he used to and for sure, Billy never heard him say he had the "best job in the world" any more.

The work load in the late sixties doubled and tripled with the nationwide increase in arson, civil disorders and harassment of fire fighters. Finally, Steve decided it was time to go. Even the most fervent pleas by Spanky and the boys couldn't dissuade him this time. He had to leave.

His departure and the huge testimonial he received marked the start of the end of the road for Freddie.

Billy often wondered if scientists would ever really know how cancer starts in people. Is it always physical or could it possibly be caused by the stress some people experience in their lives? In '69 it showed up in Freddie's lungs. For a short period, he wouldn't tell anyone and kept coming in to work. After awhile though, he asked for a transfer to the Training Division at Headquarters, telling the chief of department it was just temporary. But, the chief and all of his friends knew he couldn't continue.

Oh, he'd keep coming in and sitting at his desk and Steve, the retiree, would periodically arrive at noon to take him out to lunch. He'd keep telling him the most outrageous tales to try to keep his spirits up, but the most he could get was a small smile.

Finally, on August 3, 1970, the magnificent heart stopped beating and he was gone. He was fifty-four years old. Reflecting on it now, so many years later, Billy still remembered being relieved that Freddie's journey had ended. It had been a long, long road.

If historians ever start looking up the careers of outstanding fire chiefs, they'll note the date of his death on the department records. But, Steve, Billy and all of his surviving friends know those archivists will be mistaken.

While he wasn't eligible for the Medal of Valor, because the system doesn't work that way, Chief Frederick P. Clauss really left with five other jakes and a spark, on October 1, 1964, the night the wall came down on Trumbull Street.

3

Billy glanced up at the clock in the office and realized he had been daydreaming while he should have been reviewing the commendations. It was after 7 P.M. and he realized he'd better eat something before he continued his work.

He knew the evening meal in the kitchen of his station at Fort Hill Square was well under way because he had heard Nellie announcing it was ready a while ago. But Billy wasn't in on the meal anyway so it didn't matter. A recent visit to his doctor for a checkup had resulted in the advice that Billy drop about ten pounds. He knew it would never happen if he kept eating in the firehouse the nights that he worked.

Jakes are experts at producing the most delicious meals found anywhere. However, any dietician would have a stroke if he or she ever counted the number of calories available at the average dinner that was served soon after the night tour began. The latest nationwide frenzy over reducing cholesterol levels and fat content hadn't impacted the cooks and diners who developed the menus in firehouses.

The way the groups or shifts system operated in Boston, the same people who were on duty today would work the night tour tomorrow night so the meal planning could be arranged without difficulty. On this group, in the Fort Hill Square house, Nellie was in complete charge. Although he's only a fire fighter assigned to the heavy duty Rescue Company, he has as much authority as the commissioner in making the final decision on the various culinary choices that were proposed. He would then appoint various cohorts to pick up the necessary ingredients on the way into work the next night, instructing them on the quantities and how much to spend.

Since the house was fairly close to the Italian North End section of the city, the markets and grocery stores at which they were to make the purchases were clearly spelled out by the chef/maitre d'. These particular merchants were very friendly to the jakes and could be relied on to exceed the requested portions while granting the "firemen's discount" that Nellie had developed over years of sob stories about these brave men who laid their lives on the line constantly for the safety of the citizens and who required good meals to maintain their strength to perform these Herculean tasks.

As Billy entered the kitchen, an intense argument was going on about the price of the just completed meal. He went to the refrigerator, withdrew his lunch bag containing a salad with low-cal dressing, a dry chicken sandwich and a container of yogurt. The smell of cheese and tomato sauce assailed his nostrils but he fought off the hunger pangs, poured a cup of black coffee, and retreated to the back of the room to consume his relatively tasteless tiny meal.

He could tell right away the argument was fraudulent because Porky was yelling at Nellie about the price of the meal. The pair of them were as close as any other pair of thieves could be, so the screaming had to have an ulterior motive.

It didn't take a genius to determine they were trying to suck Eddie into the conversation, but so far they weren't having much luck.

"Lissen, Nellie, I'm sick and tired of this five dollar meal shit. You charge the same price if we have hot dogs or steak and it ain't right, don't you agree, Spider?"

"Leave my pal, Eddie, alone and stop callin' him Spider. The man's parents went to a lot of trouble to come up with his name. I know he's kinda scrawny, but enough's enough. Right, Eddie?" Nellie slid his arm around his pal's shoulders but Eddie refused to be drawn in and said to Billy, "Good evening, Deputy."

"Good evening, Deputy," Porky whispered in a mimicking voice. "Whyncha kiss him, Spider?" Turning back to Nellie he continued, "I know for a fact you got the bread at Quinzani's and it's that day-old stuff. You told us you went to Bombaderi's and I know you're lyin'. Let's face it, you've been makin' a killin' on these meals for years and it's just not right."

The reason Eddie remained mute, Billy thought, was because it was a little bit too soon after the last episode. Porky should wait awhile until the Spider's notoriously short memory span made him forget last month's meal confrontation.

All of these guys have been together for years, thought Billy. I've been watchin' them ever since I got here and they're at least equal to the characters I met in all those other houses I was in. Maybe even worse, or better, depending on your point of view.

Eddie, or the Spider, was just completing his third decade on the job, on the same ladder company, and he was just as gullible now as when Billy had been stationed with him when he was a rookie and Eddie had been on a few years.

In those days, as now, most captains of companies kept a couple of the best workers on their own work group, human nature being what it is. It was the duty of the tillerman back then to be responsible for keeping the tools on the truck clean and ready for use. The driver was responsible for making sure the front end of the tractor-trailer was properly serviced with fuel and water, and both members had to keep the overall vehicle as clean and polished as the captain demanded. The other on-duty members were responsible for cleaning various sections of the firehouse during the couple of hours required each morning.

Of course, the Spider would routinely exceed the normal work period and would be grinding the axes, shining the fenders and painting tool handles until lunch time. He was a workaholic who liked to be complimented by all of the many captains he served under throughout his career. And, he frequently was praised by them because no self-respecting leader would want to slight a guy who didn't know when to quit. It was difficult enough trying to motivate those non-workaholics to push the brooms around.

Everyone he worked with liked the Spider because they understood how he thought. But they also knew how easy he was to get pissed off and they would do it as frequently as possible, "just to keep their hand in"—a kind of practice for those guys who required more sophisticated strategies to make them lose their cool.

It seemed to Billy, looking back, that no day went by without someone casually mentioning that the Spider was an ass-kisser or brown-noser and the battle would be joined.

The tillerman's job at a fire was to climb the aerial to the roof and provide overhead ventilation, and Eddie took great pride in his real talent in accomplishing this objective. It also took a lot of courage to frequently be operating above serious fires, but no one ever questioned his courage in performing this task. Of course, when it was over, and the companies were safely back in the house, someone would occasionally mention how difficult it had been in on the fire floor because of the delay in the Spider getting the roof and the smoke that kept banking down and smothering them. Eddie, with fire in his eyes, would jump up and confront the accuser and the shouting match was on.

The department had changed to rear-mounted aerials a couple of years before, thus eliminating the tractor-trailer vehicles that had the rear wheels controlled by the tiller wheel.

This eliminated the tillerman position on the ladder trucks, much to the Spider's despair, although he still retained the job of roof-man. Porky had inferred that the commissioner had to get rid of the tiller trucks because the Spider's numerous accidents had made them cost-prohibitive and that was good for ten minutes of screaming and finger pointing.

Until last month's confrontation, the Spider, who was quite frugal, or as Nellie would say, "a cheap prick," would frequently complain about the five dollar-no change charge for each meal—urged on, of course, by Porky and his co-conspirators.

Over a period of time they convinced him he could probably buy the ingredients himself and provide better meals. As long as it stayed under five bucks, he could keep the profit and no one would be the wiser.

"Lissen, Spider," said Porky, "ja ever notice that the stuff Nellie gets has no name brands? Or if it does," he continued, "it's names no one ever heard of. Remember last week? We had ice cream that said 'Chevron' on it. For cripes sake, that's the name of gasoline, not ice cream, right? This guy is robbin' us blind. I know you can do better, pal. I think you can get real quality stuff and make Nellie look like the bum he is."

Eddie was reluctant because he wasn't sure he could do any better and he hated to lay out any money in advance. The next night they worked Nellie announced they were going to have Bluefish for supper instead of the meatballs they had agreed on the day before.

Eddie loved fish so he didn't object and the meal was really very good. When it was over and they were clearing away the dishes, Porky said, "Hey Nellie, how much?"

"Five dollars-no change, just like always."

"O.K. that's it. I've had it with you. No way I'm paying a fin for them lousy fish. I know you caught them out Castle Island this afternoon. You didn't pay shit for them and neither am I. Right, Spider? This guys been stickin' it to us for years, but not no more."

"Wait a minute, wait a minute, Porky. Be fair. We had pork chops last week and it cost me a bundle. I'm just tryin' to make up the difference."

"Oh yeah? I think you overcharged for them, too. I bet my pal, Eddie, could gets us lamb chops, cook them better and still charge less. Right pal?"

Eddie was really upset when he thought about how much Nellie was making on the free fish and he believed every word Porky said. This had been going on for a long time and someone said Nellie had a beautiful home in Dedham that he bought just from what he cheated them out of over the years. Dammit, Porky was tellin' the truth.

"Well, I think I could come up with somethin'," he said hesitantly.

"'Course you can. You get the stuff and I'll cook it for ya," said Porky. "Get name brands, too, Spider. I love that Howard Johnson's Ice Cream, don't you?"

As Billy recalled, the Spider's meal met everyone's expectations because Porky kept urging him on during the week to get the very best quality to prove that Nellie was the fraud they all suspected. Eddie had been shocked by the price of the various items; as his day to cook approached he realized that his costs were going to run over the amount he had estimated by quite a bit. The dinner was actually going to average about nine dollars per man, but after all, this is the best meal these stiffs will ever have and he was sure they'd get it up. Porky would help him, he knew. Porky was his pal, not to mention the guy who really wanted to get Nellie, so he'd support the higher price.

When the meal was over, Eddie glanced around the room with satisfaction. Everyone had eaten their fill and the dessert was the final touch. He had gotten Table Talk pies to go with the name brand ice cream and nobody could eat another bite.

"Gee, that was terrific, Spider," said Smitty, who also had been part of the get Nellie campaign. "How much do I owe ya?" Well, here goes, thought Eddie.

Before he could speak, Porky rose up and shouted, "Smitty, whadaya mean how much? This is my pal, Spider, you're askin'. He told ya he could feed us better than that asshole." He nodded towards the supposedly subdued Nellie, sitting in the corner. "That five bucks-no change bullshit is over. My pal would never hit us that hard. Right, pal?"

"Well, how much then?" Smitty persisted.

Eddie could feel them all staring at him. "Er, ah, four, seventy-five."

"What a guy! That's my pal."

Yeah, Billy thought, Porky won't get him again for awhile. Spider may forget a lot of things but not when you get him in his wallet.

4

As Billy crossed the main floor to return up the stairway to his office, the house alarm sounded and he paused to listen to the announcement: "Both companies respond to a building fire at Arch and Franklin Streets," the loud speaker blared. Billy changed direction and walked toward his car because he realized he would be responding to the alarm.

The system was designed so that whenever Fire Alarm, the central dispatch office, received a telephone call for an actual fire in a building, the operator would immediately dispatch the nearest engine and ladder company to the location. The procedure then required Fire Alarm to sound an alarm over both the radio and the wire system using the number of the closest street fire alarm box for location identification.

The striking of this series of numbers resulted in additional assistance being dispatched to the fire to complete the one alarm response. In this case, because the building is downtown and considered a high hazard location, a total of three engine companies, two ladder companies, an aerial tower, a heavy duty rescue company, a district fire chief and a deputy fire chief responded. Billy, as the deputy fire chief, or division commander, would be in charge of the assignment which totaled, including his own and the other chiefs' aides, thirty-six to thirty-eight personnel.

The routine on arrival, according to the Standard Operating Procedures, required the first arriving engine and ladder companies to operate at the front of the building, the second arriving to take the rear and the other companies to be assigned as the situation required. This constantly proven method of attack was ideal for normal fire fighting operations.

However, the constantly evolving procedures, which are periodically reviewed and altered, grant wide-ranging latitude to the officer in command. This is due to the unusual nature of the business where the ability to adapt to developments is an extremely valuable asset that is frequently used.

Engine 10, arriving first at the scene, reported heavy fire was showing from the fourth and fifth floors of a six story office building. The company also reported Arch Street was dug up and inaccessible to fire apparatus.

Billy absorbed this information while enroute and his mind started clicking off what he knew about the area. His years in the division had made him very familiar with hundreds of the old structures that were erected soon after the Great Boston Fire of 1872, which had wiped out most of the downtown district.

He briefly recalled a serious cellar fire he had in the building presently involved but the short distance to the scene didn't give him much time to think about it. He knew it was located on the corner of Franklin and Arch with a restaurant on the first floor, offices on the next couple of floors and office supplies on the top three.

It fronted on Arch Street, curved around to Franklin and was joined by a fire wall to a similar structure on that side.

A small alley to the left of the building provided a fire break on the left hand side but there was no access to the rear of the building, which closed off one method of attack.

He could see heavy clouds of smoke and sparks rising dramatically above the buildings that were blocking his view as his car turned into Franklin Street and sped toward the scene.

The building came into view as he passed Federal Street; he could see the fire was blowing several feet across Franklin Street. It was obvious he would need additional assistance at the scene so he reached for his radio mike, pressed the button and called, "C-6 to Fire Alarm, strike second alarm, Box 1443, Chief Simpson."

"Yessir, second alarm on the box. Please be advised the Aerial Tower is not available, engaged at an attempted suicide."

Billy realized this would eliminate one of his best tactical weapons at the scene as he alighted from the car on arrival.

The fire was also blowing across the much narrower Arch Street and exposing St. Anthony's Shrine on the opposite side.

His immediate evaluation was to direct the use of a hose stream to cut off the possible extension to the church and to then have several heavy stream appliances set up to try to drive the fire back into the building.

There was so much fire blowing out throughout the two floors that he realized it would be impossible to raise his aerial ladders through the flames on Franklin Street so his ability to provide overhead roof ventilation was restricted.

As he turned to start giving appropriate orders from his size-up of the situation, the officer on Engine 10, whose crew was stretching a large hose line, shouted, "Deputy, I can see three people on the top floor. Lookit," he pointed overhead.

It was true. Three heads were visible, two at one window on the left hand side and one in the middle of the top floor.

This immediately changed the possible attack method. An all out attempt would have to be made to reach them, even though the odds of success were slim. The huge crater in the street, which eliminated the placement of an aerial ladder, also prevented the deployment of the huge, air operated life net that might have worked.

Nope. The only way was an inside attack up the stairway through the front left entrance. "O.K., Engine 10, big line, up the front, try to cut it off. Rescue 1, Engine 7 get on the line with Ten." He wheeled around and shouted, "Engine 4, get a portable gun, right in front here." He directed the ladder truck crews to attempt to gain access from the adjoining building because they couldn't get past the fire on either street, although he was not optimistic about their chances of reaching the occupants by that method.

Billy ordered a third alarm to be struck and directed one incoming engine company to run an additional line up the stairway behind Engine 10, assisted by two extra alarm ladder company crews. Two more engines were ordered to run lines up the stairway on the Franklin Street side while additional companies were to hand carry portable heavy stream appliances into Arch Street and set them up for an eventual outside attack.

Had there been no one trapped, it was an obvious outside job because of the amount of overlapping fire on both floors and because of the contents, age and construction of the building, but the situation required every attempt to be made to get the people, even though the dangers to the fire fighting forces could be considered extreme.

Engine 10's line was extended up the winding staircase, floor by floor, with the crews spaced to keep passing it up.

Lieutenant Morrow, the officer in charge of Rescue 1, along with Nellie and Porky moved upward in advance of the approaching hose line, hoping to be able to bypass the fire on the two upper floors and reach the victims on the sixth. Because the ladder companies couldn't open the roof, the smoke and heat banked down and enveloped the three men. They slipped on the facepieces of their breathing apparatus and kept going.

When they reached the third floor it was obvious they couldn't get past the fire because it had burned through the fourth floor entrance door and was attacking the stairway, so they descended to help Engine 10 get into position.

An identical situation was developing on the Franklin Street stairway; no way past the rapidly extending fire.

Under the SOPs, the use of heavy stream appliances is discouraged whenever occupants or fire fighters are in a fire building. The reasons for this caution include the fact that the powerful streams, while attacking the fire, can also drive it further into untouched areas of the building before gaining control. The actual volume and force of the water under high pressure can also sometimes damage parts of the involved building and, depending on its construction, render it unsafe, with the possibility of collapse becoming a serious consideration.

However, while Billy was aware of these dangers, he could observe that it would be sometime before the hose lines advancing up the stairways could possibly be effective. He sent his aide up Ten's stairway and radioed the district chief who was operating on Franklin Street and advised them both to make everyone aware he was going to try to protect the victims by using heavy streams and to be alert for orders to get back down if it became necessary.

The victims were waving and yelling and gasping from the smoke that was pushing out around them. Billy had a spotlight directed at them to let them know they could be seen and he kept shouting to them to hang on.

When the water arrived for one of the portable heavy stream devices, he directed the officer to hit the fire just under the victims. He told the second unit that received water to start hitting the windows in the sixth floor, away from the victims, in order to break the glass and relieve the pressure of the smoke that was building up rapidly on the floor. He knew that if the floor wasn't vented, it may ignite all at once and certainly kill the occupants. His orders could also cause enough air to intensify the fire, but he had to take the chance.

As his aerial ladder was being raised to the roof of the adjoining building on Franklin Street, Spider was donning his breathing apparatus and slinging his gasoline-powered saw over his shoulder. He jumped up onto turntable of the truck and started climbing rapidly upward towards the top of the building some eighty feet above him.

He swung over the parapet of the building and dropped onto the roof, then moved rapidly across the surface to the fire wall that separated this structure from the fire building. He climbed up and looked downward. It was about a ten foot drop. He realized that if he jumped down, he couldn't get back up. Yeah, but there's people down there. Without hesitation, he swung his legs over, hung by his hands and dropped.

He called the captain on his roof radio and told him they needed to bring a short ladder over the aerial to gain access to the roof, then he headed for the skylight over the Franklin Street stairway. He pulled his axe from his belt and smashed the heavy glass panels as rapidly as he could. He was pleased to see heavy smoke, punctuated by sparks and brands, shoot upward past his face.

Next he moved as rapidly as he could across the roof, hoping the fire wasn't directly under him. He tried to determine if the roof had any weak spots but he couldn't feel any sags with his feet and kept going. He bypassed the elevator penthouse and headed for the other stairway. The penthouse door was locked from the inside and he tried to force it open with his axe but it wouldn't pop.

The smoke was starting to surround him, but he knew he had to keep trying. He dropped to his knees, swung the power saw off his shoulder and pulled on the starter cord. It caught on the first pull as he knew it would because he tested it every tour of duty he worked.

He rose to his feet and made two horizontal cuts above and below the spot he felt the inside hasp and lock would be. One vertical swipe joined the two lines and he then punched out the metal with the peen of his axe.

The door burst outward from the force of the heat and smoke built up behind it and huge tongues of flame swept upward.

Engine 10's line was now almost up to the top of the fourth floor stairway landing and the officer pressed his mike and directed his pump operator to start the water and fill the line.

As the air escaped from the empty hose, he told his crew they had to try to drive the fire back through the doorway and kill the flames in the stairway so the Rescue 1 crew could attempt to continue upward. The initial burst of water succeeded in cooling off the landing and Lieutenant Morrow and his crew sped past as Engine 10 first hit the fire above them on the stairway and, as it diminished, swung around and pushed the fire back into the fourth floor, trying to penetrate down the corridor.

The second line Billy had sent into the stairway with Engine 7 followed the rescue company up towards the next landing, the officer requesting water as they continued the stretch.

On the roof, Spider could hear the sound of water hitting the fire somewhere down the stairway, but he could also hear the people screaming on the floor below him and he knew he would have to try to get to them. He figured the rest of his company was coming but it would take awhile and they could be too late.

The initial burst of fire out of the doorway had now turned to dense smoke; he put on his mask facepiece, turned away from the door opening, and began descending backwards, step by step, down the stairway.

The heat was intense, but he knew it was only a short distance down to the sixth floor landing. He moved along the hallway towards the sound of the voices and burst into the second door he came to. He could see two figures leaning out the window and he managed to grab both of them by the belts on their pants and pull them inside. He pulled off his facepiece and shouted, "Come on", choking as he inhaled the smoke. He clamped his facepiece on the guy who looked the worst, told the other guy to grab his belt and ran as fast as he could to the opening at the stairway.

He told them both to get up on the roof and headed back in towards the sound of the other voice he could still hear.

This time it was even more difficult. He could see fire coming up the stairway and entering the floor at the opposite end of the building. He knew he had only one shot left.

He kept kicking in doors, trying to spot the victim. After two fruitless attempts, he was able to enter a third room he reached and grabbed the last occupant. They both staggered back to the stairway, and Spider pushed him up ahead until they both collapsed on the roof.

The captain and the rest of his crew were just descending the short ladder Spider had requested and they rushed over to offer their assistance. Billy had directed another ladder company to take rappelling ropes and tools to the adjoining roof in a desperate attempt to try to reach the victims if all else failed, and they were just now arriving at the top of the fire wall with the equipment that now would be unnecessary.

The fire continued to spread across the sixth floor and started pushing out both the penthouse that Spider had entered and the skylight on the Franklin Street side. It even began to show at the elevator shaft which the rest of the crew had opened.

After Billy was notified that the occupants had been removed and were being transferred to the roof of the adjoining building, he ordered the inside attack lines to be abandoned, directed all fire personnel to leave the building rapidly and commenced setting up ladder pipes and other heavy stream equipment to use the attack he would have preferred on arrival if the building had been unoccupied.

The aerial tower had completed its other mission and arrived at the scene where it would play an important role in knocking down the heavily involved top three floors from the accessible side of the building.

Of course, it was possible the lines in the stairways could have controlled the fire successfully, but the same possibilities of structural collapse still existed; prudence influenced his reversion to the safer outside approach to protect the operating force.

The battle consumed a couple of more hours until the heavy streams penetrated all of the concealed spaces and knocked down the fire. It was then possible to declare the incident under control and begin bringing in additional fire companies. Their duties would be to relieve the fire fighters at the scene and start the overhauling process that would continue until final extinguishment was accomplished, probably during the next day.

Billy ordered an additional district chief to the scene to assume command of the fire detail companies, and he and the regular chief of the district were finally able to leave the fire. The district chiefs would control the remainder of the tasks to be performed; Billy would not return to the location unless requested. Details of the investigation by the Arson Squad, the cause of the fire, condition of the occupants, why they were in the building and other particulars would all reach his desk in due time, but basically, his job was done.

Yeah, he thought, that's what's nice about the deputy's job. Go there, put it out and then dump it.

By the time he arrived back in quarters, the three companies had been there for awhile so they had been able to repack the hose on Engine 10 and get everyone back in service. It was about 4 a.m. and most of them were in the kitchen having coffee.

Billy crossed the floor to join them and as he approached he could hear a full bloom argument in progress.

Nellie was standing with his hands on his hips, shouting down at Eddie, who was sitting at the table clasping his coffee cup in both hands.

"Whaddya think you are, some kind of a fuckin' hero? What a showoff. You're right up the deputy's ass. That was the worst grandstanding show I ever saw." He looked over to Porky, "Right pal? We'd've picked off them guys like nothin' and knocked the fire down easy if you hadn't got in the act."

Billy leaned against the doorjamb and folded his arms so he cold watch the show.

For once Eddie didn't bite. He felt so great because he had got those guys that he wasn't going to let Nellie get to him. He'd been in on several rescues in the past but this was one time he was sure those guys would have died if he hadn't got to them.

Nellie kept up the harangue but for once, nobody else joined in. Finally, when he saw he wasn't getting much of response from Eddie, he turned once again to Porky and said, "Hey pal, ain't I right? What about this stiff?"

Porky, who could see the deputy standing in the doorway out of Nellie's view, replied, "Nellie, you're an asshole. My pal Eddie not only saved those guys, he saved me and you. I was watchin' you in that stairway and you were shittin' your pants—just like me. When they said to get out, you beat everyone down the stairs. If it wasn't for my pal, Eddie and my very good friend, the deputy, we'd a got killed. God bless them both."

For the first time in his career the absolutely unflappable Nellie was speechless, and Spider just smiled, raised his cup to the deputy, nodded and winked.

When Billy returned to his office, he picked up the stack of commendations he was supposed to review and put them back in his box to be studied on his next tour.

I have no idea which guy I'll be recommending for the most meritorious act of last year, he mused, but have I got a candidate for this year.

5

"That wasn't so bad, was it, Jim?" Billy said to the young fire fighter standing in line in front of him.

"No sir, but I'm glad it's over," came the response.

They were both edging forward to the Boston Sparks Canteen truck which was dispensing coffee to the operating force at the multiple alarm, now that it was under control. This unit, staffed by volunteers, came to all major fires, not only in the city but in the surrounding communities, to supplement the Red Cross and Salvation Army personnel who provided similar services.

Billy had met many of the sparks or fire buffs in the area during his career and was still amazed at the diverse types of people who not only chased fires but enjoyed the whole concept of the fire service. Most of the buffs belonged to one or more of the three major associations in the metropolitan Boston area. Billy, along with the other deputies, was occasionally invited to speak to any one of the groups after some major incident he had commanded.

The first time he was a speaker, he was startled by the somewhat military conduct of the meeting. They had roll call, which was certainly more professionally handled than any he had conducted when he was a captain. Absentees were duly noted and those who had missed a few consecutive meetings would receive warning citations. General orders were read, lists of fires since last month's meeting were entered into the record, and news about changes in various departments was noted.

Billy remembered learning at one session that Boston was getting some new ladder trucks, and at another he got a rumor about who the new chief of department would be that proved to be accurate.

While Billy was waiting for the business meeting to be concluded, he glanced around at the audience. A few jakes were in the crowd, guys who never seemed to get enough of the job. But there were also priests, lawyers, doctors, accountants and other professional men along with many people from the blue collar sector.

When Billy finished speaking, there was a question and answer period. He realized from their knowledge of the incident he had discussed and the intelligence of the queries from the audience that these guys knew as much or more about what had transpired at the scene than he did. He enjoyed answering whatever he could but made a note to be fully prepared the next time. Saying, "Gee, I don't know," as much as he did on his first visit was not great for the reputation of the deputy fire chief business.

But as he drove home from that first outing, he thought, yeah, they're impressive, but they are not our best fans.

It was a little disquieting that the people most attracted to the fire service and who loved fire fighters the most were mentally handicapped kids and adults. Disquieting because these folks also seemed to possess considerable knowledge about the fire service, which forced Billy to wonder if perhaps it didn't take a lot of smarts to advance through the ranks. After all, if these less fortunate folks seemed to have no difficulty in learning the business—how the hell tough could it be!

The guy everyone called "Johnnie Dirt" was a prime example. From the time Billy was appointed until Johnnie's recent death, the man was a fixture in the department. But a movable fixture, if there is such a thing.

He would show up at a different firehouse every day and stay at the patrol desk, reading magazines and looking at the assignment cards. No one ever bothered him because he never interfered with anything. Oh, once in awhile, in the summer, if it was real hot, you could get a pretty good whiff of his unwashed body, which was the reason for his nickname, but, hey, just turn up the A.C. Dirt's o.k.

Of course one reason nobody minded having him around was his knowledge of the assignment or "running cards" as they are called. Billy had once seen a TV program about people who are called "idiot savants." He looked up the description of the phrase and saw that an idiot is a feeble-minded person with the mental capacity of a three year old child. A savant is a person with detailed knowledge in some specialized field, such as science or literature. One of the people shown on the program could play an entire symphony on a piano after only hearing it once; another could do any complicated mathematical equations instantaneously; a third could tell you what day of the week any date in history was.

Billy figured Dirt was a kind of idiot savant because of the complications associated with the running cards.

There are about two thousand fire alarm boxes located around the city of Boston. Most of the boxes are on street corners and have a red light on top of them so they can be seen at night. In recent years, these devices have been eliminated in some cities as a means of saving money—the theory being that everyone has phones now, so who needs them? But, in cities like New York, Boston and other major population centers, the alarm boxes are retained for a few excellent reasons. First of all, not everyone has a phone, certainly none of the homeless that are everywhere. Not everyone speaks English, and few fire departments have multi-lingual dispatchers.

One thing is certain, however: if someone pulls that red box on the corner, some firemen are going to show up in a few minutes and they can help you, or get you the help you need, whatever it is.

Each one of these boxes has a numbered wheel on it and is part of an entire system of closed, all metallic type, series circuits. When someone pulls the lever on the box, the wheel turns and each spoke on the wheel breaks the circuit, transmitting the complete number to the central receiving and dispatching station called Fire Alarm Headquarters. The guy who receives the alarm looks up the location and then sends the nearest fire fighters.

Simple, huh? Yes it is. The first fire alarm system in the world was put in service in Boston in 1852. Since then there have been some changes, including the use of computers and word processors and other sophisticated technology, but the basic mission is the same: pull the box and firemen show up.

In each firehouse there is a narrow metal box about three feet long. The box contains the numbers and locations of every one of those street fire alarm boxes in the city, each on its own individual card that is a foot wide and eight inches long. The card lists every movement of fire apparatus that is necessary to handle any alarm sounded for that box location, from a one alarm response, up through the entire nine alarm complement that is the maximum the department uses.

Between the companies dispatched to the fire and those who are required to move to covering assignments, including other fire departments who come into the city under the Mutual Aid Plan, the number of items on each card is enormous.

Of course, each fire station has a list directly in front of the member on watch that lists the first alarm responses and locations for the fire companies in the station. But if no one in the house is assigned to a transmitted first alarm, the member at the desk pulls out the card and checks to see how it affects his station if it becomes a multiple alarm.

To expect any fire fighter to learn all of those cards and all of the movements listed would be ridiculous; no one ever even attempts it because it's not required in the job description. But Johnnie Dirt knew them all, every movement, every change— everything. He was amazing.

Guys would constantly pull out cards during his visits and shout a number to him and he'd rattle it off like a machine—First alarm: Engines 5, 9, 56, Ladders 2, 21, Rescue 1, District Chief 1. Engine 8 cover Engine 5, Ladder 1 cover Ladder 2, Chelsea cover Engine 56. He would continue through the entire assignment and when he was finished he'd wait anxiously until the guy with the card would say, "Dirt, you did it again," and he'd give a small grin and return to his magazine.

There are thirty-three firehouses in the city containing fifty-eight fire companies. Since fire fighters work a four platoon system, the chances of Dirt visiting when you were working was 1 in 132 so no one really grew tired of seeing him, because it wasn't often.

Besides, if you were on watch, whenever an alarm came in you didn't respond to on the first alarm, you just turned to Dirt and said, "Whadda we do on that one, John?"

His reply would be immediate, "Cover Engine 2 on second alarm, go to the fire on third...."

Billy reached up to the counter of the canteen truck and grabbed the styrofoam cup of coffee. These guys came to so many fires he didn't even have to tell them what to put in it, they knew.

Bob Sangster had the assignment this night and he said, "Nice job, Deputy. Thought it might jump across the street at first."

"Yeah, a chance it could've. Bob, I want you to meet Jim Travers. He just got out of drill school. This is his first tour of duty."

"Glad to meet you, Jim. Nice way to start your career. If you're lucky, we'll see you later on tonight."

As they walked away, Billy shook his head. Hope we don't see him, he thought. Those guys never get enough. Oh, well, let the kid learn for himself.

Shortly before they had responded to this fire, Jim's officer had introduced him to Billy and they had a brief talk about the job. The kid was very enthusiastic about being a fire fighter but, like everyone else before him, was nervous about how he'd perform at a fire and was very anxious to get the first one behind him.

When the alarm struck for the fire, Billy was immediately aware of the potential for a major incident. It was in an area of the North End that had many vacant buildings, several of them in the same blocks with densely populated tenements. The vacancies were created when the food distribution businesses that had occupied them had moved to new locations in the South Bay and across the city line to Chelsea.

In the past year there had been a half dozen multiple alarms in these old, mill constructed structures. The fires were very intense but since the buildings were designed for heavy storage and had huge wooden carrying beams and supports, they still remained relatively intact.

Billy's route to the area was on the road that passes under the elevated Central Artery so he couldn't see the tops of the buildings in the district initially, but Fire Alarm announced they were receiving several calls for a fire, which was always a clear indication that this was not a minor incident.

When his aide swung the car out onto Atlantic Avenue, the view was much better; Billy could see heavy smoke pushing over the tops of the buildings that were between him and Commercial Street, the announced location of the fire.

On Cross Street, speeding towards the intersection, Billy spotted Big Joe standing on the corner, waving furiously with his arms. Big Joe was another one of the fire fighters' top fans. Oh, he'd never be mistaken for a savant, like Dirt, but he had his own standards, which never varied.

He was a very powerful six footer, about forty years old, balding, with a broad chest and hairy, muscular arms. He would show up at the quarters of Engine 8 and Ladder 1 on Hanover Street every morning at 0800. He'd nod at the fire fighters who were gathered in the kitchen, pass by to the broom closet, and pick up his personal push broom, which was properly labeled, "Big Joe the Broom," which was actually his full title. He would then go upstairs and begin to sweep the entire firehouse, passing through the officers' rooms, the bunk room, locker room and shower room. He would also empty all the waste baskets and then continue down the stairway to the apparatus floor.

By the time he completed gathering all of the accumulated debris from the just ended night tour, the fire fighters were starting to stir from the kitchen, from which, of course, none of them would have departed until Big Joe finished his chores, which were really their chores.

"It's ready, Big Joe," one of them would yell as they could see he had finished, and then he'd enter the kitchen, say "Good morning," in his gentle, slurring voice and sit at the table in front of the huge cup of steaming cocoa with the two lemon and strawberry Danish on the plate beside it.

They'd invariably ask him how his job was going and he'd tell them it was fine. If the Bruins or the Celtics were in town, someone would kid him about how lousy they were this year, but he'd just smile and finish his snack.

The firehouse was located in the heart of the North End, just a few blocks from the Boston Garden, which is home to both of the pro teams. During the season, Big Joe performed similar sweeping duties in the corridors of the ancient sports arena and got to know all of the players and maintenance workers.

His biggest task, however, was to try to stay ahead of the mountains of trash that accumulated at the Haymarket, which is located across the street from the Sumner and Callahan tunnels, two traffic tubes that pass under Boston Harbor, connecting the downtown area to the East Boston district and Logan Airport.

Haymarket has been an outdoor market where fresh fruit and vegetables have been sold by pushcart vendors for over a hundred years. It's open every day but Sunday and does a fairly brisk business daily because of its low prices. It is considered quaint by the tourists, and the mostly Italian vendors who sell their wares do nothing to discourage this characterization. They can be as charming and forceful as their counterparts on San Francisco's Fisherman's Wharf, and equally adept at selling the visitors more than they intended to purchase. There is a constant din of shouting and screaming that only ends when the last visitor leaves.

Friday and Saturday are the two big days, however, and by Saturday night there are enough empty boxes and piles of rubbish to discourage the most dedicated public works crew, which is responsible for the cleanup.

Big Joe would complete his chores for the night crew at the firehouse. These tasks were identical to what he did each morning, and his reward was to participate in the evening meal, accompanied of course, by his huge cup of cocoa. He would then meander down Hanover, wander down Richmond Street to Commercial, up Cross Street, under the Central Artery and into the Quincy Market. He loved to pass through the crowds that were always present as he killed time, waiting for the nearby Haymarket to close so he could go to work.

Even though he loved the firemen and the athletes at the Garden, he had no interest in or understanding of fire fighting or sports. If he had been asked to select a profession from all of those he associated with, he would have immediately chosen public works, because, let's face it, Big Joe loved to sweep. The public works crews, certainly as wise as the fire fighters or Garden maintenance men, provided him with the best tool of all for his tasks. It was a stiff, straw broom, ideally suited for pushing dirt from the cracks of the cobblestoned streets. They also had emblazoned his name and title in multi-colors along the handle with four stars to indicate his rank—"Big Joe, Broom General." He liked that.

Billy rolled down the window of the car as they neared the Broom and said, "Whaddya got, Big Joe?"

"Deputy," he shouted, "you need a second alarm."

Billy alighted from the car, reached the corner and looked down Commercial Street. He could now see the fire that had been blocked from his view by the other buildings. The three top floors of the building were fully involved, with heavy smoke and flames showing from every window.

He turned to Big Joe and said, "Big Joe, I think you're right." He yelled to his aide, who was parking the car, "Tell Fire Alarm, second alarm, box 1251."

The intensity of the fire and the fact that this building had been the site of a couple of other serious fires, combined with the fact that there was no apparent life hazard in the vacant structure, precluded the possibility of an interior attack. The companies already at the scene were setting up for an outside attack and Billy continued this strategy.

His main concern now became the possibility of extension to the adjoining structures and to other buildings in the rear. The massive fire walls that separated the old warehouses from each other reduced the potential for fire spread to a minimum, and steel shutters on the windows in the rear buildings eliminated the danger out back.

For the deputy this incident became a freebie as far as the normal decisions that had to be made at every fire were concerned. He and the district chief used it almost as a training exercise by utilizing all of the massive heavy stream punch the department possessed, with little or no danger to the operating force.

As Billy entered his car to return to quarters, his aide observed that the new guy who was just appointed seemed to be pretty sharp and was a good worker. He had the makings of a "good jake," an accolade not easily come by.

"Yeah, well, maybe you're right. It's a little too early to tell," Billy replied. "I sure hope he's not too smart though," he added.

"Whaddya mean?"

"Well, if he ever finds out who told me to strike a second alarm, he'll know Big Joe the Broom's as smart as I am and he'll wanna get promoted right away."

"Maybe you're right, Deputy. I'm, just glad he'll never meet Johnnie Dirt, or he'd find out he was smarter than all the rest of us."

6

O.K., Billy thought, I'm gonna spend the whole afternoon reading these cases. The Board of Merit meeting's coming up and I've gotta review them all or get outsmarted when the vote comes for awards. I know one thing, there's gonna be a big battle for the top medal. Yeah, and I'll be right in the thick of it.

More often than not, the deputies who make the recommendations for the commendations are not actually at the scene when the act takes place. This is because the rescues that are made usually take place early in the fire, before the deputy arrives in response to a multiple alarm or call for additional assistance.

The incident with Spider the other night was one of the exceptions; Billy was at the scene when the events transpired.

And he was also there last year for the one he'd be recommending at this year's meeting.

All the deputies were in agreement that to be considered for a medal, the determination of "extreme personal risk" would involve a situation where the member who attempted the rescue had performed the act knowing there was no way of determining if he would survive the actions he was taking at the time.

This usually involved going beyond a fire with the full realization that immediate action was necessary to save a life and with the complete understanding that no protection was available.

Spider's act the other night would certainly fall into the proper category. He had jumped down onto the roof, with no way of getting back up and with two fully involved floors underneath him. If things hadn't gone as well as they had, he'd have qualified for the Medal of Valor instead of one of the ones given to the living.

Yeah, but he's not up 'till next year. Concentrate on those being considered this time.

The act he had witnessed the previous year involved two members of Ladder 15, located in the Back Bay, near the Prudential Center.

Billy had just left a fire in that district and was in the general area when an alarm was struck for a fire on Commonwealth Avenue, in an apartment complex near Mass Ave.

It was around 0200 hours and Fire Alarm announced the calls being received indicated many occupants were still "in the building." This was a recent change in phraseology. In the past, radio announcements that "people are trapped" were often made and in most cases, this was incorrect or an exaggeration of the circumstances. So the deputies, in their questionable wisdom, had recommended a less dramatic pronouncement to avoid the adrenaline build-ups the doctors said were increasing the stress attacks on the responders.

Billy had voted for the change but was puzzled when he got the same reaction from "in the building" that he had gotten from "trapped." Maybe we ain't always brilliant, he reflected.

Engine 33 was first at the scene and the officer ordered a second alarm, reporting people hanging out the windows of a six story apartment house.

Billy acknowledged receipt of the information and that he was responding as his aide, Joe, swung the car up Dartmouth Street from Boylston and moved towards Comm. Ave.

The district chief of four, on his arrival, ordered a third alarm and requested two extra ladder companies in addition to those already committed on the multiple alarms.

When Billy reported off at the fire a couple of minutes later, he could see Ladder 15's aerial was just being placed at a top floor window where three people were frantically waving as heavy smoke was engulfing them.

Fire was pushing out all of the front windows on the fourth floor and appeared to be extending rapidly. There was no access to the building from either the left or right side because both adjoining buildings were only four stories high and windowless walls ran the length of the involved building in the two floors extended above the exposures.

Huge elm trees to the left and right of the fire building prevented the placement of additional aerials in front.

Billy knew that in this area buildings that were six stories above the street in the front were seven or eight stories high in the rear because of the way the terrain dropped off. He directed the district chief to assume command of the rear of the building and sent Joe up the front stairway to attempt to determine if anyone else was trapped.

He could see Engine 33's 2-1/2" line led up the stairs but it wasn't filled with water yet, so it wasn't in position and wasn't affecting the fire. He ordered the next arriving engine company at the front to stretch an additional big line up the same stairway to try to cut off the fire.

The district chief reported the building was seven stories in the rear. He also said there were occupants at the rear windows of all three floors above the fire and he had two aerials in the alley being raised to try to pick them off. Fire was showing on the same floor as the front and appeared to be extending upward.

The next call Billy received was from Joe, his aide, and he reported the lieutenant of Ladder 15 and one of his crew had gone up the front stairway, past the fire on the fourth floor because they had been notified two women were in a fifth floor apartment towards the middle of the building.

He could see Thirty-three's line starting to swell with the water being pumped through it and he hoped they'd be able to hit the fire hard to prevent its extension up the stairs.

He ordered a fourth alarm and as he finished his message he heard the district chief call, "Urgent," a message that stopped all other radio traffic. "We have two women trapped on the sixth floor—fifth from the front. They are visible from the courtyard that faces inward. There's no way to get them from the court because no ground ladder will reach them. I'm trying to get a life net down the stairway into the court, but I think they're both unconscious."

"O.K.," Billy replied, "how about a rope from the roof?"

"Can't get to the roof yet. The trucks are bringing down people over the ladders. I got two lines going up the back stairway, but there's heavy fire between them and the victims."

Billy ordered a ladder company to get to the roof of the four story building on his left, taking a ground ladder with them. He told the officer in charge of the unit, "Lissen, the roof isn't open yet, so try to get it as quick as you can. I'm sending a rappelling team up from the rescue company to try to get these people so stay with them and give them a hand. But be careful, this fire's really taking off. Make sure you can get back off the roof."

Up on the fourth floor, Engine 33's line hit the fire in the stairway leading upward, succeeding in cutting it off and preventing further extension into the fifth floor. The additional line that reached them on the landing was operated by Engine 37's crew; they managed to darken the fire in the front rooms and then turn and crawl down the long hallway leading to the rear, driving back the flames and moving deeper into the building.

Joe raced ahead of Thirty-three up the stairway, realizing the two members of Ladder 15 hadn't been heard from. The intense heat flattened him to the floor as he reached the level and he kept shouting, but there was no reply.

The lines coming up the back succeeded in knocking down the fire in the stairway and one unit entered the same level as Thirty-seven and worked towards the front.

The second company continued up to the floor where the women had been seen, and the district chief, who had joined them, said, "O.K. now. Move along the corridor. Kick in every door. There's a couple of bodies up here somewhere and we gotta find them."

He didn't know it but his search would be fruitless.

At the front, Joe and Thirty-three's crew could hear glass breaking over their head and they realized someone was getting the room open. The change was immediate. The tremendous heat was reduced and the visibility improved dramatically.

They thought they could hear sounds coming from the corridor leading to the rear and they crept forward. They stumbled into the officer of Ladder 15 who had one woman's arms locked around his neck with her body draped along his back as he crawled towards them. Right behind him was a fire fighter with the second victim in an identical grasp.

Joe and Thirty-three's crew were able to grab all four people and get them over to the stairway, where other companies Billy had sent up the front joined in removing them.

Joe managed to relay the information to Billy who had requested several paramedic crews to respond.

The company coming from the back was puzzled that they failed to find the victims and the district chief was astounded when he learned someone had gotten above the fire to get them.

Once they were dispatched to the hospital, the attack on the fire moved ahead rapidly, particularly with the additional personnel that had arrived in response to the fourth alarm.

The two women survived the incident and recovered completely, although they were hospitalized for a week. Both the lieutenant and the fire fighter were burned on the hands, ears and neck due to passing by the fire to reach the upper floor. They both suffered from exhaustion and smoke inhalation also. They had clamped their mask facepieces on the women when they dragged them out of the window and compromised their own air supply while doing so.

The officer had also broken one hand, although when Billy interviewed him, he couldn't remember how it happened.

Both members were released from the hospital after a few days, but their recovery from the burns kept them off duty for two months.

Billy was recommending the lieutenant for the most meritorious award, because of his more severe injuries, with the fire fighter recommended for one of the other extreme risk medals.

Billy shuffled the stack of reports aimlessly in front of him. Now I gotta read all this other stuff and see what all those other deputies are putin' in. They'd better have some miracles if they expect to beat my guys. Well, at least Beano's gone. Boy, would he be on my back for the story I'm gonna tell.

Come to think of it, with these two fellas this year and the Spider next year, that Redhead will be calling me "Son of Beano."

7

Billy stepped out of the shower, grabbed his big towel and rubbed himself vigorously. It felt good. He finally felt warm again. He had stood under the stream of hot water until the chill finally got out of his bones.

It had been a long afternoon but at least he'd be home tonight. His partner, Jerry, had relieved him at the fire, but he shouldn't have to stay much longer; everything looked good when Billy had turned over command to him a while ago. Just a matter of setting up a fire detail, having the companies pick up all their gear and return to quarters. Oh, there'd be units at the scene all night, but the department policy of changing the guard every three hours when it was extremely cold insured no one would be overexposed to the horrendous weather.

Once again, Billy had postponed his review of the high commendations. He had completed all of his regular paperwork earlier than usual this morning just so he could spend the entire afternoon conscientiously reading the stack of reports. If you went over them all thoroughly, especially when you had guys of your own you were pushing for, you had more arguments to use in the stories of the other deputies who were pleading a case for their members.

But, no luck today. Have to try again tomorrow night.

Yeah, but if he didn't get to them then, they'd have to wait until he got back. He and his three golfing partners were heading for Bermuda, along with the wives, for a week beginning next Saturday. What a deal they had! It was a package including plane, hotel, meals and golf. This would be Billy's first visit as it would be for Ron and Larry Peterson.

But Nifty Richards had been there many times and had a connection with the travel agent.

Nifty got his nickname from his golfing ability. He was one of the best players on the job and had a three handicap, which was about fifteen strokes better than Billy and the two brothers.

They had reservations at the Belmont, which had its own course. It should be a great week. Hey, anything was better than Boston in the winter, he thought.

The fire he just left was a perfect example of why any excuse for leaving town should receive serious consideration during January and February.

Shortly after he began reading, Box 6166 was sounded over the alarm system. This location was in District One, the East Boston section of the city and part of Billy's responsibility as division commander. It was not part of his first alarm response assignment but if the fire required extra assistance, Billy would then go and assume command.

Many boxes are struck for fires in the course of a tour of duty; if the deputy doesn't respond on the first alarm, he only displays mild interest until the first report is given either by Fire Alarm or by the first personnel arriving at the scene.

If it's not in his division, he has no interest in it and wipes it out of his mind. Let the other guy think about it.

But today, with the bitter cold weather, the district the alarm came from and the fact there was a brand new acting district chief working, Billy paid closer attention.

District One has been the scene of many serious and even disastrous fires in the history of the department. It has so many three deckers wedged into its residential areas that they look like a continuous unbroken chain of buildings, although they are actually sub-divided by many small and narrow streets.

The streets have great names. Whoever laid out the town put a little thought into it. None of the 1st, 2nd, 3rd or A, B, C shit like in Southie. They say a jake working over in South Boston only has to be able to count up to nine and know the alphabet from A to P to find his way around.

Naw. Eastie sounds pretty classy: London, Paris, Bremen, Frankfort, Berlin, Chelsea and other major European cities identify some area streets. Lexington, Trenton, Saratoga, Bennington, Princeton and other famous American Revolutionary War sites constitute others. Birds get into the act with East Eagle, Condor and others.

Yeah, they even got a street that circles the whole town that's called Border Street. Makes sense.

But great names do nothing to reduce the hazards over there. These rows of wood frame structures are often lacking fire walls between each occupancy, and as many as eight are frequently interconnected in one block. Since each separate unit contains three floors with seventeen rooms, as many as twenty-five families may occupy the section.

Another problem, which also exists in some other parts of the city, are the electrical wires that crisscross the streets and hamper normal ladder operations. Access to the roofs to perform vertical ventilation has to be done by hand raising forty or fifty foot ground ladders because the aerial ladders can't be elevated through these overhead obstructions.

Shortly after the box stopped its toll of numbers, Fire Alarm announced over the radio, "Receiving calls for a fire at Brooks and Morris Streets." Yeah, thought Billy, the heart of the tenements.

His concern with the acting district chief didn't stem from any lack of confidence in the guy. Hell, he didn't even know him.

Previously, when a chief was absent for any reason, the senior captain in the district would assume his duties. Although the assignment was unpaid, it insured that an officer familiar with the district would be directing operations at fires. However, the latest city-union contract had changed that procedure dramatically. The fill-in position was now funded so that the member assuming the job would receive the pay associated with the permanent rank. The contract also required that the member to take the job must come from the top of the current Civil Service promotional list.

Billy agreed wholeheartedly with the concept. First of all, it meant the members who studied hardest for promotion and beat the competition in the exam would be compensated for their success. But, more importantly, they would be detailed around the whole city, covering absences in all of the districts, thus gaining a wide range of experiences that had never been available to young chiefs in the past. Yeah, they might start off in a new place not knowing anything about the area, but the fact that they had studied so hard usually indicated they would learn rapidly.

It was also great to see the city finally had to pay for all the free work they used to get in the past. Many times, chiefs or company officers would be off sick or injured for months at a time and the fill-ins were for nothing.

But, that didn't mean you weren't a little concerned when a new guy was in charge. Oh, the fire companies are very experienced, but the head guy has to make the decisions.

This particular man was named Roger Stanley and his permanent assignment was as captain of a ladder company out in the Roslindale section, which was not in Billy's division and where the hazards were completely different from Eastie. Today was his first day in the assignment and Billy hadn't got to meet him yet although he had talked to him by phone in the morning.

The next message over the radio was, "Car One to Fire Alarm. We have a fire in a three decker, corner of Morris and Brooks. Heavy smoke showing." Fire Alarm acknowledged the message.

Billy thought, hope he don't fool around. He didn't. Next message was, "Car One. Strike second alarm, orders of Acting District Chief Stanley." Billy left the room and descended to the garage where he could hear the wall speaker rattling. "We have just had an explosion in the rear of the building, strike third alarm."

As Joe, his aide, drove the car out of the garage and headed towards the expressway, Billy thought, it's great when a guy knows enough to call for help. Nothing pissed him off more than a chief who would have a serious fire in progress and allowed his ego to make him think he could "handle this without help from those other guys." Yeah, while the fire fighters worked their asses off trying to contain the fire. The chiefs who regularly worked with Billy were well aware of his views and didn't waste any time getting additional assistance. That was preferable to getting your hide ripped off in his tirade.

The philosophy of "send them back if ya don't need them" is much more intelligent than "Jeez, they're startin' to drop like flies. Maybe I better get some more help now."

But Billy didn't have that concern now as the car rose up the ramp onto the artery leading to the Callahan tunnel.

By looking across the harbor, he could see huge clouds of smoke pushing up to the low, overcast skies and he could hear the radio blaring as Car One ordered a fourth alarm.

The car raced down the ramp and into the tunnel where the traffic was fortunately rather light for this time of day.

Smoke formed a haze over the entire district as they turned off at the exit and crossed over to Chelsea Street. They could see red lights flashing several blocks ahead and it was obvious from the increasing density of the smoke as they approached, punctuated by sparks and brands blowing towards them, that there must be more than one building involved.

It flashed briefly through Billy's mind that he seldom responded to a fire in this district that didn't involve more than one building, so what else is new?

As they turned off Chelsea Street he had a fairly good chance to observe the extent of the fire; it was working its way down Brooks Street towards him. He could see at least three triple deckers were involved on this street, and it was probably extending down Morris Street as well.

He was moving rapidly along towards the intersection when he spied two fire fighters in dress uniform. He knew them both.

"Strangler," he shouted to the taller of the men,

"Yessir?"

"You and Davey get a line in the top floor of that building and let me know if it's in there," he shouted, pointing to the fourth three decker, which had some light smoke pushing out around the upper floor windows.

Billy arrived at the front of the original fire building and was met by the acting chief. "Deputy," he reported, "the fire's moving down both streets and is also going through the backyards along the fences. I'm sending portable guns into the rear to try to cut it off but I don't have anything coming in down the other end," he finished, waving his arm down towards the buildings extending eastward down Morris Street.

"O.K., Roger, I'll get some more help. You take command of the rear and ask for anything you need directly to Fire Alarm."

"C-6 to Fire Alarm."

"Fire Alarm answering."

"Strike fifth and sixth alarms, Box 6166, Chief Simpson."

When he heard the alarms striking over the principal radio channel, he used the separate fire ground channel to have Fire Alarm direct the incoming units and also to provide Car One with anything he requested.

He directed that the aerial tower attempt to maneuver into position from the opposite end of Brooks Street, getting as close to the intersection as possible.

The original fire building and the exposure on the right were fully involved so no interior attack was possible; heavy streams would have to be used to try to kill the tremendous heat build-up that was threatening another row of three deckers directly across the street.

He could hear Roger Stanley requesting more lines in the rear and giving specific instructions about how they should be stretched through alleys and over fences. Hm. Sounds good.

Billy's primary concern, however, was to cut off both ends of the extension and, as additional district chiefs arrived on the extra alarms, he told them his needs via radio and assigned them positions on both streets.

The roads and sidewalks were becoming increasingly icy and Fire Alarm was advising incoming fire companies to proceed with caution while announcing that the temperature was 12 degrees Fahrenheit. Public works crews were being dispatched with salt and sand to try to improve vehicle and foot traffic.

Billy was bent over, one ear blocked by his gloved hand, the other with the remote radio receiver jammed against it, trying to hear the various messages, when he felt a hand on his shoulder. He turned around and was delighted to see that the aerial tower had maneuvered its way down the icy streets and was positioned almost perfectly to operate on the two most heavily involved structures.

The captain who had tapped him said, "Deputy, we got our own feeder connected and we'll have water in a minute. Whaddya want?"

Billy could have hugged him. "Both those buildings, Cap. Hit 'em with all you got."

Once he saw the crew up in the bucket start to operate the powerful stream, Billy was no longer concerned about possible fire spread across the street. However, he ordered seventh and eighth alarms sounded to provide sufficient lines for all of his needs.

He eventually was able to walk along the front of the involved structures and see how far the fire had gone. He was gratified to see the building he had sent the two uniformed fire prevention inspectors into had been saved, although the fire had extended across part of the top floor.

Another line was stretched up the front stairway into this building from one of the extra alarm companies, and it was obvious the fire had been effectively cut off from further extension at this point. It never reached the fifth building on this side.

Similar efforts had been effective on Morris Street, resulting in a successful attack and fire containment. Roger Stanley reported that the spread through the yards had been halted and he was placing hand lines up the rear stairways of all except the two buildings that were fully involved. He was hitting those structures with the small, lightweight portable guns that had been hand-carried into the yards.

The tower was rapidly knocking down the visible fire at their position and hand lines were being effectively moved through the involved floors of all the other buildings from both front and rear entrances.

A total of eight structures were damaged and over twenty families would be homeless in this bitter cold. Billy knew, though, because he had seen it many times in the past, most of those driven out would be taken in by neighbors in this tight-knit, working class Italian neighborhood. For those who couldn't be housed, the Red Cross would find them accommodations.

Now that the incident was under control, Billy issued orders permitting the Red Cross, Salvation Army and Boston Sparks Canteen to open and dispense coffee to the operating force.

He was becoming increasingly cold himself and went over to pick up a container. There were the Strangler and Davey, covered with ice and shivering in their dress uniforms, with ice caked over their low-cut shoes.

"You guys did great. Didja find much fire up there, Strangler?"

"Yessir, we sure did. We ran an inch and three quarters offa Engine 5 and Davey brought a rake with him."

"Yeah," said Davey, "when I drove it up in the ceiling, we could see it movin' right across. Strangler opened the pipe and we were hittin' it but we couldn't hold it."

"We thought we'd have to bail out," said Strangler, "but Engine 22 showed up with a big line and we were able to catch it before it got inta the next building. Jeez, I'm freezin'."

"Yeah, well I'm gonna give you both commendations and I'll tell your boss up the street what a good job you did. I'll also call George up in clothing and get you some new suits."

Billy pulled on his underwear and sat on the bed in his room, putting on his socks and thinking about Strangler and Davey. Both of those guys were excellent fire fighters and both had transferred into the Fire Prevention Division out of necessity. They had been out investigating complaints in the district when they saw the apparatus responding and followed the fire companies to the fire.

Davey had to get a day job because his wife had a debilitating disease that required him to be home every night and prevented him from working the rotating shifts required on a fire company.

Strangler, however, whose real name was Thomas, had to work days so he could be available for his other job as maitre d' of the restaurant at Wonderland Dog Track. This facility is located in Revere, the city adjoining Boston at the Eastie line, and quite handy to get to when his daily department duties were completed.

His nickname came from the fact that he resembled Albert DiSalvo, who was known as the "Boston Strangler" and who had murdered several woman in the Beacon Hill section of the city.

He got life at Cedar Junction in Walpole but eventually, one of the other inmates sent him early to whatever reward awaited him in the next life.

Tom was no murderer but his reputation as a lothario in the department, combined with his prominent nose like Albert's, gave him his name. At first he was upset by the cruelty of the Hoss, who christened him with the title, but in due time he grew to like it and probably wouldn't respond if anyone remembered and called him by the name his mother gave him.

His need for the extra job was prompted by his alimony payments to his wife and support of the gang of kids he had fathered before she got wise to his extra-curricular amorous activities and threw him out on the street.

Besides, his continued pursuit of the ladies was quite expensive. At the restaurant, he cut a dashing figure in his tux when he was seating people with his suave flair; the endless opportunities that were presented to him were more than he could resist.

But God, he was a terrific jake, thought Billy, and he had just proven it again. The line he and Davey had stretched, the 1-3/4", was a gamble with the amount of fire potential in the building, but it was a common sense approach by both men who realized the safer and more effective 2-1/2" line would probably have been too difficult for them to get in position fast enough. Good judgement under the circumstances.

Yeh, and that acting chief did a great job too. Before leaving the scene, Billy had made certain he told him his initial actions and his effective performance throughout the fire had stopped what could easily have become a conflagration.

Billy reflected on how the equipment on the job had changed since he was appointed at the beginning of the fifties. There was no such thing as 1-3/4" in those days. Nope. Just booster and big line. A booster line was a hard rubber 1" hose that could be stretched rapidly but was only effective on small fires such as mattresses, auto fires or rubbish fires.

A big line is a 2-1/2" diameter hose with a 1-1/8" nozzle that is still used as the main inside attack on serious building fires and for many outside operations as well.

Yeah, but in those days, each length weighed over fifty pounds and it was so tough to drag it around. Now, the hose they used weighed half that amount and was much more maneuverable and effective. It didn't have to be dried either. After it was used at a fire, you just packed it back on the apparatus again and it was ready to go. The jakes loved it.

Those lightweight portable guns were also a great new innovation. They certainly had stopped the fire in the rear at the just completed fire.

And the big, light, four inch feeder lines let pumpers supply more hose lines to companies than was ever possible in the past.

The 500 or 750 gallon water tanks on the pumps made the possibility of a strong, immediate attack on the fire a reality. In the old days the system was so complicated, it seemed to Billy he was always laying in a hallway somewhere, waiting for the water as the fire advanced towards him and drove him and his partner back down the stairway.

Hm. What else had changed? The aerial tower jumped right into his mind. Before its invention, the distribution of water to the upper floors of buildings was a haphazard affair involving a lot of guesswork with the use of heavy streams directed from the street along with ladder pipes controlled by guy lines; no one really knew where the hell the water was going but it looked great in the pictures. Now jakes could operate with reasonable safety at heights up to a hundred feet and could actually see where they were putting the water. It was so much more effective and used so much less water that it had become Billy's favorite weapon at big fires.

The tower also had tremendous rescue capabilities if it was at the scene early enough. It was so much easier to get occupants to enter the bucket than to climb onto the rungs of an aerial ladder when they had to be evacuated from the outside.

The aerial ladders were so much better with their all metal construction and hydraulic power. And they reached so much higher, too. When he came on they were all made of wood, spring raised and hand cranked and could reach only eighty-five feet, which usually meant the roof of a six story building. Now, most of them reached 110 feet—some even went up to 135—and the overall strength of their construction allowed them to be used at angles that would have been impossible in the days gone by. Aluminum hand raised ladders were also much more practical than the enormous wooden spars and rungs that had been the standard.

Yep. Pre-connected deck guns, much better hose nozzles, foams and chemical additives as extinguishing agents for flammable liquid fires.

How about the better masks, personal lights, turnout gear, radios and overall better communication systems?

And the tools! Jaws of life, hydraulic forcible entry tools, power saws and resuscitation equipment and medical supplies.

Billy shook his head as he realized he was lost in his daydreams. Don't get too cocky with all of this reverie. The way you're thinkin' you sound like you believe the job is easier. Well, it ain't.

In those days, the equipment was primitive but we had a lot more help on each fire company. As salaries increased over the years, the city managers kept reducing the number of available personnel and they're still doing it today.

There had been three major so-called reorganizations during Billy's career. A reorganization in the fire service is never initiated by the chief who leads the department. It originates at city hall, usually involves some hired gun consultant and always ends up with a reduction in uniformed forces. They frequently cite the improved equipment as the reason for the ability to eliminate jobs, but the truth usually is the table of organization reduction is premature and excessive. The bureaucrats seemed to think fire fighters are getting bigger and stronger like the NFL recruits. The reality is they are getting smaller and weaker due to the influx of many smaller ethnic groups and women fire fighters.

Billy had no quarrel with the latest arrivals. What the hell, our folks weren't allowed on the job by the old Yankees back at the turn of the century. It's a natural progression and good jakes have no particular nationality or gender.

But please, don't tell us we need fewer people when the tasks that have to be performed require a certain number of bodies to do it right.

The magic pill you throw in the window and the fire disappears ain't made it to the scene yet.

Billy, for cripes sake, he thought as he finished dressing, go home will ya? Remember, one more night and you're in Bermuda and if they need any help while you're away, it's too long a run.

8

Billy cranked the paper into the typewriter. Gotta get that commendation in for the Strangler and Davey before I forget it.

He hadn't had time following the fire yesterday, but if he didn't do it tonight, he wouldn't get to it until he returned from his trip and by then, so many other things would have happened that it wouldn't be important anymore. Yep, they both deserved recognition for holding that fire and cutting it off.

The commendation itself doesn't mean an award at the Annual Ball or anything; it simply means they did something noteworthy enough to put their names in orders and put it in their records.

Their use of a 1-3/4" line got Billy thinking again about the old days and the arguments that raged back in the fifties over the size of line to be used. The department had a new civilian commissioner who was appointed specifically to cut the fire department dramatically and he was very successful in doing so. Of course Billy was a private at the time and wasn't familiar with the decision-making process. He was just one of the guys that had to implement whatever was sent down because he was a "user."

A fire school run by the Memphis, Tennessee Fire Department had done extensive work on the use of feeder lines, 1-1/2" hose and fog nozzles which resulted in major changes in their operating procedures. It was being tried in several other cities and towns and got plenty of publicity in the trade journals.

The new commissioner hired a consultant and then carefully selected a staff that he knew would implement his program without a mur-

mur of complaint. The whole objective of the changes he desired was, naturally, to reduce the number of fire fighters and fire companies.

The smaller hose didn't require as many people to move it into position and if you did this with every company, you could get rid of a lot of help. He even had orders issued that the first attack line at any fire must be a 1-1/2" line, regardless of the seriousness of the fire. One poor lieutenant who violated the rule because of the intensity of a fire he arrived at was transferred the following week to a company located many miles from his district, even though his attack was successful.

Yeah, Billy thought. A railroad. That's the term fire fighters frequently used for an unrequested transfer because over eleven hundred people got moved around during that guy's six year tenure as commissioner.

Once you take away the ability of the company officer or the officer in command of a fire to exercise his own judgement, based on the situation he is confronted with, your fire fighting competence and efficiency are going to deteriorate. Frequently, the decision made by that first arriving company officer determines the success or failure of the entire attack, and every wise chief officer spends a great deal of time teaching his subordinate officers what he expects of them.

To put it as simply as possible, Billy reflected, if you come into a building fire and it appears to involve only one room or less, an initial attack with a small line is fast, efficient and effective. If it's a larger fire, the bigger line must be used because it has a much stronger punch to deliver and it protects the operating force which is making the attack.

There's an old fire fighting axiom which is still true today: If you run a big line at a fire and it is larger than you need, you can always connect a reducer at the end of the line and make it smaller. But, you can never make a small line bigger no matter what you do.

Yeah, good judgment, thought Billy. Some guys have it and some guys don't. But if you do what that old commissioner did when he took it away, then nobody has it and you're gonna pay for it. Neither the buildings nor the intensity of the fires cooperated with his revolutionary program, and the numbers of multiple alarms rose astronomically along with the building losses.

Oh, he eventually died off and the years slipped by and some of the system he had implemented remained because it did have merit if it was used properly. In time, no one even remembered the old system because jakes can make pretty near anything better if you let them participate in its development.

The failures were often related to poor judgement which was sometimes a reflection of human nature.

In the districts that are primarily composed of two and three story wood frame dwellings, the use of smaller lines is very effective on the initial attack, but it is less so in the districts with the much larger apartment houses and commercial properties. Consequently, many fires are handled promptly with the use of one or two small lines in those areas with the smaller buildings and the company officers and chief officers are very adept at their proper placement and use. But, even there, a serious fire requires a big line for the same reason it does anywhere else, and that first officer must have the judgement to decide how to initiate the attack.

Of course, no one's perfect and occasionally the line that should have been big is small and if you're lucky, you'll get by o.k. If you're not, you'd better hope you work with a chief who has a little compassion in his soul. If you have to back out because your line's too small and the fire gets away from you, not only will he let you know about it while he's probably striking a second alarm, so will all the other jakes at the scene. "Yah, them assholes, lost another one," is a comment that is frequently heard following such incidents.

If you happened to work for the diminutive chief everyone called "Barry Fitzgerald" behind his back, forget it.

His nickname arose from his slight stature, his discernible brogue and his soft voice. He really did resemble the Irish actor who often played a parish priest in the old MGM movies.

He understood the business as well as anyone in it and his fire fighters loved working with him because he handled his fires effectively while never raising his voice, unlike some of his counterparts.

About the only time he would display any displeasure was if someone ran a small line when he thought they should run a big one. Oh, he wouldn't yell or shout; he'd just stare at you with those piercing blue eyes and his cheeks would redden quite perceptibly. He would then quietly inform you that you were lazy and neglecting your duty to the citizens, to your company and to the department, and you would feel yourself shrivel as you tried to slink away, knowing you had let him down.

Of course, no one on his own work group ever ran the wrong line because they knew him and had no intention of facing that censure. Naw, if you're gonna get chewed out let it be by someone like the "Greek" or "Fearless Frank" or one of them guys who would forget who they yelled at once it's over.

You knew if Barry gave you the word, you could never look at him again.

Billy was never stationed in the district and didn't work much with any of those guys, but once, when he was a private, he was detailed for one tour of duty to Engine 24 in the Grove Hall section of Dorchester. This entire area is densely populated, mostly by blacks and hispanics, and has more fires and multiple alarms than any other area of comparable size in the city.

Billy knew several of the members on duty because they frequently saw each other at union meetings. The lieutenant, Gus Sweeney, had been a couple of years ahead of him in high school and they were good friends.

It was a routine tour of duty. The morning was spent doing in-service inspections in their area of the district, a chore all jakes hate with a passion and consider a nuisance. The duty consists of the company travelling to an assigned street and going through the buildings looking for blocked exits, piles of rubbish, defective wiring and heating systems and other violations and checking to see if the smoke detectors are functioning. Of course, the worst offenders of all the fire regulations just don't answer the doorbell until the less than persistent jakes move along to the next occupancy, so not much gets corrected.

The only real value of inspection duty, then, is that it lets you get a look at some of the access problems you may have when you come to a fire in the place, but in most cases, in this particular district, a three decker is a three decker. Stairway, long hallway, living room, bedrooms, kitchen, rear porch, with two more identical floors above.

Cellar, lots of storage, three huge oil tanks, three boilers, hot water heaters. What else ya wanna know?

Inspections were cancelled if there was a multiple alarm in progress or if the temperature exceeded 85 degrees Fahrenheit or dropped below 40 degrees. Or if it was raining or snowing.

Suspicions of collusion between the Fire Alarm Office and the fire companies on announcing temperatures that leaned towards cancellations and the relative inclemency of the weather were never pursued. In other words, if you could get out of it, good luck.

On this particular tour, however, no reasonable excuse could be found and they went to the designated street. The inspections were routine but Billy was struck by the number of vacant and burned out buildings in the area. They go to plenty of jobs here, Billy thought.

At 1100 hours they were dispatched by radio to a fire in a school but it proved to be minor and they were dismissed soon after arrival. Gus decided it was too late to return to inspections so they stopped by the bank to cash their checks, went to the sandwich shop to pick up spuckies for themselves and the truck company in the house, and returned to quarters.

Lunch was interrupted by a fire on the second floor of a two and a half story, occupied house; they ran and operated a 1-1/2" line. It did a nice job of knocking down the fire in the partially involved room and a small line run by another engine company was stretched up into the attic overhead and caught the fire as it was extending up through the walls.

When they got back to the house, Billy said to Gus, "That was nifty, Lieutenant. You guys really can move with the inch and a half."

"Yeah, we use it a lot out here. Not down your way, huh?"

"No, I guess we're kinda conservative. Big line, big line, that's all ya hear them yellin'."

"Yeah, but that seems to be whacha need. Big buildings, big hose. That's why I stay out here. Plenty of work, no strain. Got a good boss, too. Chief Roy and I connect pretty well. I know what he wants, he knows what I'll do."

At 1530 hours in the afternoon, Fire Alarm directed both companies in the house to respond to a building fire in the 300 numbered block of Blue Hill Avenue, which was only a fairly short run from the station. Billy could count Box 179 being struck over the radio as they sped out the door and turned right on Washington and rolled up to "Blue", the nickname for the famous avenue that ran for miles through the Roxbury, Dorchester and Mattapan districts. The avenue had once thrived with many shops lining its route, most of them with apartments overhead, but it had seen its share of changes over the decades as the mostly Jewish population had departed for the suburbs. Now many occupancies were boarded up and burned out and the deterioration was continuing.

As they moved down through the square, Billy turned his head and could see smoke drifting out of a couple of wood covered windows towards the back of a four story brick and wood building on the right hand side, near the corner where Warren Avenue branched off to the left.

"Drill tower," said Frank Jackson, the black fire fighter seated between Billy and Mike Tracy on the padded bench that abutted the driver's cab. The term was used by jakes throughout the city to describe a place they had been to many times in the past for fires, usually vacant and frequently boarded up, as this one was.

The driver stopped at a hydrant about a hundred feet from the location and Frank jumped off with the tool bag as Billy pulled the end of the feeder line from the back of the pumper and looped it over the hydrant. Billy got back on.

The pump then was driven down the street, passing by the entrance to the building with the feeder line dropping off into the street, pulled from the hose bed by the vehicle's movement and guided by Billy and Mike.

Ladder 23 pulled directly in front and some of its members prepared to raise the aerial to the roof while one jake went over to the sealed front door and began springing it open with his forcible entry tool.

Gus shouted to Billy and Mike as they slung their breathing apparatus onto their backs, "Inch and a half, right up the front. Smells like a mattress."

Yeah, thought Billy, as his nostrils caught the distinctive odor, grabbing the nozzle attached to the preconnected hose and draping it over his shoulder. He moved rapidly through the doorway and up the stairway, the small line trailing behind him as Mike fed it to him from the crosslaid flaked pile of attached lengths on the apparatus.

Light smoke was pushing towards him as he continued upward and he hoped the laddermen got the roof skylight off quickly.

It's probably boarded over like the rest of the joint, he thought, but if it's only a mattress it probably won't matter.

He turned at the second floor level and climbed up the next flight, noticing some of the stair treads were charred and cracked from previous fires.

He continued up the final set of stairs to the top, where it terminated at the front of the building. It was pretty dark because of the plywood covering the windows but he dropped to his knees, donned his mask facepiece and moved down the long hallway as Gus and Mike joined him.

After they travelled about twenty feet, the heat increased dramatically and Gus shouted through his mask, "We got more than a mattress. Mike, go back and tell them we need a big line and get the water."

It became obvious at least one room was fully involved in fire and possibly two or three.

Billy could hear the air rushing through the open nozzle and felt the line swell as the water burst through the pipe.

"Just try to hold it, Billy," said Gus, but the heat made them scamper backward. Billy swung the stream upward, hitting the ceiling, and even hit directly overhead to cool them off but they couldn't make much progress.

Mike crept up behind them and said, "Lieutenant," in a frightened voice, "Barry's back there and he says we ain't getting a big line."

"Oh, shit," said Gus, his voice quavering.

"Keep hittin' it, Billy, I'll be right back." Mike and Billy did the best they could and at least it didn't seem to be getting any worse. They could hear an axe striking the roof and also the sound of a power saw overhead but so far, there was no opening above and the heat and smoke kept them enveloped.

Just when they thought they'd have to abandon the line, the laddermen broke through and the smoke and heat rose upward, noticeably improving conditions.

Gus was back behind them and they were able to wriggle along the corridor and swing into a room on their right, knocking down the fire that involved all of the contents, which consisted of mattresses, broken chairs, couches and tables.

They could see another company approaching the next room down by way of the corridor from the rear stairway; they could also see they were dragging a 2-1/2" big line with them.

The fire was contained with both lines after several minutes and Billy was puzzled by the worried looks on the faces of Gus and Mike.

"Jeez, Lieutenant," he said to Gus, "we did o.k. I never thought we'd make it with that inch and a half. Nice job."

Gus didn't react because he was staring past Billy at the doorway, where Billy could see a tiny chief officer standing and crooking his finger at Gus. Gus walked out into the corridor and Billy moved over so he could find out what the hell was going on.

"O.K. Lieutenant," said the chief in a gentle voice, "how come?"

"Er, I thought it was a mattress, sir."

"How could you determine that in a boarded up building with all the windows covered?"

"Ah, I guess I was wrong, Chief. But, honest to God, sir, I didn't know you was in yet."

"Lieutenant, do you mean if you thought I had already reported in for the night tour you would have run a big line instead of a small one? Is that because you're afraid of me?"

"Well, not exactly, sir. I never thought of it like that. Yeah, come to think of it you're right. When I saw you at the top of the stairway, I figured I'd rather burn to death than have you starin' at me. I nearly shit my pants, sir."

"Your fear aside, Lieutenant, what did you learn here today?"

"Well, I learned if I'm not sure what I got, I'd better run a big line and believe me, sir, that's what I'll do from now on."

"Well, that's fine, Lieutenant. You should never base any of your decisions on who you think's working. Just use your own judgement on the fire. Got it?"

"Yessir."

When they had returned to quarters and completed getting the equipment back in service, Billy was relieved from duty by a member arriving for the night tour and he stopped by the officers' quarters to ask Gus if he could go home.

"Yeah, go ahead Bill. Whatcha think of Barry Fitzgerald?"

"Boy, he don't fool around does he?"

"Naw, and I hate to admit it but he was right. My only excuse is we've had so many rubbish fires in that dump I thought we'd be o.k. I also forgot he and Chief Roy relieve each other early in the afternoon."

The speaker over the desk announced a phone call for Gus and he picked up the receiver on his desk. "Lieutenant Sweeney," he answered and listened to the voice on the other end.

"Ah, fuck you, Ned," he said as he slammed the phone back on the hook.

"Who's that?" asked Billy.

"That's Ned Holt on Twenty-one. He just wanted to remind me he saved my ass again."

He went on to explain to Billy that Barry had immediately ordered Engine 21 to run a big line up the back stairs and Engine 42 to run another one up the front when he had arrived at the scene. Once he had determined the fire was confined to two rooms on the top floor and he was sending a powerful enough attack to confine it to the area, he thought it would be a good opportunity to teach some young officer a lesson.

He told Twenty-one to go up the back and hit the fire from the rear but warned them not to drive it towards the hallway that Gus, Billy and Mike were laying in.

Next he kept Forty-two with their charged big line at the top of the front stairs with him in case Engine 24 really got in trouble.

"Well, he succeeded," concluded Gus, "he sure taught me a lesson. See ya later Billy."

Yeah, thought Billy, as he yawned and stretched in his office chair. That was twenty years ago and he taught me one, too. I'm still using his logic and it's not bad, either.

Of course, he thought, the 1-3/4" inch lines used today are much more powerful and effective than those 1-1/2" lines were back then. But judgement is still judgement.

9

He completed the commendation report, signed it and put it in his out box. Kinda cold in here, he thought. Yeah, it's always pretty drafty but tonight seems worse than usual. 'Course that Montreal Express is still blowing down here outta Canada and it's supposed to get down near zero tonight but I'm chilly. Think I'll go down and get some coffee before I get on the Board of Merit stuff, but I'm gonna check with Charley about the heat.

He walked down the corridor that divided the various company officers' rooms from the fire fighters' quarters and stopped at Engine 10's room.

Charley Powers, the lieutenant on the company who had been working with Billy for years, had his feet up on his desk and was reading the paper. He had on a heavy woolen shirt and a black sweater.

"Charley, is the heat screwed up again?"

"Yeah, Deputy. I just called the maintenance and they're checking with Edison."

"Well, if they can't get it fixed, let me know and I'll move you guys to other houses. Too damn cold tonight to fool around."

"O.K., sir. Good job yesterday, huh?" he said referring to the East Boston fire.

"Yeah, great. How'd you guys do in that third building?"

"Terrific. We had the whole top floor to ourselves and everything went swell. We knocked down a lot of fire."

"What's the status of Fire Fighter Goddard?"

"He's still incarcerated, sir. But thank you so much for your concern, Deputy."

This was an ongoing piece of drama between the two men and they both played their parts to perfection.

Fire Fighter Goddard was a constant headache to Charley. Sure, he periodically had a bit of a booze problem, but when he got on the sauce, he started chasing the ladies and this caused him considerable financial difficulties as well as domestic confrontations.

When this happened, he usually arrived at work with some facial bruises that indicated his dear wife, Jeannie, had beaten the shit outta him. He'd be well behaved for a few months but then the old double-edged temptations would get the best of him and he'd be gone.

The latest episode, however, had been too much for his beloved spouse. She had gone to court and the judge sent him down Deer Island for thirty days, where he joined many other non-support perps.

He wasn't one of Charley's better fire fighters either, but the compassionate lieutenant accepted him as an ongoing penance for his own shortcomings.

"You know, lieutenant, I heard it's nice and warm down there, plus he ain't going to any fires."

"Well, that's true, sir. But he ain't gettin' paid either. He's goin' in on charges when he gets out, too. But worst of all, Jeannie's waiting for him. She forgot when she got him put away, his dough stops. She'll kill him."

Billy went down the stairs and passed by the patrol desk towards the kitchen. The man on watch at the desk was also wearing warm clothes, and the portable electric heater in the room was glowing.

He met Porky outside the kitchen entrance and he whispered to him, "Deputy, don't ask Nellie about his hat, okay?"

"O.K." They must be on the Spider again, he thought as he entered the room.

Nellie was sitting at the table, a black knitted woolen hat on his head. It had a Boston Bruins logo on the front and a price tag dangling by its plastic cord and hanging over Nellie's right ear.

Billy realized without asking that the logo was new but the price tag wasn't. It was just Nellie, doing his thing—confusing people and irritating them. Every year, he would buy a new hat at the start of the winter and leave the price tag in place as he rode the subway into work. He was most happy when any kindly old lady would tap him on the shoulder and say, "Excuse me, sir, but you have a price tag on your hat."

"Thank you ma'am," he would reply, "I know it."

He'd then return to his newspaper as the puzzled woman moved to another seat much further away.

When he'd walk towards the firehouse from the train station, he'd stop into the gay ladies bar on Broad Street, arriving at around quarter of five. The stout, muscular, woman bartender would ask him for his order and tell him he had the price tag on his hat. "Thank you, sir, er ma'am, I know it. Could I please have a beer?" He'd then sit there and nurse it until about two minutes of five, then signal for another drink.

His whole purpose in being there was to piss everyone off, just like he did in the firehouse because it was a well known fact in the neighborhood that starting at five p.m. only lesbians were allowed in the bar. Oh, not officially, of course, because it was a licensed Place of Assembly and no one could be excluded —but in reality, no one else came in.

The bartender would come over and say in her somewhat gruff voice, "I'm sorry but there's a private party here tonight, sir. We're closed at five o'clock."

"My word, is that legal?" he'd ask. She'd fold her tattooed arms across her chest and reply, "Yeah."

"I'm going to see about that," he'd say, indignantly. "I know Mr. Chasen at the Alcohol Beverages Commission and I'm going to check that out."

"Lissen, pal. Don't do that. We have enough problems with the ABC. Have a beer on me, then just move along. We don't want any more grief."

Nellie would drain his second beer, wave thanks to the glaring bartender and saunter out the door, price tag firmly in place, ready to return next winter.

Billy could see the Spider was having difficulty keeping quiet as he stared at Nellie. "Hi Eddie," Billy said, "how the Bruins doin?" The Spider worshipped the local team and knew every player and their individual records. He had been following them long before Bobby Orr had played for them and never missed watching them play on TV. His frugality prevented him from purchasing seasons tickets but that didn't mean he wasn't dedicated. Just cheap.

Of course, they hadn't won a Stanley Cup since Bobby retired, and some years they never got very far in the playoffs.

Naturally, Nellie rooted for anyone they played against and spent much of his time ridiculing Eddie's devotion to the team. This year, though, they were knocking everyone dead and had a four point lead in their division.

"Hi, Deputy," said Nellie. "I was talkin' to my pal Ray Bourque of the Broons the other day and he says we're goin' all the way this year."

"Wow," answered Billy, immediately joining the conspiracy. "I didn't know you knew him."

"Sure. He and I are pals. I go to all their games when I'm off, you know."

"Isn't that a lot of dough?"

"Well, yes sir, it is, but when you're as loyal as I am, what's money, right Spider?"

That was enough for Spider. "You're fulla shit," he shouted. "Whaddya mean loyal? Last week you had on a Blackhawks hat and the week before Montreal. You don't know Bourque and you ain't never been to a game."

This was what Nellie was waiting for. "How would you know, you paltry galoot."

"What's that mean, Deputy?" asked Spider, turning to Billy.

"Gee, I dunno Eddie," replied Billy, "I'm a golfer, I don't know a thing about hockey."

"Deputy," answered Nellie, "it means he's a cheap prick, sir."

As the shouting intensified, Billy filled his cup with coffee, walked out to the patrol desk where Pimples McIntyre was on watch. Pimples hated his nickname because he felt it was unjustified so Billy always called him by his real name. "Hey, Mark, aren't you cold? It's freezin' in this joint."

"Yessir, it is. But I got on my thermals. I just talked to the lieutenant and he says the heat's comin' back on pretty soon. An Edison steam line ruptured up on Milk Street and they had to shut down the system. But it's back on now and we'll be warm in a while.

Not soon enough for me, thought Billy. I got sixteen other firehouses in the division I can visit; I'm not staying here, freezing to death. Come on Bermuda.

He dialed the department phone on the desk and it was answered, "Mellen, Ladder 24."

"Yeah, Andy, put the Captain on will ya?" He could hear the voice over the P.A. system, "Captain Otis, department phone."

"Captain Otis," came the answer as the extension was picked up. "Yeah, hey Duke, this is Chief Simpson."

"Yes, Deputy, how ya doin'?"

"I'm freezing. You guys got any heat up there?"

"Sure, come on up."

"Good. Whaddya got to eat?"

"Why? I heard you were on that rabbit food and yogurt."

"Well, I am, but I think I need more than that tonight it's so goddamned cold."

"We got beef stew and we got plenty for you and Joe. Throw that other stuff away."

As he hung up he said to Pimples, "Call my aide will ya, Mark? We're goin' out."

He walked across the main floor thinking about the nickname and how Mark was christened by Nellie and Porky.

There's a firehouse in Division Two at Ruggles and Huntington Avenue that houses Engine 37 and Ladder 26 and the District Chief of District Five. The house is kind of famous nationally because it has frequently been listed as number one in the country in the number of responses to alarms per year. This annual survey in *Firehouse Magazine*, with its enormous circulation, is supposed to be the bible on such information, although some references to dummy runs and poor mathematics in determining the leaders, have been made. In any case, the legitimate combined turnouts of the three units totals about 15,000, and that is an impressive number on anyone's calculator.

But that isn't what gives this house its reputation because several other stations are almost as active. Nope. The place is known for the fact that on the top floor, where the kitchen is located, candy, peanut butter, jam and other goodies are always kept in the open and available for anyone who wants any. Whoever takes something simply puts the money in the cigar box next to the food, and the member in charge of the house fund will use it to buy additional supplies.

This honor system has been going on for decades; theft of either food or money has never been reported. In a country where there are occasional reports of violations of the honor codes at West Point, Annapolis and the Air Force Academy, this is astounding.

The other thirty-three firehouses in the city are awed by this successful program. So much so, that even when companies cover at the house when Thirty-seven and Twenty-six are at a fire, no one would even think of touching the stash.

An honor system had been tried from time to time in every other house but never seemed to last very long. In the house Billy worked out of, it had been a spectacularly short attempt.

Every station has a house fund that is run by one member, usually an honest jake who has been conned into the thankless task. It requires each member pay so much a week, around five bucks, in order to keep the station supplied with coffee, tea, sugar, salt, pepper, dishes, knives, forks, pots and pans.

A list is prominently posted on the bulletin board with lines drawn for each week of the year. Check-off marks are made beside each member's name to indicate he has paid for the week. When a guy occasionally falls behind, the evidence is there for everyone to see and a lot of yelling and screaming usually gets the recalcitrant offender to get it up. But the money and check-off stamp are protected like Fort Knox in every house but Thirty-seven and Twenty-six.

Porky and Nellie tried the honor system in the house, which was probably a bad start because neither one of them was noted for integrity. There was a young Asian immigrant who stopped in the house all the time on his way to his job as a night cook at the Kei Tak Kee Restaurant on Essex Street. He was a funny little guy whom everyone liked, particularly because he would drop off a load of Chinese food when he was on his way home after midnight on Saturday nights.

One night he had arrived just as the companies were being sent to a fire on Summer Street. It turned out it wasn't much of a burn but the engine and truck company were kept at the scene while Rescue One was dismissed and returned to quarters.

When the two companies arrived back in quarters, no food could be found, and although the rescue members swore it had been stolen while they were out, suspicious evidence was later found in the trash barrels out in the parking lot.

The pay as you go system with the exposed delicacies and the cigar box lasted about a week. In that time, no money was really stolen, that anyone knew of, but the supply of candy dwindled rapidly with a total cash intake that was not commensurate with the number of missing Snickers, Milky Ways and Baby Ruths.

The investigation by Porky and Nellie failed to produce a suspect until Mark showed up with a couple of suspicious-looking zits at the corner of his mouth. The poor guy was actually a diabetic who wouldn't dare touch anything with sugar in it. But, while he denied his involvement in the candy caper, he didn't want to reveal his medical condition, so he suffered his fate, although he hated the name.

Whenever Nellie was having a meal, he'd use chalk on the blackboard to list the names of whoever was going to eat. Mark was startled the first time he saw the name Pimples MacIntyre on the board, but he eventually got used to it and simply erased it each night and replaced it with Mark.

Yeah, thought Billy, there's some real ball-breakers on this job and a skin like leather is not a bad thing for a jake to have. Maybe it should be in the civil service application.

His own record was not spotless in this regard, he mused. Take the case of Captain Otis, whom he was on the way to visit, and Andy Mellen, who was presently on patrol.

Duke Otis had a reputation as a tremendous jake. He had spent the early part of his career on an engine company in Roxbury and was described as a "dog"—a jake who will never quit and would rather burn to death than retreat at a fire. Stubborn? Yeah. But good to have around when it's really a tough job.

He made lieutenant and was assigned to another engine company in the same area, the result of an unusually perceptive decision by the personnel division at headquarters, which is not noted for its common sense.

When they appointed Andy Mellen to the company, right out of drill school, they reaffirmed everyone's belief that Duke's assignment was an aberration because Andy was certainly the wrong guy to put there.

This frail, frightened little guy probably would have made a swell sales clerk in Jordan Marsh's, but a jake? Not hardly.

One night during a fire in a four story brick tenement their company was assigned to stretch a line over a ground ladder into the top floor. Duke took the nozzle, slung it over his shoulder and told Andy to come behind him dragging the hose.

Normally, the fire fighter would take the lead with the officer close behind him, but in this case there was a report of people trapped and Duke wanted to get water on the fire as rapidly as possible. The on-the-job training of Andy Mellen could continue at the next fire; this one had to get done quickly and properly.

At the top of the ladder, Duke took off his leather helmet and smashed it through the top pane of glass, which permitted the smoke to gush out of the opening and relieve the tremendous pressure that was building up from the fire.

He next broke the bottom pane by the same method and ducked down as the smoke poured out, but with less force because of the higher venting that was occurring. He slipped on his facepiece and dropped into the room; he could feel a significant amount of heat, although no actual fire was visible in the area.

Duke told Andy to call down for the line to be filled with water, then dragged the hose across the floor of an empty bedroom, reaching the closed door that led to the rest of the apartment. The wood was warm to his touch, even through his glove, but he knew he had to open it and search for victims, although the water hadn't filled the line yet.

When he reached up from his prone position and turned the knob to the right, releasing the catch, the fire blew into the room, completely enveloping Duke in flames, even igniting the outer shell of his turnout coat, which was a much more primitive design than the equipment currently in use.

He tried to get back to the ladder but had to drop to the floor because of the heat; he could feel his flesh cracking and splitting as the flames attacked his ears, neck and exposed portions of his face.

Duke practically dove out the window and Andy managed to prevent him from falling right to the street, hitting the flames with his hands. Andy leaned against Duke as he attempted to guide him to the ground, managing to make progress although Duke's upside down position complicated the effort.

Other jakes came up under Andy, and the group succeeded in reaching the bottom, where Duke was rapidly removed to the hospital.

Ironically, as frequently happens, no occupants were trapped on the floor, and the fire was contained by a couple of big lines that were being stretched up the front stairway as Duke was making his rescue attempt.

The burns he received were both second and third degree and the recovery process consumed several months. The department medical examiner advised Duke that his fire fighting career was over and he could retire with the pension he had earned. While Duke was devastated by the report, he had no intention of retiring if he could be retained at some other job.

He was assigned to the Fire Prevention Division and served as an inspector of hazards for the next several years.

Andy was awarded a medal for his assistance in getting Duke out, although the act didn't actually constitute "extreme personal risk," as the criteria requires. But, a graphic and emotional presentation by Beano, for one of his boys, who was so grateful that Duke had survived, coupled with a shortage of high commendations that year, resulted in the award being voted at the Board of Merit meeting when the cases were reviewed early the next year. Some of those present would have preferred a less prestigious recognition; Andy never was required to enter the building or pass through the fire to render his assistance. But, hey, Duke's alive and when you get a look at the deep burn scars that were still healing, it was a good job to get him down safely. Yeah, if Mellen didn't grab him, he'd probably have died when he hit the street 'cause he was coming head first.

Every year, the New York City Fire Department, or the FDNY as it is called by everyone in the fire service, has an annual Medal Day that takes place on city hall plaza. The event is the biggest day of the year for the department members, and the place is thronged with family, friends and fire fighters who enjoy witnessing the public acknowledgement of those who performed so bravely during the previous year.

Many other departments around the country pay similar tribute to their own members, although the ceremonies are not as well known as what occurs at the largest fire department in the world.

In Boston the event is really a classy affair, usually held at the Park Plaza Hotel in Park Square. The hotel is noted for its gorgeous ballroom and it has suitable function rooms to handle the event.

The ceremony takes place at the end of May, a few months after the Board has made its determinations, and it, like the FDNY ceremonies, is jammed with well-wishers, although it begins in the late afternoon and continues throughout the evening.

The entire evening is conducted by the Boston Firemen's Relief Fund, which was founded in 1879 to provide assistance to any needy fire fighter and his family from the time such member is appointed until he retires. The fund also continues to assist widows of members when required until such time as she is also deceased.

The trustees are all members of the uniformed branch who are elected by their peers.

When it was first established, the fund was vitally important to fire fighters because they lacked medical insurance, injury and sickness pay and most of the other benefits that have been negotiated in modern times through the efforts of the union.

Currently the fund is extremely healthy because there is less of a demand for its resources, although it continues to operate with intelligence and compassion. But, its solvency allows it to conduct an annual awards presentation and ball that will match or exceed that held by any other fire department, including FDNY.

The evening begins with a dinner in one of the function rooms where each award recipient is provided with an entire table for his family. The balance of those attending the banquet is composed of the mayor, the fire commissioner, the deputy chiefs who comprise the Board of Merit, the trustees of the Relief Fund and the wives or close friends of all of the dignitaries. It also includes the department chaplains, with or without wives, depending on their religious affiliations and rules.

It goes without saying that everyone is dressed impeccably, the uniformed personnel in their best dressed uniforms, their wives magnificent in the latest fashions, the kids of the award winners on their best behavior.

The Master of Ceremonies is usually chosen from the ranks of retired fire fighters and it is a great honor to be selected for this task. He, the mayor and other civilian dignitaries are in black tie and tux, suiting the dignity of the presentations.

Of course, as happens in the military and in police forces, some of the heroes are reluctant to be there. These guys contend the act they performed is "just part of the job," and they are embarrassed by the unwanted publicity and notoriety.

But as Billy said one time to one of his friends who was horrified when he learned he was getting a medal and promptly stated he'd refuse to attend, "Lissen, you nitwit, shut up and show up. Remember, this may be the only time in your whole life your kids can really be proud of you. And it will improve your image with your lovely wife, whom we both know thinks you're a real asshole.

"Besides, knowing how you usually perform, which is less than heroic, you're probably gonna be in on charges some day and the fact you got this medal may save your job. I can visualize the Hearing Board now as they consult on your well deserved punishment: 'Well, at least this shithead had one good day on the job—let's not fire him.'"

"Hey Billy," his close friend replied.

"Yeah?"

"Fuck you."

"Thank you."

Following the invocation by one of the chaplains, the denomination being rotated annually, the meal is conducted without delay.

About the time it is concluded, the main ballroom is opened to all members who are not receiving awards as well as their guests. In recent years, an Irish band begins playing at around 1900 hours and it will continue until 0100, interrupted only by the ceremonies which commence at 2000 hours.

A Grand March consisting of the mayor, the commissioner, the trustees and the Board of Merit with their spouses or significant others, leads off the program; after it passes in review, the "National Anthem" is sung by a retired fire fighter.

The Medal, Roll of Merit and other award recipients are then led into the hall single file, escorted by the Department Gaelic Brigade with their kilts and bagpipes.

The Master of Ceremonies reads the high commendation which describes the actions of each hero, commencing with the lower award recognitions and climaxing with the Most Meritorious Award.

The deputy fire chief of the member's division makes the presentation, except for the highest award which the mayor presents on behalf of the citizens of Boston.

The fire commissioner also presents an award to the top man; then after he and the mayor speak, the ceremony is concluded and the band resumes its chores.

Andy didn't get the highest award but he did receive one of the three medals, and it was amazing how much taller Beano appeared to be on the stage as he fastened the medal to his tunic.

Duke was in the audience looking up at his pal on the stage, and he whispered to Jimmy Felton who was standing next to him.

"Jeez, Andy's so nervous, I can see him shaking."

"Yeah, he thinks he's shrinkin'," said Jimmy.

"Whaddya mean?"

"Well, he's usually taller than Beano and he doesn't realize his boss got his elevator shoes on."

"You're shittin'," said Duke.

"No I ain't. Lookit his hair, too! Ja ever see anyone that old with that golden color? This is his big day. That's why he's always puttin' guys in for awards. He looks magnificent."

Andy was never able to repeat his heroics as his career moved through the years. He was actually very timid and probably would have been better off in a much more sedentary job. As soon as his seniority permitted, he transferred to a less active company and hoped to just keep working and avoiding as much fire duty as he could.

But even the quietest house gets caught once in a while and he had some frightening experiences at the place he had chosen.

After a few years, he tried somewhere else and then another company, but each time he ended up at some major incident, frequently enduring injuries that he was attempting to avoid.

About ten years after the fire, Billy was surprised one day to read in the General Orders that Duke was transferring out of Fire Prevention and back to fire duty.

He was assigned to a ladder truck downtown and on Billy's work group. He explained to Billy on his first day that he couldn't stand it anymore. In spite of his burns, he wanted to get back to what he loved.

"Everything's healed," he said when Billy asked him.

"Besides, if it ever happens again, I'm way ahead of the rest of ya."

"Whaddya mean, ahead?"

"Well, lookit my face. Nothin' can make it any worse than it is. But you pretty boys, you gotta watch out all the time. I think that's why the Strangler went up the street. That stuff about alimony is the shit. If he looked like me, he couldn't make out in a whore house."

Duke was a terrific addition to Billy's division. He had never lost his courage, his fire fighting instinct or his good judgement during his long absence. And, he really loved the job. He was content to do what he was doing until his time was up.

A couple of years after he was back, he had his own surprise in orders one day when he read that Andy was being transferred to his company. While he certainly was grateful for what Mellen had done for him at the fire, he also knew he wasn't getting the most aggressive guy on the job and this irritated him somewhat because the Duke was all business. He expected a major effort from anyone who worked with him and Andy didn't fit that mode.

He could have assigned him to one of the other officers on the company so he'd work a different tour and Duke would seldom have seen him. But, unlike many other captains, he didn't believe in sticking his lieutenants with a stiff, so he kept Andy with him.

Besides, fires seemed to follow Andy wherever he went, so maybe the work load would pick up. And it did, too.

Since his arrival several months ago, Duke's group was constantly on the move and made all the major incidents.

Yesterday in Eastie was a prime example. His driver, Joe Fitz, had managed to snake the ladder truck down through the narrow approach streets while responding on the multiple alarm. The members then managed to raise a ground ladder up between the overhead wires connected to a three decker, open the roof and draw the fire straight up in the air, allowing an engine company to make the top floor and cut off the extension to the next building in the row. Nice job. Of course Andy cut his thumb and sprained his neck, but that was pretty routine for Duke's ill-fated hero. He was wearing a bandage on his hand and kept rubbing his neck tonight, but since Duke wouldn't acknowledge the minor bruises, Andy remained on duty.

When Duke heard Andy announce that the deputy was in quarters, he slid the pole to the main floor and greeted Billy and his aide. "Hi, Deputy, Joe, can't you guys stand a little cold? Keeps ya alert you know."

"Sure, Cap, I know it," replied Billy, "but I'm not warmed up from yesterday yet."

"Well, Joe Fitz will fix you up pretty soon. I saw him inserting the secret ingredients into the stew a while ago."

Fitzy, besides his expertise with driving and maneuvering the huge ladder truck through the horribly congested Beacon Hill area that encompassed the firehouse, had culinary skills unmatched as far as beef stew was concerned.

Billy always felt that part of the duty of a good division commander was to know where the good cooks were in the area he commanded. This way, he rationalized, whenever visitors came from other parts of the country and even overseas, the image of the department could be maintained by making certain they were well fed. The reality was he did a lot more visiting than any outsiders and that was the reason he was on his current stringent food fare.

But, if a guy wanted Italian, he obviously would drop in on Engine 9 in Eastie, where Franco Pasquarosa did pasta Bolanese, or to Broadway, where Timmy Collins cranked out corned beef and cabbage by the ton. Walter Whitney produced soul food at Engine 29 in Brighton, Stan Zukavitch was famous for kielbasa at Ladder 19 in Southie and, his personal favorite, sauerbraten from that Nazi, Otto Rotenberg on Ladder 15 in the Back Bay.

He knew there was a new guy who cooked Thai meals in Charlestown but he wasn't adventurous enough to give it a try yet. Hm, diets don't last forever. Maybe next month.

Billy waved acknowledgement to Andy at the patrol desk where he had risen to attention and saluted, and said, "How's it goin', pal? What's that blow-out patch on your hand?"

"Er, it's nothin', Deputy," he replied glancing fearfully at Duke.

"Captain," Billy said, "you must be thrilled to have Andy on your company, after all he did for you."

"Yeah," mumbled Duke, "it's a real thrill."

"You know I was in China during the big war," Billy continued, as they walked down towards the kitchen.

"Yeah, I'm pretty sure you mentioned that quite a few times before," replied Duke.

"They have a lot of philosophers over there, like Confucius and those guys. It's the oldest culture in the world you know."

"How interesting, sir." Why don't he get to the punch line? I know he's got one, he always has, thought Duke. Yeah, and they usually suck. But, what the hell, he's a good guy and a good jake, plus he's the boss, so you gotta have patience.

"They believe that when a man saves another guy's life, like Andy did with you, he then becomes responsible for you for the rest of your days. I'm so pleased you asked Andy to come back with you, 'cause now I know you'll be safe."

Jeez, he's getting worse. "Thank you for your concern, sir. Now, do you wanna keep this shit up, or do you want some stew? The Bruins are playin' Montreal tonight and we all wanna watch it. You and Joe are welcome to stay, although hockey doesn't really lend itself to those marvelous theories you expound. They are more of the neanderthal type, sir, and may be a little too crude for your taste."

Boy, thought Billy, that's what I like about the Duke. He just zinged me much better than I did him. I love that challenge.

The stew was up to Joe's highest standard and it sure took the chill out of Billy's bones.

They repaired to the recreation room to watch the game and it was equal to many of the past battles between these two teams that were vying for first place in their division to gain the advantage for the play-offs.

Billy wasn't as great a fan as he used to be when there were only six teams altogether, never mind these various divisions. Yeah, Boston, New York, Detroit, Chicago, Montreal and Toronto. Those were the days. Now they got four divisions, twenty-four teams, and they're playin' in places like San Jose and Tampa, for cripesake, where they didn't even know water freezes in the winter.

The teams were deadlocked at two to two in the second period, Montreal with the faster skaters and more skillful stick-handlers, Boston with its Big Bad Bruins image intact as their roughing penalties rose.

At 2100 hours, Andy hit the house alarm in response to the message announced by Fire Alarm over the communications system, "Engine 4, Ladder 24, District 3, respond to a report of a fire in Snyder's Army and Navy store, corner of Washington and Avery. We're striking Box 1471."

Andy made the same announcement as the members arrived at the apparatus, and it was a slightly slower response than usual because of the bitter cold.

Everyone pulled their boots up all the way, made certain every snap on their coats was fastened, pulled the flaps out of their helmets and down over their ears and, finally, pulled on the long woolen mittens whose use was reserved for this kind of a night.

Billy and Joe did the same thing as the fire companies roared out the door and turned right up Cambridge Street, led by the district chief's car.

They sped through Government Center, past city hall and along Tremont Street. In spite of the early hour, they didn't see a soul out on foot because of the frigid temperature and the driving wind that funneled between the high-rises they were passing.

The wind seemed to blow even harder as they passed Park Street Station and traveled opposite the wide open Boston Common, swinging left onto Avery Street and down towards Washington.

While they were enroute, Fire Alarm announced they were receiving additional calls including some reporting that the Hotel Avery was involved. Billy started evaluating what he knew about this section of the district. It was pretty well run down and had been for several years. The buildings were all historic but neglected and they contained many vertical openings as well as serious exposure hazards.

The army and navy store was fully occupied and in business but the Hotel Avery was closed, although it was usually a haven for a lot of homeless guys who hung around the nearby Combat Zone all day and huddled in the unheated rooms at night. There was still plenty of old bedding and furniture in the place, and it had been the scene of several fires in the past.

The water supplies were very good in the area with both high pressure hydrants as well as regular post hydrants, although the possibility of some of them being frozen was always a factor at this time of year.

When the district chief arrived at the intersection, he reported heavy fire showing from the store. He would probably have ordered a second alarm but he knew Billy was right behind him and would no doubt do the same.

Billy had come down another side street to Washington because he rightly guessed that Duke would probably position his ladder truck on Avery Street, opposite the ten story hotel.

Duke always used good judgement; and his position left the front of the department store free of apparatus so the aerial tower could be positioned for an outside attack, which seemed quite possible.

His own position opposite the hotel would allow him to use the hydraulic aerial ladder to rescue anyone who might be trapped on the upper floors. He knew he couldn't hit the roof because it exceeded the 110 foot limit of his truck, and past fires had taught him the ninth floor of this building was his maximum reach.

Sure enough, Duke could hear yelling from up above and as he looked upward there were people at a half a dozen locations, waving and screaming.

At the front of the original fire building on Washington Street, it was obvious to Billy the store would soon be fully involved and he could see where the fire was jumping across the alleyway into five or six floors of the hotel.

He commenced ordering additional alarms struck, assigned the district chief to take charge of the operation at the hotel and concentrated on positioning the incoming companies to set up heavy stream devices, including the aerial tower, which was his best weapon for this kind of a fire.

Washington Street was wide enough to permit the tower to be safely placed at a distance that wouldn't endanger it or its crew in the event the department store collapsed, which was a distinct possibility, as the fire spread rapidly throughout the interior.

The district chief requested additional ladder companies on Avery Street to assist in making rescues but also reported he was attempting an interior attack with hand lines being stretched up the main stairways.

This sounded proper to Billy; the hotel was of first class construction and would thus restrict the spread of fire; it was also strong enough to make the chance of collapse a remote possibility. However, he cautioned the chief by radio that he could see quite a few rooms showing fire from the rear and it would require a major inside effort to get the job done.

He sent his aide, Joe, down through the vacant lot to the left of the store to check for any further extension and was pleased to hear the fire building abutted another structure in back, but both buildings had massive fire walls between them.

In spite of the massive streams that were plugging into Snyder's, the fire continued to grow, eventually involving all four floors with sheets of flame leaping outward and upward.

Billy figured the upper floors must be overstocked with clothing and other goods and it would be some time before the streams were able to gain control. But he was confident they would succeed in protecting all of the other exposed buildings in the highly congested area.

He assigned one of the multiple alarm chiefs to assume command on Washington Street and moved his own position to Avery Street. He was pleased to see that three aerial trucks had been squeezed into the narrow street and their ladders had been extended to three different floors.

A few occupants were being guided down the ladders, but a far larger number were streaming out the front doors.

Billy notified Fire Alarm to alert the Red Cross and Salvation Army many people would probably require shelter, particularly because of the weather.

The district chief told him that as far as he could determine, about twenty rooms on the upper floors of the hotel were involved and he was making progress but needed more big lines.

Billy eventually struck a total of nine alarms for the fire and the interior attack became a prolonged process.

The operations on the upper levels caused the stairways to become solid masses of ice, and Billy used some companies to spread salt on the treads to try to improve traction.

When the fire was finally knocked down, his first objective was to try to get as many companies dismissed as conditions would allow, while still continuing the work. He returned to the front of the original fire building and saw the streams, particularly from the aerial tower, turn the heavy fire and black smoke to steam and light smoke and he directed that as many companies as could be released be allowed to leave the scene.

The success of the operation now permitted him to enter the hotel to examine the situation. The corridors were black and the footing was icy but he managed to get up to the top floor where he could look down and see hose streams from the hotel striking into the department store fire from several effective angles. Great.

As he started working his way down, he was really impressed with the amount of fire that had attacked the ancient furnishings but even more impressed with the number of lines that had been moved and advanced down the hallways. Conditions had to have been really tough, and he felt the same admiration he always did when his jakes accomplished such difficult tasks.

He saw Nellie, Porky and the Spider in one room and he managed to eavesdrop on the conversation.

"Hey, Porky, ja hear my good pals the Montreal Canadians, knocked off those asshole Broons after we left?"

"Jeez, Nell, I thought you were with our guys this year. You got that new hat, ain't cha?"

"Naw, I never liked them jerks. Lookit this." He slid his hand inside his coat and pulled out another woolen hat, emblazoned with the shield of the Frenchmen from up north and with the price tag dangling from the side.

Billy shook his head as he continued down the hallway, that Nellie's ready for anything. He could hear the Spider screaming, "You got no sense of loyalty. You fair weather prevert," his voice fading as Billy moved rapidly away.

On the sixth floor he was met by Joe Fitz, who pulled him into a room that hadn't been touched by the fire.

"Hey, Deputy, wanna hear somethin' good?"

"Sure."

"Well, when we got up to this floor, we could hear someone yellin' down the end of the hallway," he indicated the direction pointing to his left. "The captain and me crawled down to the room on the end. Boy, was it juicy. But in the back we found an old geezer, trying to make it out of the bed."

"What happened then," Billy said.

"We picked him up o.k. 'cause he didn't weigh nothin', but when we tried to come back this way, the fire broke outta one of the rooms into the hall and cut us off."

He continued, "Duke, er, the captain, told me to head for the front of the building where we might get on an aerial, but when we got there, none of the sticks were near us. We went back to the hallway, with the poor geezer lookin' terrible and sucking on my mask facepiece. It was pretty bad. But, all of a sudden we could hear a big line comin' down the hall and it cut right through the fire and then knocked it down. We really moved outta there fast."

"Sounds like you did a great job, Fitz," marveled Billy.

"Oh, yeah. But that ain't the best part," he chuckled. "Guess who was on the pipe that saved us?" He couldn't wait to continue. "It was Andy," he burst out laughing. "He was slow as shit comin' up the stairs, like always and when he got up here, we were gone down the hall. Then when the fire cut us off, he yelled down to Engine 10 and they brought their line up fast. He was in the best position so he grabbed the pipe and opened it."

"Well that's terrific. But what the hell's so funny?"

"Don't cha get it. Duke's always complainin' about Andy draggin' his feet and now he saved his life again. When the captain realized what happened he said, 'Oh Jeesus, now I'll have to lissen to that deputy with his chink World War II shit all over again."

The work of getting the companies relieved at the fire while continuing to conduct the attack continued for several hours, but finally, as the sky was growing lighter, Billy turned the operation over to a chief who was brought in specifically to supervise the overhauling operation.

Throughout the operation, Billy never noticed the cold because his mind was constantly occupied but now as he was preparing to leave the scene, he started shaking uncontrollably.

A spark handed him a steaming cup of coffee but he had difficulty in getting it to his lips because of the quiver in his hands. Boy, I'll be glad to get out of here, he thought.

Joe tapped him on the shoulder and said, "I started the car about ten minutes ago and it's all warmed up."

"Great. Let's get the hell outta here." The car swung down Essex Street to Atlantic Avenue and headed toward High Street, then under the expressway down Oliver Street and onto the apron in front of the firehouse.

Shit, thought Billy, wonder if that damned heat is back on. But as he got out of the car, he could feel the warmth envelop him. Joe grabbed a couple of spanner wrenches from Engine 10 and they whacked away at the snaps on their coats that were encased with ice.

When he had removed his outer clothes, Billy raced up the stairs and headed for the shower.

The hot water beat against him, driving away the cold and he mused, didn't I just do this nonsense the last tour of duty?

Yeah, but not next week. When my relief gets in, I'm gone and Bermuda's waitin'.

10

Shit. I'm back, Billy thought as he went into his office after relieving his partner. Winter's still here. Wish I coulda stayed for the month.

Jerry told him as he was leaving that it had been a fairly busy week but at least the worst of the cold weather was gone for awhile, although the temperature was still below freezing.

"That ice palace you created up at Snyder's and the Avery was a beautiful job. Not your fire fighting skills so much as your ability to enhance the scenery. Photographers have been showing up from everywhere to capture the stalactites you produced with your excess use of water. It's a veritable winter wonderland. The *Globe* had a great color shot in the Sunday paper and they commented on your artful placement of streams."

"Yeah, well lissen, Jerry I may not be as articulate as you just were, but you're fulla shit."

There was a note on his desk from the commissioner requesting him and his counterpart in Division Two to go to the Department Fire Academy at 1000 hours to witness a demonstration of a new life net. Both Rescue 1 and Rescue 2 were also going to be there to participate in the test of the device.

This was good news to Billy; he hoped it was better than what they were currently using. When he had been appointed back in the fifties, a state law required a life net be available at every fire. Consequently, all twenty-one ladder trucks were equipped with a net made of rope that was about eight feet in diameter. Fortunately, they were never used at fires, although they were occasionally placed in position for attempted suicides.

Every rookie fire fighter was required to jump into the net from the second floor of the drill tower during training. Once you'd done that, you realized it was a pretty ineffective way of trying to save anyone. The rope was stiff and your back ached after you completed your turn. As a matter of fact, a few guys had received serious injuries from the short fall. And it was no fun holding the damn thing either. The force of the jumper hitting the net pulled the holders violently forward. Imagine if a poor victim jumped from any higher up. Forget it. He'd probably get killed and take a couple of jakes with him.

The rope nets were replaced with canvas in the sixties and they weren't a hell of a lot better, but the law required that they be carried and every new ladder truck had to be designed with a compartment large enough for these cumbersome tools.

The company that made them went out of business in the past couple of years because of the inevitable lawsuits they produced. Consequently, no replacement parts were available and when one got broken, it was gone. But the law wasn't and it was sure worth looking at something new.

When Billy was departing for the Academy, he glanced into his in box and noticed the sheaf of Board of Merit papers. Oops. Forgot about them again. Well, maybe tomorrow night.

While riding the ten mile journey to the drill site, Billy kept glancing up at the overcast skies, which were pretty constant throughout the winter months. *Two days ago, I had to leave that beautiful island to come back to this. Why the hell did my grandparents have to settle here when they left Ireland?*

You'da thought they would have been more considerate of their descendants. 'Course they didn't have any dough to continue on to anywhere else. Just get off the boat and go to work.

And, he had to admit, he really liked the area most of the year. If they could just eliminate January and February, he could adjust to the rest. Sure. Keep makin' a trip each year to break up those gloomy times and it would be o.k. But, the first day back is depressing, especially with the very fresh memories of the trip.

The morning they had departed from Boston, the temperature had been 6 degrees F. when they got to the airport. They even had a short delay because it was so cold that the maintenance crew had some difficulty in starting the plane.

As soon as they were airborne, however, their spirits were lifted when the jet passed rapidly over Cape Cod and headed out into the Atlantic.

Nifty was like a tour guide because he had visited Bermuda several times, and he assured them it would be a hell of a lot warmer there than Boston.

"To tell you the truth, though," he said, as the flight attendants were distributing breakfast, "it's not the Caribbean. This time of year, it's always cooler than in the summer. But, it's at least in the sixties and if we're lucky, in the seventies, every day. Gets kinda windy too, and an occasional shower, but its terrific for golf."

Billy's wife, Phyllis, said, "What about us, Nifty. We hate that stupid game. If you guys think you're gonna play all day, forget it."

Nifty was always a charmer. "Phyl, how could you possibly think we'd neglect you wonderful ladies?" he replied.

"Easy," she replied, "we've been married to you fanatics a long time, remember?"

"Lemme give you the plan, will ya? We chose the Belmont for a couple of good reasons. Sure it's got its own golf course, but that doesn't delay us in getting to play. No travel time, see? So we get finished early. Next, it's got a ferry stop right at the foot of the street. This takes ya on a beautiful boat ride across the harbor and deposits you right in the middle of Hamilton. It's almost like a scenic cruise.

"Wait'll you see the shops they got; Trimingham's, Archie Brown's, A.E. Smith's and the rest. You'll forget we're alive.

"I figure if we start playing as soon as it gets light in the morning, you lovely girls can sleep in, rise and have a leisurely breakfast in the gorgeous dining room. By then your heroes will be done. The rest of the day will consist of our complete devotion to each and every one of you. Your wish is our command. Whether it be sightseeing, shopping, swimming or horseback riding."

"O.K. Francis," (which was Nifty's real name) said his wife, Margie, "cut the crap. I've suffered through your days of devotion in the past." She turned to the other ladies and said, "I've got to admit though, a lot of what he says is true. I think you'll all love the place. It's gorgeous and it's also really laid back. The people are wonderful, with a great sense of humor. You know what's really nice is there's no unemployment and no crime. The kids all go to school in uniform and they're really cute. So polite, too. The rest of the world could take a lesson from this place, believe me."

The flight from Boston is less than two hours because it's only about seven hundred miles to that speck in the Atlantic, but following breakfast, Nifty gathered the other men at the back of the plane. "Now lissen," he said, "we'll do a lot of that devotion shit, see, but not today. The problem is that Bermuda's on Atlantic time and that's an hour ahead of us."

"So what?" said Larry, "what's the difference?"

"The difference is we gotta tee off as soon as we can because it gets dark about five o'clock this time of year."

He explained that the plane would land at Kindley Field in St. George parish about eleven, Bermuda time. Then they had to go through customs and grab a couple of cabs to get to the hotel. He told them the ride was very scenic but kind of slow because the streets are narrow and there's usually a horde of tourists on mopeds screwing up the traffic. He said most of them couldn't handle the bikes very well and the fact that the traffic was on the left hand side, like England, nobody from the States knew what the hell they were doing.

"But," he said, "as soon as we get through customs, I'll call the Belmont and get a starting time, see?"

"But what about the girls?"

"Well, that's the hardest part. We gotta grab our clubs, get the first cab and talk them into following with the luggage. Whaddya think?"

"I think you're outta your fuckin' mind, is what I think," said Ron. "Helen will kick the shit outta me if I drive off and leave her in a foreign country."

"Naw, it's not like that down here. See, I got a plan. The cabbies are good guys and real honest. So, I'll arrange to have them take the girls to the Hamilton Princess. They can go to lunch there, as long as we buy, and then they can take a ride on one of those horse-drawn surreys along Front Street. The cabbie will drop the luggage at the Belmont and in the meantime, we'll be whackin' the ball right down the middle."

Billy thought it over for a couple of minutes. "Well, Nifty, I dunno, but it's worth a shot. It's gonna cost us plenty if they go for it. Phyllis has been conditioned over the years, just like the rest of them, that we're basically assholes. But we've kept them in food and clothing, so she might go along. But it's up to you to sell the plan. Me and Ron and Larry want to look like innocent bystanders."

Son of a gun, mused Billy, they had pulled it off. The plan was flawless—almost. Nifty returned to the front of the plane and the others remained in the back but they could see his arms waving about as he described the wonders they were to see.

What made it work so well was the island itself. When it first popped into view over the horizon, it was a magnificent sight, starting with the blue and green water that swept over the reefs on the approach to the runway.

There's only a handful of flights every day from England, Boston, New York, Atlanta and Dallas, so the immaculate terminal building isn't overcrowded and the customs people are polite and efficient.

Nifty dashed for a pay phone in the lobby and came racing back to the others as they reached the cab stand where the sky cap had lined up their luggage. He wisely negotiated with a charming, elderly cabbie to transport the girls to downtown as Billy, Larry and Ron piled into the cab in front, and in a few minutes they were off.

The trip to the Belmont was fascinating. The narrow road was lined with the most beautiful flowers and plants they had ever seen and the homes were white stucco with multi-colored pastel roofs. And immaculately clean! A little different than back home.

The cabs separated as the girls circled the roundabout and swung down the main drag to Hamilton, while the men continued into Warwick Parish and then up the driveway to the Belmont. The doorman had their clubs taken right to the clubhouse while they were checked into the hotel. Just as Nifty had predicted, they were standing on the first tee at one o'clock, looking around at the marvelous setting while waiting to take their turn.

One view from the hotel looked down on Hamilton Harbor from its majestic perch on the top of a hill and another faced the magnificent rolling hills. The course was sprinkled with small but beautiful homes as it wound its way up and down the gentle slopes.

About the only thing Nifty was wrong about was how they would hit their drives from the first tee. His went right down the middle because he was a great golfer, but the other three hackers hit their shots over the trees and into the adjoining fairways.

Billy and Joe got hung up on the expressway on their way to the Fire Academy and the blowing horns and cursing of the commuters brought him back to reality. But, he thought, as they inched their way along, it had been a terrific week. Their golf had improved as they played each morning; they even beat Nifty a couple of times when they negotiated enough strokes from him. The meals at the hotel and at its partner, the Harmony Club, were sumptuous. The ferry ride became a favorite with the ladies and they traveled into the city many times.

Their efforts with the mopeds were failures, although Nifty and his wife were experts and would wave merrily as they sped off to some remote beach. But the island bus service was great. They published a schedule which they managed to adhere to and the open, airy vehicles took the tourists from one end of the twenty-one mile spread to the other. They saw everything from St. George to Somerset, and even managed to swim at the hotel beach club when the temperatures reached the seventies.

Each evening, following the six course meal, they saw a show, either at their own hotel or at the relatively close Inverurie or Elbow Beach complexes. The shows were mostly steel bands and limbo dancers and the rhythmic beat was infectious.

The ladies, of course, were enchanted with the afternoon tea that was a cultural constant in every hotel, and they managed to stop at different locations each day for the charming tradition.

The final night, as they were finishing dinner, Nifty said to Billy, "You know how I knew this was the last night?"

"How?"

"I noticed you cut down to two desserts. Your conscience must be starting to bother you."

"Yeah, you're right," answered Billy, glancing down at his expanding waist line.

The traffic jam dispersed and Billy thought, back on the goddamned yogurt. This time I mean it. But, the guy who wrote the song is right: "Bermuda is another world," and I'm gettin' back there again.

They exited the expressway in Neponset, went up the overpass and down into the city of Quincy through which they had to pass in order to reach the Fire Academy. It's located on Moon Island in Boston harbor and is connected to the mainland by a bridge.

It's about ten miles from downtown and didn't seem like a very good choice when it was opened back in the sixties.

The main problem is that the distance from Boston proper limits the number of fire companies that can be out of service at one time to attend any kind of special training. It's too far away when a major fire occurs in Boston. But, and it wasn't thought of at the time, it's distance from other habitation allows fires to be set for drill purposes that the environmentalists haven't discovered yet. Oh, no doubt a Greenpeace crew will pull up to the breakwater some day, and the ball game will be over. But, until then, it's a great place to practice.

As they traveled through the Squantum section of Quincy, Billy started thinking about the department drillmaster who ran the Academy—Spanky, one of Steve's crew from so many years ago.

The guy amazed him. He had a difficult time with the books but he was persistent. Over a period of several years and many examinations he had been promoted to lieutenant and then to captain. He had attempted the district chiefs' test on a few occasions but never got high enough marks to get a job.

It was ironic because he frequently served as an acting chief when he was on the promotional list as required by the contract. Billy thought Spanky was the best acting chief he had ever seen and was at least equal to most of those who had been promoted. He had served on only the busiest companies throughout his career and had paid attention all the way through. This not only gave him the experience that is so essential to being good, he had a natural fire fighter's instinct that is very rare.

Spanky had, however, received more of his share of injuries because of the staggering number of incidents he had worked at. He had decided to retire a couple of years ago.

But the commissioner, who had served with him many times, prevailed upon him to accept the training post at the Academy because the last drillmaster had just been pensioned.

The most amazing thing about this exceptional guy was that he still was as humble and possessed the same innocence he had as when Billy first met him. He declined the appointment because he felt he wasn't knowledgeable enough and he knew how important it is to start new recruits off properly. The commissioner was wise enough to call several of Spanky's closest friends and they finally convinced him he was worthy enough for the position.

Billy laughed to himself. In the time since then, Spanky had become the most beloved leader at the school that anyone could remember, much to the surprise of no one except himself.

In addition to possessing the knowledge the position required, Spanky also had the personality a good teacher needs to get the message across.

His reputation as a teacher loved by his students eventually reached City Hall, and the city's public access cable station sent a film crew to record the journey of the recruits from one drill class, from their appointment to graduation. When the one hour program was shown on the local station, it became an instant hit, primarily because the director was astute enough to capture Spanky's character, compassion and leadership qualities in her story. Since the station doesn't produce many programs of outstanding quality, it was run many times during the next couple of years, much to Spanky's chagrin.

His friends naturally accused him of being a showboat, just to watch his face redden and listen to his apologetic explanation, which started off, with, "Jingoes, I never meant for this to happen. I just figured it was good for the department and...."

When Billy arrived at the Academy, it was still pretty cold, with the temperature in the twenties and the northeast wind creating a wind chill factor in the single numbers. He glanced down the length of the drill yard and could see the new recruits climbing in a file up over a ground ladder, across the top of the three story, pitched roof practice fire building and down another ladder to the ground.

One of Spanky's lectures was about the fact that fire fighting was a non-stop business. The Academy was located directly below the flight path to one of Logan Airport's runways and he would say, "See that jet goin' by. They fly in almost any kind of conditions. They gotta keep the planes movin' to keep their schedules. But every now and then, because of fog or ice or heavy snow, they have to close the airport for awhile.

"They may advertise that they are an all weather business, yeah, but not quite. Fires are definitely all weather, and so are fire fighters. So I don't want to hear any squawking when I get you outside." Yep, thought Billy, he's down there doing his thing.

The members of the two rescue companies were huddled around the coffee pot inside the classroom building; they didn't have the same view as Spanky. As a matter of fact, Nellie was talking to the members of Rescue Two, in a voice purposely pitched high enough for Billy to catch the words, "Well I don't know about your deputy, out in Division Two, but I know that our close friend, Chief Simpson, won't let them take us outside today. It's brutal out there and he takes great care of us."

The deputy in charge of training, Nat Tracey, who was to supervise the demonstration, greeted Billy and said, "You listenin' to that bullshit, Bill?"

"Sure. When you ready start?" completely ignoring the attempt at seeking his compassion.

"Right now. Everyone outside," Tracey shouted.

The demonstration was a huge success. The device consisted of an air bag that was rapidly inflated by two fans that were powered by a gasoline motor. In less than two minutes, it could be positioned and ready to catch a victim. Its fifteen foot diameter made an inviting target for someone who had to jump, and the landing was like hitting a soft mattress. A video tape that the manufacturer showed included stuntmen jumping from the hundred foot level of a tower, which made it about ten times better than the existing equipment carried on the ladder trucks.

When the manufacturer invited anyone to try a jump from the roof of the building, Nellie casually suggested to Porky that he give it a try because if he could make it, with his rather rotund figure, the rest of them would be safe.

Jumping into the air bag was so easy and semi-enjoyable that pretty soon everyone was getting into the act.

Spanky brought the new class down to watch and many of them asked if they could try. The rules had been changed over the years, because of the occasional accidents that had occurred, so now the jump into the net by recruits was voluntary rather than mandatory. But this was a piece of cake! They all lined up on the roof in their brand new gear, their black coats with luminous yellow stripes making them look like bumblebees from a distance, and plunged, one after the other onto the neoprene surface.

Nellie's jump was anticlimactic because the demonstration had gone so well, and nobody bought his claim of a ruptured disk as he limped away after climbing out of the bag.

After the rescue companies were returned to the city, Billy and Jackie Franklin, the deputy from Division Two, stood talking to the training chief. "That was a good show, Nat," said Jackie, "how many of those ya gonna get?"

"Oh, just that one, for now. They cost about eight grand and I only go so much dough in my budget. But they have a smaller version that's only eight feet in diameter and is a little bit less. What I'm gonna do is put this one on the downtown rescue company and the other one out with you, Jackie.

"The big one can catch them from higher up, but the small one will fit in a lot of places you don't have room enough for the fifteen foot spread."

"Whaddya gonna do with all the old nets?" asked Billy.

"Junk 'em."

"Jeez, what about the state law?"

"Well, the way I figure it, Bill," Nat answered, "one or the other of those rescues goes to every building fire in the city, and just the fact that they are responding should more than cover the law. Besides, Bill, how many times you ever used one at a fire?"

"None. Yep, Nat, you got the right logic." He could see Jackie also nodding.

"You guys wanna come up for coffee?"

"Sure, can we get a seat?"

"Yeah, they'll let you in, I think."

This exchange was due to the fact that the Liars Club met every Wednesday at the Academy, and the sound of their many voices talking at once had been growing as they were arriving and trudging upstairs to the kitchen.

The club was in its twentieth year and most of the charter members had died off, but it didn't seem to make much difference.

Retired jakes all sound alike, and after awhile they all seem to look alike, and their most common denominator is they all talk at once. The din is unbearable to the uninitiated, but Billy and Jackie had been there before. They understood that while the retirees would be fairly respectful of their rank, there was no way anyone of them would sacrifice their seat to them. Nat wisely brought in a couple of extra chairs.

About the only one these guys would acknowledge was the commissioner; when he showed every month or so, John Barrett, the current and unquestioned spokesperson of the group, would demand they stand at attention while the boss was seated. This respect, of course, did not extend beyond the tenure of the department head. The most recently retired commissioner returned for a visit and was not surprised to find everyone calling him by his first name and regulating him to the rear of the room in the place reserved for the newest arrival.

Barrett was never elected to his place at the head of the table. He had just slid into the chair following the death of his predecessor and, because he could talk faster than the rest of them and used words they couldn't understand, no one challenged him, although he was the object of much of their loudest shouting.

His 250 pound body weight on his short-statured figure seemed to belie his tales of cat-like movements he had made at fires while rescuing literally hundreds of citizens throughout his career. Even though his rank was fire fighter, he was an expert at describing how the deputies would frequently consult with him at fire scenes, desperately seeking his advice on how to proceed with the attack.

How this would come about was never quite made clear, what with his position, laying up on a floor with the heat so intense that the nozzle was melting and his ears were burning while the deputy was attempting to direct the operation from outside. But, since most of his stories were punctuated with cries of "you're fulla shit" and "you're a fuckin' liar", these situations were never properly resolved.

What made him such a leader, however, was his ability to stare with his piercing eyes at those malcontents who attacked him and wither them with a tongue-lashing that would have seemed more appropriate at institutions of much higher learning than the Fire Academy.

While Billy and Jackie were being seated, Barrett was just commencing to answer a critic's crude remarks: "It is still inconceivable to me why a profession as noble as the one we were engaged in would accept such an ill-mannered, rude and slovenly lout as yourself. Were I the appointing authority, I would have exercised every cogent modus to hinder your engagement in this field of endeavor. Isn't that correct, deputies?" he concluded, turning to the two division commanders. "Yeah, sure," they replied in concert. "What the fuck did he say, Jackie?" whispered Billy. "Beats me, but I'm not getting in an argument with him." Most of the other guys in the room had ignored the exchange because they were all pursuing their own views on various subjects related to politics, sex, sports and fire fighting.

The use of loftier vocabulary did startle Saul Garter from his reverie. He spent a lot of time dozing now that he had reached the age of seventy-nine, but he still liked to make the meetings in case there was any lively discussion about women, who had been his avocation throughout his somewhat troubled career.

Sports, politics and fire fighting had never been of much interest to Saul. As a matter of fact, Saul wasn't his real name, but hardly anyone remembered what it was. He had retained his pseudonym following its appearance in the *South End Journal*, a gossipy rag that pre-dated such national publications as the *Star* and *Enquirer*. A weekly column by a guy dubbed "I. Ben Snoopin" updated the readers on who was doing what to whom, and Saul was a frequent item because of his adventures in that modern day Sodom and Gomorrah section of the city.

He had arrived in the city from the woods of New Hampshire following the war, amid rumors—which he never denied—that a posse was looking for him as the result of the impregnation of numerous farm girls in the rural outlands. He was appointed during the "Chinese Exclusion Act" era of Steve's promotion to lieutenant, when one of the principle requirements was the ability to breathe.

Much to the surprise of his instructors and classmates in his drill class, he excelled at two things on the job. He was an excellent chauffeur and could handle and place a ladder truck into positions that less skilled operators would never attempt. Of course he never bothered to learn the routes to the fires and his officer had to constantly tell him which turns to make to reach the location of the incident.

He was also a marvelous axe-man, a result of his lumberjack experiences up in the frozen north. He could make short work of any wooden floor that required opening and was like a surgeon in the precise and effective cuts he would make.

This ability would piss off the other jakes on the company, who were far better workers and much more highly motivated, because Saul wouldn't make a move unless ordered. It was almost a regular routine for his long-suffering officer to turn to one of the other members when a difficult job of chopping was encountered and say, "Go out and get that goddamned hay-shaker and tell him to bring his axe."

Usually the messenger would find Saul standing on the turntable of the elevated aerial ladder, leaning on the pedestal control box and gazing at the passing ladies.

He would enter the room like a true specialist and bow to the officer, "Yessir. You wanted me, lieutenant? I was making certain no one attempted to move the stick."

"Yeah, yeah, Saul, knock off the shit. Just open the floor," and he'd indicate the spot he needed opened.

"Certainly sir. Would you please ask these amateurs to step aside?"

With a few deft strokes, he'd accomplish more than the efforts of the entire crew, an achievement that never endeared him to his peers.

In addition to his lust for the opposite sex, Saul loved playing the numbers and spent much of his time ducking the local runner for the North End bookie who controlled the play in the area. The runner had the firehouse on his regular route and would only succeed in collecting what Saul owed him when he delivered less than veiled threats from the big guy on Hanover Street about possible knee-capping.

The two vices, sex and gambling, kept him broke throughout his career. His two failed marriages resulted in court ordered automatic withholding from his weekly check; the bookie got a good share of the rest and the balance was used for his current amorous pursuits. He would occasionally prevail upon his lieutenant and any other unsuspecting jake that submitted to his inventive stories for a loan. Most of the men he worked with regularly had been burned by him in the past, and after a while they came to the conclusion that it was better to have Saul owing you a couple of bucks because then he was afraid to hit you for more. Just write it off and forget it. You'll be ahead in the game.

He'd usually approach the lieutenant with a heart-wrenching tale of desperate need that would commence, "Lieutenant, sir, my mother is ill in New Hampshire and she requires some financial assistance. Could I prevail upon you to advance me some cash, pending the arrival of my holiday check?"

The lieutenant's gruff reply would be, "Lissen Saul, your mother died five years ago. Twenty bucks and no story. Pay me back Thursday or I'll detail you to Brighton for a month."

One time, though, he made a big score on a four number lottery play; he even had plenty left over after all of his debtors caught up with him. He took the remainder and went on a cruise with another charmer, "Dirty Book" Driscoll, or DBD as he was known.

Dirty's nickname came from the fact that he not only had a locker full of raunchy books and magazines, he always had one in his back pocket. When he was busily engrossed in the text, the outline of his rear pocket retained the shape of the latest steaming novel. His nickname was certainly appropriate.

The trip they had taken had stopped in Trinidad, Aruba and Caracas, Venezuela; DBD, who was primarily a voyeur rather than a participant, returned with nothing but admiration for his far more active hero. He swore that the prostitutes in one bawdy house had given Saul a standing ovation when they were departing, but since neither man was noted for his integrity, the report remains unconfirmed.

Billy remembered asking a friend of his when he was going to retire because he had recently turned sixty. The guy replied, "Deputy, I'm going all the way. If Saul Garter can make it to sixty-five on this job without being fired, anyone can. They'll never get rid of me."

When Saul first joined the Liars Club, he frequently participated in the discussions, particularly if any conversation seemed to be heading towards his favorite subject. But now he spent a lot of time brooding and reflecting, ever since he had gotten in an argument with Barrett who quoted some scientific article that reported a rapid decline in the regenerative abilities of men approaching their eighties.

While Saul privately admitted he had noticed some slackening of his participation in the hunt, he hated to hear anyone say it, particularly that wise-ass know it all. But as he started to protest, Barrett went on to describe another article he had read about what the hereafter would be like. He said it was clearly understood that man had only so many, to put it delicately, sexual encounters he was capable of in the course of his life. "Yeah," said Saul, his attention riveted on Barrett, "what's that mean?"

"Well, it also said most men, like myself, fail to use up that tremendous number we are allotted because we do not display the same satyriasis abnormalities you do."

"Huh?"

"Well, to put it more crudely, we don't get laid as often."

"Shit I know that. You guys are pathetic."

"Yeah, I admit it. You ectomorphs seem to attract the opposite gender without any difficulty, which is a sad commentary on the judgement of the ladies. But, the learned man who wrote this article, I think he's one of those gurus from Calcutta, seemed to know what he was talking about.

"In the great beyond, all of those who haven't used up our allocations will be mandated to do so, using maidens of our choice."

"What about us?" Saul asked with some alarm.

"Well, unfortunately," was the reply, "because of your excesses here on earth, you fellows will be required to abstain but watch the rest of us, possibly throughout eternity."

"Yeah, well if that's how it's gonna be, I'd rather go to hell. You assholes amateurs won't even know what to do. That's terrible. Whoja say wrote that?"

From the other end of the room, Bridgie shouted above the din, "Hey, Billy, you got anyone up for a medal this year? You guys are meeting pretty soon, ain't ya?"

"Yeah, coupla weeks. I got those guys from Fifteen. Gonna be tough to beat them I think."

"Well that's because Billy Shea and Pero and all those other guys like them are pensioned. The new breed just ain't the same."

"Oh, I think I'd give you an argument on that Bridg, although I agree they were terrific. But some of these new kids are great. We'll never run out of heroes, believe me."

With most of the fire fighters who performed an exceptionally brave act, it was a once in a lifetime act based on the circumstances that confronted them at the incidents.

But the two Bridgie mentioned, and a handful of others, were just so fearless that they earned the respect of the most callous jake.

Pero had been decorated a number of times; each job involved rescues that seemed impossible to others at the scene.

Billy didn't witness any of these lifesaving incidents, but recalled one fire where his own company had managed to grab a couple of trapped occupants over ladders from the upper floors of a six story apartment house. Once they had gotten the victims to the street, they raced up a stairway to the top floor in an attempt to find others who were missing. The fire had extended up through the middle of the building via an atrium from the lobby to the roof. When his company reached the top floor, they couldn't find anyone on the side of the shaft they were on and couldn't reach the other side because of the intensity of the flames that were coming towards them across the ceiling.

Billy could see through the fire in the shaft and thought he saw a figure on the opposite side. He shouted, "Hey, mister, are you alright?"

"Yeah, I'm fine, Cap," came the reply in a voice as normal as if they had been down in the street.

"Who's over there?" Billy cried, because it looked like a civilian who was cut off and there was no way he and his crew could reach him.

"Oh, it's me, Pero, Ladder 3," came the calm answer. "I came down through the roof and there's nobody trapped over here. I'm leaving now. Why don't you fellas go back down?"

As he disappeared from view, the room he was in lit up from the spreading fire and Billy and his company were forced to retreat as their own side became engulfed.

When they reached the street, Billy notified the chief in charge of what he had seen and he answered, "Yeah, I know it. There he comes now down Three's aerial." Billy shook his head as he remembered.

Billy had been at the fire that involved Shea's most memorable act. It had been in January, too. Just as cold as it's been lately, he recalled with an involuntary shiver.

Billy had been the captain of Ladder 17 and they were dispatched to the report of a fire in the Hotel Paramount on Boylston Street in Boston's famous Combat Zone. The Paramount was a ten story edifice attached to the six story Plymouth Hotel, and while both buildings were well constructed, the clientele consisted mostly of short term visitors whom the ladies of the evening gathered from the numerous strip joints that crowded Boylston, Essex, Washington and LaGrange streets.

There had been an occasional mattress fire in the buildings and once in awhile a fully involved room, but no major incidents that Billy could recall.

Tonight, however, they had all they could handle. Fire Alarm reported receiving calls for an explosion while they were enroute, and for once, the people making the reports were right.

A massive gas main had ruptured underground and since the surface of the street was sealed by ice and frozen snow from the intense cold, the highly flammable fumes were trapped and accumulated rapidly. They seeped into the basement of the hotel and were ignited by the flame from the boiler, creating a tremendous blast that blew a huge hole in the sidewalk and the street. The flames rose as high as the buildings themselves and entered several windows on each floor of the Paramount.

The fire also entered the occupied lounge in the basement, immediately killing a bartender and some customers.

When Billy arrived at the scene, he knew the collapsed street would make it impossible to position his truck in front of the Paramount, so he directed the operator to raise the aerial at an angle to the sixth floor where he could observe several occupants gathered at the windows.

He could also see an arm waving from the fourth floor window over the front entrance stairway nearest to him and he ordered a ground ladder to be raised to that level.

He could hear extra alarms being sounded over the Fire Alarm radio and knew the chief in charge was not hesitating to order the maximum response the department could provide.

As Billy and his crew were positioning the heavy fifty foot ladder to elevate it, he glanced up and saw two bodies draped over the second floor ledge; since they were not moving and badly charred from the fire, he knew they were beyond help.

Looking to his left and downward, he had a clear view into the basement lounge where he could see other unmoving figures laying on the floor with heavy fire spreading through the area.

He concentrated on guiding the ladder into the screaming person they were now reaching, and as soon as the tip hit the ledge one of his laddermen scrambled upward and grabbed the leg of the guest who wasn't wasting any time getting out.

He was startled by the district chief who yelled, "Ladder 17, quick. Drop a ladder into the cellar." He looked around and saw the chief pointing downward. A jake was down on the floor of the lounge with the figure of a girl in his arms and he was bent over protecting her as the fire seemed to encircle them both.

Billy and his crew grabbed a twenty-eight foot straight ladder from the side of the truck, ran over and shoved it into the hole as an engine company directed a stream of water down towards the flames. The jake scrambled rapidly up and Billy and his crew managed to grab the victim as the fire fighter collapsed into the street.

A couple of police officers dragged both people away and Billy and his company returned to the attack. Because of the extent of the fire and the number who died or were rescued, Billy didn't ask about the incident until a couple of hours later.

The chief told him that when Rescue One arrived at the scene, Billy Shea had looked into the hole, observed the bodies but thought he could see one of them moving. Without hesitation, he jumped down through the flames that were blowing out of the torn gas main, landed on some debris, crawled over to the edge of the basement floor and pulled himself up to the girl. He gave absolutely no thought to his own safety and actually had very little chance of getting out alive, but he made the move anyway.

This was even more amazing because Shea had been badly burned on both wrists when he had been trapped at a previous fire, which was so intense that the rubber on his turnout coat had melted into his flesh. After suffering the agonies of the burns and the lengthy treatments and recovery period, he had returned to work as though nothing had happened and performed his duties with the same disregard for danger he always had.

The operating force managed to evacuate many occupants from both hotels safely, but a total of eleven people died in the fire, the most in the city since the Coconut Grove back in 1942. The extreme cold and the water streams turned the area between Tremont and Washington into a skating rink with a thick layer of ice covering the entire front of both buildings. The fire damage was so extensive that the structures were torn down. Yeah, thought Billy, and they've never been replaced either.

That damn Combat Zone is the one area of the city that has resisted the efforts of every new administration to revitalize it. The most recent attempt involves the adjacent Chinatown section but in spite of their growing political influence, so far the Asian community has had little success in making changes.

Even though this fire took place during the first month of the year, there was little doubt throughout the department that no one would exceed Billy Shea's performance during the remaining eleven months; for once, the view of the membership was accurate. He received the Fitzgerald Medal for Most Meritorious Act of 1966 at the Annual Ball the following year. His selection by the Board of Merit had been unanimous.

As Billy took leave of the Liars Club, he mused, if this group had existed back in those days, I think even they would have approved this award. Yep, and since they were far more critical with their evaluation of heroics than any Board of Merit deputies, Shea would have been pleased.

11

Billy skipped lunch and went to work on the reports from the districts when he arrived back in his own quarters. The air bag drill, combined with the lengthy session at the Liars Club, had taken much longer than he expected. It was essential that the routine paperwork, including the allocation of company strengths for the next day and night tours be done as rapidly as possible. It was probably true, Billy reflected, that if the city were to be destroyed by fire, flood, war or famine, they wouldn't get too excited in the commissioner's office, but if those papers weren't on his desk tomorrow morning, panic would set in and the phones would start humming. Directives would be composed and messengers would be dispatched, because it was a well known fact that the whole complex would be vaporized instantly if the trail of minutia was ever interrupted.

Billy and his counterparts in the divisions would frequently shake their heads in wonderment when they would be engaged at a fire of historic proportions and get an apologetic query from an embarrassed Fire Alarm operator forwarding a message from Disneyworld wondering where the overdue monthly reports from District X were. The reply from whichever division commander received the message would occasionally border on insubordination, depending upon the timing of the inquiry.

Billy reached the bottom of the pile and spied a letter that had been concealed by the stack of papers. He passed everything over to his aide, Joe, who would indiscriminately use Billy's signature stamp to approve everything in sight. Billy was pleased to see the letter was from his old friend, Nigel Banks, who was a captain in the Toronto Fire Department.

Their relationship reached back into the sixties and they communicated at least a couple of times each year.

Billy figured, if nothing else, since they had become friends, his knowledge of geography had improved. He used to picture Toronto as being up around the Arctic Circle somewhere and was surprised to learn that while it was about five hundred miles west of Boston, it was only a little bit north on the map. Actually, the two climates were similar, probably due to the Canadian city being on the waters of Lake Ontario, while Boston is on the Atlantic. For some reason, though, Toronto always seemed to be much colder and get a lot more snow than Boston, but the meteorological records disproved this theory.

The cities were approximately the same size; so were the fire departments; they also used the same type of breathing apparatus, as well as other personal protective equipment.

Billy remembered the marvelous experience he and several other Boston jakes had when they had attended the International Association of Fire Fighters Convention back in 1980. While none of them were elected delegates to the IAFF meeting, they had volunteered to go and work for the Hoss who was running for Secretary-Treasurer of the organization.

One of their major assignments was to run the Boston hospitality room for their candidate and make certain any visiting delegates received as much food and drink as they could possibly handle, night and day.

They were not permitted to ever enter the convention hall because, after all, no one had voted for them for anything. They were regarded as scumbags by the proud delegates, some of whom were not noted for their fire fighting expertise, aggressiveness or motivation in their home communities where they had been chosen to represent their membership.

The first day they were in business, Nigel came to see his friend Billy and introduced him to the two Masters-at-Arms who were charged with the responsibility of making certain that no non-delegate swine ever slipped through the huge entrance doors to the auditorium whenever the convention was in progress. They were both tall and muscular men, in their early sixties and appeared to be quite stern and well aware of their awesome responsibilities at the convention.

When Nigel explained to them that Billy was one of the guys who had shown him and nine other Toronto fire fighters such wonderful hospitality when they had traveled to Boston to see the 1967 World Series between the Red Sox and the St. Louis Cardinals in the days before Toronto had its Blue Jays, both of the guards immediately loosened up and smiled as they crushed Billy's hand in their huge paws. He asked if they might be interested in a taste of Wild Turkey, which the hospitality room had stocked in appropriate quantities. They allowed that they might be, and Billy signaled Frankie Manning, who was serving as bartender. They also accepted a few selections from the high quality buffet that the Hoss insisted be maintained, and in a short period of time, they were seated in comfortable overstuffed chairs, enjoying an additional refreshment, to ease the pain of standing on their feet for long periods, while maintaining their vigilance.

Billy told them whenever the sessions were halted during the entire convention, he would personally guarantee similar food and refreshments would be awaiting them and they would always be the first customers.

As their smiles grew wider, he said, "Tell me, Richard, and you too, Thomas, if, in the course of this battle, it ever becomes necessary for one of us uncouth, non-delegates to gain access to the hall to reach one of our men, is there any chance you might let one of us slip inside?"

"Eh, yeah," they both replied.

"You mean you'd go in the tank if necessary?"

"Absolutely," they cried in unison as they emptied their glasses.

Yeah, Billy reminisced, the brotherhood of jakes knows no international boundaries.

The evening following the Hoss's victory, which was achieved with the complete cooperation of the Toronto delegation, was a momentous celebration for the Boston group. Nigel, Richard and Thomas were toasted into the early morning hours and the friendships were sealed forever with Canadian beverages as well as Wild Turkey.

In spite of the fact that Boston had its first race riots in '67, when the racial climate was rapidly deteriorating nationwide and other major cities were facing similar civil revolt, the year was very exciting in a more positive way for the city.

The Red Sox, those stiffs who still haven't won a World Series since 1918, Billy recalled, had the "Impossible Dream" team with Yaz, Jim Lonborg and the rest of the Cardiac Kids capturing the attention of the country with their miraculous and successful drive for the American League pennant.

Naturally, he remembered, the Cardinals would beat them in seven, just as they had the last time the locals made the finals, back in '46, but it was fun while it lasted.

Billy was stationed in the South End in Twenty-two's house on Tremont Street, which is near the district line that encompasses Fenway Park. One of the company officers in the house was a former secretary-treasurer of the International who had made friends with many fire fighters during his tenure in office. He had been in touch with his fanatical baseball compatriots from Toronto who were coming to town en masse in spite of their inability to get tickets, which naturally had been scooped up by all of the scalpers in the traditional Boston manner.

The ten jakes were scheduled to stay at the firehouse and their friend, John, who was an outstanding chef, was going all out to prepare a sumptuous repast for their first night. It didn't turn out as well as he had hoped because the companies responded to a multiple alarm at the beginning of the night tour and the food was ill-prepared by the time they managed to sit down shortly before midnight.

Billy was at his desk in the office shared by both companies, doing the report for his ladder company's activities at the fire, when John entered to perform the same chore for his engine company.

"How's your guests doin'?"

"Oh, they're having a good time. They say the meal was swell but you and I know it sucked. They enjoyed going to the fire, though. It'll give them something to tell the folks back home if they don't get in the game."

"Can't get tickets, huh?" asked Billy.

"Naw, this town's goin' nuts. All my sources have been wiped out by the demand. I didn't know they were coming until it was too late."

"Jeez, I like these guys, John. That fella Nigel and I hit it off great. I'm gonna keep in touch with him."

"Yeah, well, I met plenty of good people everywhere I went and believe me, a jake is a jake, no matter where they come from."

They both concentrated on completing their paperwork and as they were finishing, John said, "Er, Bill, I gotta plan I'd like to run by you. See what you think."

"Go ahead."

"You know the detail at the ballpark?"

"Sure. We never get a shot at it 'cause it's in District Five."

The discussion was about the number of off duty fire fighters who were being assigned to the game because of the overflow crowd that would be inside the park with its small seating capacity.

Cops were paid to be at every home game but no fire fighters were ever included in this plum assignment.

However, the World Series and its attendant hoopla had resulted in the district chiefs from the area negotiating a sizable presence of uniformed fire fighters, to be paid by Mr. Yawkey, in order to keep the aisles and exits clear in the event of emergency. Of course, the fortunate jakes would only be selected from the district, in accordance with the department paid detail procedure.

Billy's district union representatives had complained that the men from their side of the line had to respond to any fires that occurred in the park as part of the first alarm response, but their pleas fell on deaf ears.

What a deal! See the series and get paid for it. It was the type of assignment that warmed the hearts of all those jerks from Thirty-seven, Twenty-six, Four and Fourteen that were at the top of the district detail rotation list.

"Well," said John, "you're workin' for Frank Cummings tomorrow, aren't you?"

"Yeah. I owe him a tour of duty."

"Whaddya think about me borrowing the dress uniforms of the guys on duty and suiting up my friends."

"Jeez, I dunno, John. Lemme think it over." He paused for a couple of minutes. "What if one of them gets bombed and gets pinched?" He continued, "The guy whose suit he's in will be in the shit. I know they're jakes and everything, but isn't that impersonation or somethin'"

"Oh, I suppose, but lissen, I'll be with them and I'll talk to the cops if there's any trouble."

"Well, it's o.k. by me. I'll let Nigel take my stuff. But lissen, how about this? We won't give them our badges, 'cause they got our numbers on them. And you'll have to ask all the guys who are working in the morning."

"I will, don't worry. That's a good suggestion, too. Nobody will be looking for badges, just uniforms."

The day crew was a little reluctant but since John had always been pretty persuasive when he was running for election, he charmed them out of their gear.

The Canadians looked kinda funny in their ill-fitting clothes as they piled into the department van John had conned from the Arson Squad but they were very excited as they headed up Mass Ave and over through Kenmore Square.

John had arranged for them to enter through the assigned left field bleachers gate on Lansdowne Street with the legitimate members of the detail; the ticket attendant kept shaking his head as the sea of blue passed by him through the gate.

As it turned out later, the Canadians were not the only non-assigned jakes to come to the contest in uniform. By the time the game was getting underway the gateman was heard to mutter to a security guard, "What the fuck are they expecting, a conflagration in this place? I thought it was fireproof. I never seen so many firemen since the last time them assholes were parading for a raise."

The on duty jakes in the firehouse were sitting in the recreation room, enjoying the pageantry on their new color TV and the game was tied as the later innings approached. One of the network announcers suddenly exclaimed, "There's a fire, there's a fire," as the camera swung towards left field and heavy clouds of dense, black smoke rose outside and past the nets that topped the famous Green Monster Wall.

Billy and his crew were startled and the Fire Alarm radio sounded a tone, followed by the striking of Box 234, which was a first alarm assignment for the companies. They raced out the door, following their prescribed route via Mass Ave to Westland Ave and around the Fenway Gardens to Boylston, as the radio chattered, "Box 234 has been struck for an outside fire which has extended into a warehouse on Lansdowne Street. Companies responding be aware of heavy traffic and large crowds in the area."

The smoke was plainly visible in the sky when they moved down past Fenway Park on the side that encircled the right field and center field sections, but they couldn't get the apparatus onto Lansdowne because of the congestion.

The district chief from Five, spoke to Billy by radio and directed both companies to drag a line from the hydrant on the corner approximately five hundred feet to the entrance of the warehouse and then through the building to the rear section where the fire was entering through the windows and starting to engulf the stacks of boxes inside.

He ordered an additional alarm struck in order to help them make this stretch and also to assist the first arriving companies which were encountering similar problems getting to the scene from Brookline Avenue.

It's gonna take a long time to get it there and get water, thought Billy, but all we can do is keep stretching it out.

The weight of the heavy hose, combined with the illegally parked cars that blocked the street and the insufficient number of personnel available reduced progress to a snail's pace. Billy could see the smoke getting blacker and spreading wider and higher above the exposed building.

He told the crew to keep coming and ran up towards the fire to try to locate the chief because his radio was inoperative.

He found Chief Hastings in front of the building watching as four companies dragged a big line past him and into the alley from the Brookline Ave side. Billy shouted, "We're coming, Chief, but it's gonna take awhile."

"Do the best you can," was the reply. "If I can get this one line going, I can cut it off from the other buildings out back. You just get it here as quick as you can, Billy, and try to catch it coming in."

"Wait a minute," he exclaimed, "here it comes now, Bill. Nice goin'."

Billy spun around and was delighted to see his line advancing rapidly towards him, his crew moving quickly forward, and behind them, spread out like toy soldiers, were John and the ten Toronto jakes, pulling the heavy canvas line.

Billy chuckled as he remembered the incident. Yep, they got the hose in rapidly, filled the line and cut off the fire. It was a scene he'd never forget. And neither would Chief Hastings.

He said to Billy when the fire was knocked down, "Hey, Billy, where the fuck those guys come from? They all had Boston patches on their shoulders but since when did our guys keep saying 'Eh?'"

"Chief, old pal, all I can tell you is you don't really want to know. This operation couldn't stand an in-depth investigation."

"O.K., Billy, and take my word for it, there ain't gonna be one. Nice job. Make up and go home," the department phrase for dismissal from a fire scene.

John and the Canadians had dashed out of the park as soon as they had seen the smoke and jumped right on the line. It would have been a great story, Billy thought, if the Sox had gone on to win, but they didn't.

It was a certainty that it would never happen again, what with Toronto having the Sky Dome now and winning the Series last fall. Who the hell would make any kind of a journey to see our darlings who finished right were they belong? Last.

Maybe I'll go up and see Nigel in October.

12

Alright, this is it, thought Billy. Tonight I'm reviewing those commendations and I refuse to be interrupted. I'm not even going near the kitchen and get caught up in whatever intrigue those conspirators are inflicting on the Spider.

The dry tuna fish sandwich and can of low-cal pineapple slices had curbed his appetite, at least temporarily, and he was fiercely determined to be back in what he arguably called tip-top shape when the golf season starts in April.

He glanced out the window of the office and could see the big snow flakes filling the sky, but the forecast was for just a few inches, nothing major. Someone had told him an old Indian proverb years ago and while he wasn't sure he understood it, the big flakes always called it to mind. Sitting Bull, or one of those guys, said, "Big snow, little snow. Little snow, big snow." He thought it meant if the flakes were big there wouldn't be much accumulation, and if the flakes were little, watch out, you're gonna get buried. He had immense respect for the real Americans, much more than for the local forecasters, but even the Redmen screwed up once in a while. He could remember standing up to his hips in snow a couple of times, watching the huge flakes drifting down in a seemingly never-ending volume.

Tonight would be a good test for the new policy about skid chains on the apparatus. He hoped it worked out well.

It had been a long-standing rule on the department that whenever it started snowing, all the apparatus would be required to install skid chains on the rear wheels. The theory, of course, was to insure that the companies would be able to get to any location no matter how poor the street traction was. The problem with this conservative approach was that many times the snow would accumulate in the outlying districts such as Hyde Park, West Roxbury and other distant areas, but the downtown districts would have hardly any because the temperature was a couple of degrees warmer and the snow would frequently be mixed with rain, thus limiting the amount on the ground.

The purists always maintained, however, while that may be true, suppose a major fire occurs in the outlying areas and the intown companies respond upon the striking of the extra alarms? They would never reach the scene without chains, so they better put them on early rather than late.

There was no evidence to support this view but nobody wanted to change it. Consequently, the unnecessary chains would break on the first run on dry surfaces and would then flail the underside of the apparatus fenders until the broken links could be fixed upon return to quarters. The damage would continue throughout the winter, and the chipped fender undersides would rust, contributing more to the decline of the equipment than any other factor.

Rust is the major enemy of fire apparatus, particularly along the seacoast where rain and fog are excessive. Since the city budget requires a fire engine be in service for over a decade, it will start looking shitty about half-way through its life, in spite of conscientious maintenance attempts. By the time it's finally replaced, it is ready for the local junk dealer.

The latest administration up the street was trying a lot of new stuff, and since the commissioner had the ear of the mayor, he had been able to replace much of the ancient equipment through capital bond money. The boss, who came out of the ranks and understood the business, was taking a number of different approaches to problems; many of the recommended solutions came from the staff meetings involving all of the chief officers.

The commissioner had written to several fire departments in Canada and the snow belt areas of the U.S. and was surprised to learn that several departments had eliminated chains, most quite recently, but a few stretching back as far as thirty years. He was encouraged to learn that all of them were using the same high quality snow and mud tires he had made standard for the department; they were rated to be effective in providing traction for up to eight inches of snow.

Of the major departments surveyed, Buffalo, New York reported the highest annual accumulation at 110 inches, almost triple the 40 inches recorded in Boston. This western New York city—which got snowstorms that no one but themselves ever heard about because of their location on the eastern shores of Lake Erie—rarely found it necessary to use chains. This information convinced the commissioner to give it a try.

He was cautious enough to still provide each unit with the necessary equipment at the start of the winter, but he would only allow them to be applied on the orders of the division commanders, following a district by district survey periodically throughout the snowfall.

It had worked well at the end of last winter, although the storms were not very bad as the season came to a close in April. Tonight could prove to be a good test if the forecasters and the Indians were wrong. And they were.

By 0500 hours, the snow had reached a depth of seven inches.

As far as Billy could determine, everything had worked out well in spite of many responses during the night. But he really hadn't spent much time monitoring snow because he was so busy throughout the entire tour. Once again the commendations sat neglected in his box as more important duties rudely interfered.

Shortly after he sat at his desk, a report of a fire in a high-rise building located a couple of blocks from the firehouse pulled him away from his dedicated attempt to look at the reports. He didn't get back to quarters until near midnight because the incident developed into a major operation requiring six alarms and twenty companies before it was over. He could have returned earlier, but the commissioner, who was also at the scene and in command, told him to stick around for the eleven o'clock news shows. All three local outlets wanted live interviews from the boss and Billy. He didn't mind the task because he had learned long ago how important cooperation with the media is in a city where the size of the department budget is frequently determined, not so much by need, as by the public image, which can be projected either favorably or unfavorably by the staffs of the newspapers or the TV stations.

High-rise fires are rare anywhere in the country and for that matter, around the world, but when serious ones occur, they are as difficult a job as fire fighters can encounter. These problems, combined with their infrequency, result in extensive coverage, even in the national press, and the reasons for this are understandable.

Whenever people are trapped above a fire, it is a frightening experience; when some of them are killed, it has an impact on everyone who ever works or lives in these enormous structures or who visits them either on business or as guests in the many hotels that are erected to high elevations. Probably the most publicized modern fire was at the MGM Grand Hotel in Las Vegas at the start of the eighties, not only because over eighty people were killed in the blaze, but because so many millions of visitors were familiar with the hotel from their junkets to the town.

Consequently, when you get a serious fire in such a location, the one thing that is certain is the press will assemble in droves.

When the location was announced, Billy was encouraged by the fact that it was in one of the newer high-rise office buildings; he knew it was fully protected by a complete automatic sprinkler system.

He arrived promptly with the companies and could see a significant amount of smoke was pushing out of the exit doors from the lobby of the forty-three story structure. He was aware that the building adjoined the Meridian Hotel, which was a six story renovated, first class building and one of the most expensive occupancies in the city.

Scores of people were pouring out into the street and the security guard informed him that there was a fire in the sub-basement, some three floors below the street. The guard said all of the lights were out and many people were on the upper floors, some of them calling for help from the sixteen elevators that were in two separate banks and shafts.

The tower unit crew and Engine 10 had already disappeared down the stairs leading to the basement because they had been informed some electricians who had been working on the electrical system were missing.

Not only had the regular power supply been disrupted, so had the emergency supply when the generator failed to activate.

Billy commenced striking extra alarms and dispatched the rescue company and two ladder companies to the upper floors to assist the occupants to the street.

The heaviest smoke was apparently going up the elevator shafts, because the stairways, while they had a heavy haze spreading upward, were livable. He sent his aide to the basement to report on the situation, while he dispatched two additional engine companies down the stairway. The district chief of the district was sent up above with the duty of releasing as many people as possible from the elevators, whose location had to be determined by opening shafts since the building was completely dark except for lights shining in from surrounding occupancies. He also had to coordinate the rest of the evacuation. Billy kept sending him additional fire companies to assist in the effort.

Billy was then notified that the smoke had entered several floors of the Meridian Hotel, and he ordered its evacuation until it could be determined if the fire was extending.

He was pretty certain the fire could be contained in the basement of the office building, but until he could confirm this fact, he took the prudent action of getting people out.

Boston fire fighters of every rank are equipped with personal lights, which are presently worn on the chest of the turnout coat and have proven invaluable as have their predecessors through the years. Billy had no idea who was responsible for this vital equipment, since they had been using lights since 1920, but he was never more grateful for that wise decision than he was tonight. Of course, the earlier models were heavy and difficult to wear, but they worked. The new lights were terrific, and everyone who went to the upper floors was able to guide the terrified occupants to the stairway, down to the lobby and out to the street. He received a report that the ladder and rescue companies had released all of the victims trapped in elevators; this news eased his worst fears as he turned over command to the commissioner and concentrated on the fire attack in the basement.

He had seen someone being removed from the basement stairway earlier but had been unable to determine what was transpiring because of his concerns with the upper floors.

He now learned that the fire had originated in the electrical switching room and had extended rapidly to involve a major portion of the equipment. The electricians had been conducting some routine maintenance test when a violent explosion had occurred. Two of the men had escaped but had been burned, and another one was caught beyond the fire in the room. He had been rescued by the crew of the aerial tower while the engine company attempted to protect them with their line. This worker was very severely burned. All three had been transported from the scene.

They could attack the fire with water streams because all of the power was off. The approach, however, was cautious just in case that report was incorrect, but progress was being made.

Billy also was able to report that the smoke in the Meridian was dissipating and the evacuation could be terminated, while the lobby could be used for the evacuees from the highrise. Those who had not headed for the subway to go home were huddled out in the street, waiting to return for their belongings.

The mayor and his staff had showed up, leaving a fund-raiser in a nearby building; they were herded into the Meridian where his honor extolled the virtues of the fire department—anxiously waiting to see if this was true.

Billy reported to the commissioner at the lobby command post that he had the fire under control and as soon as the upper floors were all searched and evacuated, they'd be able to report the situation under control.

As they were talking, a voice suddenly came over the battery powered elevator emergency communications systems, which had a speaker directly over their heads. They could hear a woman saying somewhat conversationally to a companion, "Now that the smoke's gone, I wonder when they're gonna save us."

"Who the hell is that?" said the commissioner.

"I dunno, sir," replied Billy.

"Well, where's it coming from?"

The maintenance chief stepped forward, "Sir, I believe it's probably from people in the elevators."

"I thought they were all out," the boss said, turning to Billy who shrugged nervously.

"Sir, did they check out the blind elevator shafts? They go all the way up to the twentieth floor before there's an opening."

"Jeez, Billy, let's get on it," said the boss.

Billy reflected as he sat at his desk in the early morning hours, boy, whenever you think you learned this crazy business, something else happens.

The maintenance man was correct. It became necessary to open the elevator doors on the lobby floor, shine lights up the shafts and try to guess at what floors the elevators were stuck. The problem was that since the shaft walls have no openings all the way up to the twentieth floor, there are no floors that can be counted to try to make an accurate determination.

Billy tried to estimate the distance as he did when he was a ladder company officer, and his estimate was pretty good, missing the highest one, that was up 180 feet, by only a floor. The rescue companies were able to break into all three elevators that contained people without difficulty, using sledgehammers to puncture through the elevator lobbies' walls. A total of eleven occupants were removed safely.

They probably had no idea how lucky they were that the shafts they were in didn't vent most of the smoke; they all would have died.

When it was over, he and the boss agreed that there would be an immediate addition to the high-rise Standard Operating Procedures, which frequently had to be changed in this constantly evolving part of the business.

Billy got a call from the chief of the district who told him the officer in charge of the aerial tower and one of his jakes had done an outstanding job getting the victim who had been trapped. They both had received minor burns and were relieved from duty. Unfortunately, the maintenance engineer had just died. The district chief wanted to know how Billy felt about writing the officer and the jake up, because technically, they hadn't saved anyone, since the guy didn't survive.

"Jeez, Russ," he replied, "that has nothing to do with it. It's too bad the guy didn't make it, but it's the attempt that's the thing. Those guys almost got killed in the effort. You go ahead and make the papers out."

Funny how some guys think, he reflected. He knew a couple of deputies who were concerned when a guy got the most Meritorious Act award, even though he had failed to get a guy out of a room in an apartment house in Roxbury. The man was crazy and possessed the strength of the mentally deranged.

The jake wrestled with him as long as he could and then had to abandon him and leap out the window onto a ladder as his own hair ignited from the fire. Billy had no difficulty in voting him the award. The chief who had submitted the report commented to the two reluctant deputies, "You guys ever read some of the Congressional Medal of Honor awards in the service? Many of those recipients weren't able to accomplish their objectives, but at least the government recognized their bravery. If it's good enough for them it's good enough for jakes."

This silenced the critics and the award was voted unanimously.

Boy, Billy thought. Now I'm really in trouble. Wait until the Redhead gets me at the meeting when he finds out I got two guys coming up this year and three more next. He'll crucify me. He dreaded the thought of what nickname he'd get crowned with; on the department, once they come up with a good one, you own it for life.

The high-rise fire didn't end the action for the tour. About 0100 Billy responded to a second alarm on Worcester Street in the South End for a fire in a four and a half story, brick and wood apartment house. The fire involved the three top floors of the eighty year old brownstone and the first arriving companies rescued several occupants over ground ladders and aerials. Some police officers also had to be assisted to the street as gasoline cans exploded while they were trying to get the people out.

Soon after he arrived, Billy was notified that bricks were starting to drop from the rear portions of the fully involved top floor; he immediately ordered all operations inside the building to be discontinued and an exterior attack be made.

He had reports that the fire was extending into the top floor of the adjoining building on the left and he sent additional lines and jakes up the stairway. A vacant lot was on the right side and thus no exposure danger so he was confident the fire could be contained.

Just as the outside heavy streams were about to be opened, his aide, Joe, called on the radio, "Deputy, I'm in the basement of the fire building with Engine 21 and we're having a bitch of a fight with four guys who won't leave!"

"Whaddya mean? Get 'em out Joe, get 'em out."

"We can't! They're punchin' the shit outta us."

Billy grabbed two companies that were coming down the outside stairs, dragging their lines down to the street and told them what was going on and to get inside quick. He could now hear all kinds of yelling, cursing and screaming.

He couldn't send the cops in to help because debris was raining down from the upper floors and he was afraid the front wall might collapse as the fire was roaring out of every window from the second floor upward.

Fortunately, within a few minutes, the extra jakes gained the upper hand and a crowd came bursting out of the street level entrance to the basement apartment, still punching and wrestling and eventually continuing the fight in the middle of Worcester Street. The occupants were starting to get the better of the jakes when the police finally jumped in and the tide of battle turned for good.

The outside attack on the fire continued for about an hour and the fire in the adjoining building was limited to the ceilings and cockloft on the top floor.

When it was eventually knocked down, Billy went looking for the lieutenant of Engine 21. He found the company operating a portable gun in the rear yard, effectively hitting the fire through the openings in the windows and the section of brick that had come down.

"What the hell happened, Neil?" he asked.

"Those jerks didn't wanna leave so we beat the shit outta them. They're dealers and they got the coke stashed inside the walls. We caught them tryin' to take it out. Good thing I had Buckwheat and Jamal with me."

"Jeez, I dunno, Neil, Joe told me you guys were losing."

"Excuse me, Deputy, but your driver's fulla shit, sir. Them other guys you sent down were just in the way."

As soon as conditions permitted, Billy got the Arson Squad to enter the apartment and they found an enormous cache of drugs as well as guns and stacks of hundred dollar bills.

Billy clasped his hands behind his head and started smiling. There wouldn't be any commendation for this effort, particularly since the consensus of everyone but Neil and his crew was that they might be great jakes, but they were lousy fighters.

Billy didn't actually know the real names of the two fire fighters Neil had mentioned, just Buckwheat and Jamal that they were christened by their leader when they were appointed.

Neil, along with most jakes on the job, was bitterly opposed to the affirmative action program the federal courts imposed on the Boston Fire Department back in the mid-seventies. Most members felt it was unfair to use today's young white people as a means of correcting what the courts perceived as past injustices against minorities. The resentment still continues, thought Billy, but it's more towards the courts and the social planners than the personnel.

As time went on, some of the minorities became damn good jakes, and it's pretty tough to stay pissed off at an individual who works just as hard as you do and is exposed to the same dangers constantly.

When Neil found out he was getting two blacks from the latest drill class about five years ago, he was bullshit. "For cripes sake. They give me two of these beauties together. That captain of mine is only takin' one on his group. He's pretty cute. Keeps all the best guys to himself. The one he got's probably related to Colin Powell or Jesse Jackson. I bet mine are from the cotton fields or Jamaica or sumthin'.

On the day they reported for duty, they knocked on his door at the second floor office, their new uniforms sparkling with the reflection of the lights off their silver badge and buttons.

"O.K., o.k., knock of the salutin' and sit down," he said to the obviously nervous young men. They were both in their mid-twenties, and while one was slim, well over six feet tall, the other was short and stocky.

"Lissen to me. I'm not gonna shit ya. I don't like the court order and I'm not thrilled that you got assigned to me. But how I treat ya is up to you guys. If you wanna be good jakes, I can make ya as good as anyone on this fuckin' job. If you just wanna be fuck-ups, you'll be dyin' to get away from me."

He went on to explain that this was the best company in the city and his work group was better than the other three put together and he wasn't going to let that change.

When he finished his lengthy tirade, he told them to get changed into their fire fighting gear and report to the main floor.

Out in the locker room—and out of their new boss' hearing range—Jim said to Joseph, "Boy, he's just like that drillmaster, Captain Spanky, told us down the Academy, isn't he?"

"Yeah," replied his partner, "but remember, he said his bark's worse than his bite. He tried to get him as an instructor down the school but he told him he'd never leave the company. Let's hope it goes o.k."

Beginning with that first tour of duty, Jim and Joseph became the most drill happy jakes on the department. When Neil got them outside the first day and started to teach them how to connect to the hydrant and operate the pump, he said, "Lookit. We got enough Jims and Josephs on this job already. You," he pointed to the tall slim guy, "from now on you're 'Buckwheat' after that movie star in 'Our Gang'. And you, shorty, you'll be 'Jamal', 'cause I don't know anyone else by that name."

He was surprised at how quickly they grasped his instructions, not realizing that each of them had associate degrees from local colleges, which represented a couple of more years of formal education than Neil would ever have.

They were as frightened as any other rookies at their first fire and made a few mistakes, but neither one of them retreated from their positions, laying in the hallway on the second floor of a three decker, as the heat and smoke tried to drive them back to the stairway. When they talked about it later, they admitted to each other that while the fire sure was scary, they were even more afraid of their lieutenant, who leaned against them and pushed them forward constantly, yelling through his mask in a muffled voice, "Keep movin' in, keep movin'. Ya want Engine 17 to get by ya?"

The company was one of the busiest in the city; it not only responded to many fires in its own district, it was on every running card in the city for multiple alarms. It didn't take long for rookies to become veterans.

As time passed, Neil grudgingly admitted to himself, and a few very close friends, that his two stars were more than adequate jakes and maintained the image of the company, while contributing to the morale of the group because they both were funny guys. Once they settled comfortably into the work group, Buckwheat demonstrated a credible imitation of Eddie Murphy, while Jamal tried to emulate Cosby. Jamal also did a nifty take-off of his illustrious leader, behind Neil's back of course.

Like many other jakes, they also could do a good job of making certain that no scrap of food remained following the evening meal. By the time they had celebrated their second anniversary on the job, both were about twenty pounds heavier.

Neil, of course, would never admit publicly how proud he was of them both and how much he had taught them. As a matter of fact, when Billy congratulated him on their defeat of the pushers, even though it was not a certain fact, he said, "Lieutenant, you must be proud of those two black kids, you certainly praised them enough during the fight."

"Naw, Deputy, you got it all wrong. I really hate them. I'm gonna eventually kill them off."

"Whaddya mean. You're not that kind of a guy, are you?"

"Sure I am, but no one will ever prove it. See how fat they're gettin'."

"Yeah, I notice they're beefing up a little," was the reply.

"Well, the way I figure it, I'm gonna keep them on our high calorie-high fat meals and the cholesterol will get them both.

"But it's gonna take time."

Billy noticed both black fire fighters leaning over and listening intently. As he glanced up at them, Buckwheat winked and covered his mouth so his chuckle couldn't be heard, while Jamal spread his feet and pointed his index finger directly ahead in a perfect mimicry of Neil directing the movement of a line in the initial attack.

Billy had a theory that after jakes are on the job for about a decade or so, they all think alike and even start to look alike, no matter what size, shape or color they are, and tonight seemed to confirm that belief, once again.

When he glanced out the window he was surprised at the mounting snow, then remembered the no chain order, and wondered how it worked out. He had been so busy he completely forgot about the weather and the new rules.

He dialed Jackie Franklin's number in Division Two and heard him answer on the first ring. He had just returned from a one room fire but had otherwise had a quiet night. Sometimes the work was all out in his division and sometimes in Billy's. And sometimes neither of them do shit, but we'd never admit it.

"Hey, Jackie, how'd the new system work with the tires? I completely forgot about it. I never even remembered to have my districts surveyed."

"Don't worry, Billy, old pal. I took care of you like always. I had all of our districts checked periodically and every company got to every alarm without chains. We had about a hundred runs around the city while you were foolin' around with those minor incidents, and the only guy had an accident was me. My driver started to go past a street and when I yelled at him to turn, he did, but so fast that we skidded into a fire alarm box and knocked the shit out of it. Before I got this last run, I composed a fictional story about a hit and run driver that I know the boss won't believe. But he'll be so happy that the no-chain plan is working, he'll file it with all the rest of our imaginary data. He told me that most of our cover-up reports make him think he's on Fantasy Island but he admitted that he always gives a guy credit if the tale is particularly inventive. He said that indicates a man puts some time into his prevarication, rather than blatantly throwing himself on the mercy of the court."

13

Another day tour, another failed attempt to do my review. It's almost like a conspiracy to have me unprepared so some guy from the other division wins the top award instead of one of my jakes from Ladder 15.

Billy's relief had just arrived in quarters in the late afternoon and he could hear him coming up the stairs. Tonight it would be Vince, one of the three guys plus himself who rotated the duty, each working forty-two hours during the 168 hour week.

Vince was a guy who'd been a deputy for over ten years and had seen just about everything. There wasn't much that got him excited, but he loved to spread as much gossip as possible, just to keep everyone alert.

"I'm in Billy," he said as he entered the combination locker and bunk room they shared. "See ya made the news again today."

"Oh, you mean the train accident? Yeah, it was a pisser. Nobody killed but there sure were a lot of injuries."

"Naw. Not that. Some of your heroes are gettin' charged with assault and battery on some poor innocent citizens they beat up on Worcester Street the other night. I always said you and Jackie Franklin are in charge of an undisciplined herd."

"Aw, fuck you, Vince. Those innocent citizens are pushers. Besides, I think my guys came in second in the fight."

"You mean, the Striker got defeated? My, he's one of you and Jackie's super stars."

"Striker" was the nickname given to Neil because of a couple of incidents he had been involved in at major fires that were unique in the history of the department.

The rules and regulations permitted anyone in charge at an incident to take any action necessary until relieved of command by a superior officer. As a result, it was not unusual to have a lieutenant or even a senior fire fighter in charge of a company call for more assistance before the arrival of the chief of a district. As a matter of fact, the current boss was a strong proponent of such actions and took a dim view of anyone who would criticize such initiatives. His oft-stated opinion was that any member of the uniformed force in charge of a fire, no matter how briefly, was representing the department and the city and had as much authority as the commissioner to attempt to control the situation. He believed, rightly, that a guy at the scene knows a lot more about that particular fire than someone who isn't there yet, and he didn't want anyone to be so intimidated that they'd be afraid of the consequences and thus fail to make important life safety decisions.

Neil's company, Engine 21, operates out of a one unit firehouse in the Uphams Corner section of Dorchester. When no other company is in a house, the single unit is frequently alone initially at a fire close by their station and faces some desperate situations until the other responding units arrive. Neil and many other officers in similar situations will order a second alarm.

But on two almost identical occasions, when the chief was engaged at another incident at the opposite end of the huge district, Neil and his company arrived at three fully involved three deckers with the fire extending rapidly to others nearby. In both cases he ordered a total of five alarms struck before a superior's arrival. The excellent nature of Neil's judgement was confirmed by the fact that the chiefs at both incidents struck a couple of more alarms to cut off the potential conflagrations.

But at the next union meeting, fire fighters, being what they are, naturally told him he panicked and the fight was on.

Actually, after the furor quieted down, he grew to like the nickname, although he'd never admit it—and God help Buckwheat, Jamal or the rest of his crew if he ever heard them saying it.

"Yeah," said Vince, "but I admit the fight only got a small piece in the Metro section of the *Globe*. The train crash has been on TV all day. What happened?"

Billy described the frightening wreck to Vince in great detail, now that the usual kidding was ended and they got back to business.

At 0814 hours, Box 13-1546 was struck for the report of a train crash at the Back Bay MBTA station. This was at the absolute height of the rush hour, the time when the huge trains are jammed with commuters traveling to South Station and on to their jobs downtown.

Over a million people pour into the city each morning by a variety of conveyances. Of course, most of them jam the expressways with their personal cars from the North Shore, South Shore and from the West by the Mass Pike Toll Road. A couple of hundred thousand use the MBTA and its assortment of electric subway and surface trains, buses, street cars and diesel trains that are leased from Amtrak. A few hundred even fly in on the shuttles from New York, but that route not only requires a nifty expense account, it also demands almost infinite patience in then getting from Logan Airport to the city through the Sumner Tunnel. This particular two mile journey usually takes longer than the two hundred mile, thirty minute flight from the Big Apple.

A number of boats also shuttle into the harbor and dock along Atlantic Avenue, and while these are an elegant and even enjoyable means of commuting in the summer months, they ain't much fun when the winter arrives and the northeast winds churn up the seas. They stock a supply of bags similar to those used on the air shuttles when the turbulence becomes excessive.

Engine 33 arrived first at the scene, reported a train crash and requested that an additional rescue company be dispatched along with several ambulances and a large police detail.

The railroad tracks pass under Dartmouth Street at this location and the station loading platforms are about twenty feet below the surface. A nine car train had been stopped at the platform, taking on additional passengers for the remaining one mile trip to downtown, when it was struck in the rear by a seven passenger train.

The cause of the incident was still under investigation, and Billy knew it would be weeks before the truth was learned, if ever. But, he was aware how much luck played a part in whatever happens and this case was no exception.

The train in the rear had passed through a stop signal, and the two current theories were that either the brakes failed or they worked but there was still ice on the rails from the overnight rain that froze when the temperature dropped below freezing. The second theory seemed unlikely, because the first train didn't report any trouble with ice. Thank God I don't have to figure it out, thought Billy. The National Transportation Safety Board had representatives at the scene and they assumed control of determining the cause.

The moving train was only travelling at about fifteen miles an hour when it hit the rear of the stopped train, but the force of the tons of metal caused some telescoping and derailment of both trains.

Fortunately, the front train had its diesel in the rear, so the main collision was between two huge engines rather than passenger cars, which no doubt saved many lives. However, the engineer and his assistant were trapped in the back unit; one of the rescue companies cut them out with a combination of acetylene torches and Amkus tools.

Billy coordinated the procedures and was pleased with the results. The commissioner and the head of Health and Hospitals, which operates the famous Boston City Hospital as well as the ambulance service, held a series of meetings between both organizations in order to reduce the animosity that has existed between both public safety organizations for years.

This type of hostility is a natural outgrowth of two diverse groups trying to accomplish the same task. A prime example of where disagreements occur is auto accidents at which people are trapped; the fire fighters are trying to free the victims at the same time the EMTs and paramedics are attempting to keep them alive.

The meetings were bringing several problems to light, and the discussions resulted in a greater appreciation of both organizations' objectives and a growing mutual respect was developing.

Oh, it still ain't perfect, thought Billy. He remembered one ambulance driver telling him, "I've been on this job a dozen years and in that time I've never seen an EMT hit a fireman, but I've seen eight of my guys whacked by jakes." Hm.

Today, though, a new spirit of cooperation was plainly evident, probably because there was so much to be done.

Billy requested a couple of extra ladder companies in addition to the original eight units he had been assigned.

By the time the operation was completed, over a hundred injured victims, six of them in serious condition, received first aid and had been carried to the street for transportation to area hospitals. In addition to the fire and EMT personnel, the Boston, MBTA and Metropolitan police had assisted in the outstanding effort.

The commissioner responded and had no orders to give to Billy because of the professionalism he observed; he hastened to express this opinion when the job was completed.

"Billy," he said, "I think they want you on the noon news today. You're starting to get more ink than I am." He continued, "This was a real good operation and so was the high-rise the other night. I saw those reports about the two guys on the aerial tower and they're getting high commendations."

"Thanks a lot, boss," replied Billy modestly. But the commissioner, who had lived longer than any of them in firehouses, couldn't depart on such a high note.

"What about this shit with Twenty-one losin' to a bunch of dopers? I thought you trained your troops better than that."

This from the same guy who appeared so shocked when a reporter asked him about the incident and replied that his jakes would never strike a civilian, no matter what the provocation.

"Jeez, Commissioner, those guys are from Division Two. None of my men are so crude."

"Good, I'll tell Jackie Franklin you're a stool pigeon when I see him. I want the both of you up in my office this afternoon."

Oh, oh, thought Billy. Here's trouble. "Er, about the fight, sir?" he asked timidly.

"Naw. That case is going nowhere. The Arson Squad and the cops got enough evidence on those assholes to put them away for a long, long time. That was one of the biggest busts ever in the city. Striker and his crew were performing a public service whacking those shitheads. But don't quote me, just tell them to win the next time."

The meeting's purpose was to develop an addition to the high-rise SOP as a result of the blind elevator shaft rescues; the commissioner wanted to get the information out to the department immediately rather than wait for the next review of changes following the Board of Merit session.

It had been almost a great day, thought Billy, as he got into his car to drive home. The one flaw, which would probably impact on the boss' high opinion of him, had occurred when he got back from Headquarters.

The principal Fire Alarm operator called and reported he had an outraged citizen on the line who was demanding to speak to the commissioner at once. This wasn't unusual, of course; someone was always bitching about something, and the commissioner surrounded himself with competent, well-spoken assistants who could smooth over almost any complaint. But, the operator reported to Billy, the phones were down at Headquarters and the woman didn't believe him when he told her to call back later. "It's about one of your companies, Deputy, so could you please talk to her?"

"Yeah, put her on."

"To whom am I speaking?" came the shrill voice. Billy identified himself and politely said, "How can I help you ma'am?"

"I want to know what kind of men you have who teach little children such filthy language," she replied.

"Er, where'd this happen, ma'am?" he asked.

She named a company in one of his districts and said that her little grandson, whom she was minding, came home from kindergarten all excited. "I asked him why he was so happy and he told me his teacher had taken him to the firehouse to meet all those wonderful firemen. He then said, and I don't normally talk like this, 'They let us all get on the fuckin' fire engine and took us for a ride.'"

"Uh," Billy said, "I find that hard to believe ma'am. Fire fighters love little children and they'd never say anything like that." He rolled his eyes to the ceiling as he concluded.

"Are you inferring that he learned such talk at home, sir?" she demanded.

"Why, no ma'am, but I..."

She cut him off, "It's obvious I'll get no satisfaction from you, you obnoxious lout. I'll be in the commissioner's office in the morning, Mr. Simpson, and I'll let him know how you treat those who pay your salary, and his, I might add."

She slammed the phone down before he could reply. So much for our latest attempt to build our nice guy image, he thought, as he dialed the number of the district chief in charge of the district where the incident occurred.

The chief told him he'd look into it and call him back. About ten minutes later the phone rang.

The chief started off talking quite formally but commenced giggling as he continued. "What the fuck's so funny, Tom?" asked Billy. "This dame will be up the street in the morning and if she's as big as she sounds on the phone, she'll bowl over the boss's stoolies and take a poke at him. If she does, neither one of us will be laughin'."

"Yeah, I know it. But it is kinda funny, though. What happened is the nice little teacher arrived with the nice little kiddies and the nice little fire fighters were nice and polite.

"They piled them all onto the new pump with its ballroom sized front seating compartment and whipped them around the block. Just as they were backing into quarters, both companies got a run. The kids got off and the pump sped out the door because the crew members were still on the piece and the motor was running. Captain Benkis slid the pole to get on the ladder truck and, you know how he is, he was bullshit 'cause the pump beat him out. He hates hosemen, you know."

"Yeah, yeah, I know it. He's famous for it. Get on with the story will ya," Billy said to his long winded subordinate.

"Well," Tom snickered, "Mopey Casey was drivin' and you know how nervous he gets when the captain's pissed. Benkis is screamin' at him to get goin' and he can't find the ignition switches. The captain finally says, 'Get this fuckin' fire engine out the door or I'll put you in on charges.'

"What he didn't know was that all the nice little kiddies and their nice little teacher were standing at the side fascinated by the whole show." After a brief spasm of chuckling, he continued, "It was a false alarm and when they came back, the nice little teacher lined up all of her charges and told them to thank the nice little fire fighters and she was mortified when the nice little kiddies said in unison, 'Thank you Mr. Firemen for letting us ride on your fuckin' fire engine."

Billy, who was glad Tom couldn't see him grinning, said, in as stern a voice as he could muster, "Well, Chief, I am ordering you to reduce all of what you've been laughing at to writing and have the report on my desk when I get to work tomorrow night."

Yeah, almost a perfect day.

14

"We're gonna have a doctor from the Mass. Eye and Ear take a look at you. He's on his way over. I don't think you have any permanent damage, just considerable irritation, but those guys next door are the experts."

"Thanks, doctor. How're my other people doing?"

"Well, they're all o.k.—although we're holding three of them for awhile. They all showed significant carboxy-hemoglobin in their blood gases and we want to monitor them for several hours. One of them also had a dislocated shoulder. They've been admitted upstairs. The rest had cuts and bruises and have been discharged."

"How many ja get?"

"About a dozen. Must have been a bad fire."

"Yeah. A cellar. They suck."

This conversation was taking place between Billy and a young intern in the emergency room of the Mass. General Hospital.

It was about 0530 and Billy was sitting with a gauze bandage wound around his head, covering his eyes. He was filthy and had the same peculiar smell that all hospital personnel recognized whenever fire fighters were brought in from a fire for treatment. It was a mixture of smoke, sweat, dirt and a lot of unidentifiable odors that combined to produce an obnoxious scent.

He had been brought in for treatment because his eyelids were swollen almost shut and his vision was blurred as a result of the lengthy operation he had been directing most of the night.

Shortly after the night tour began, he had responded to a one room fire on the third floor of a five story apartment house on Beacon Hill, which was a first alarm assignment for him. The incident had been handled without any more difficulty than usual in the highly congested neighborhood. The streets on Beacon Hill are extremely narrow; if you're lucky, you'll manage to get a ladder truck in front of the involved building and possibly one pump into the street. Duke got his ladder truck into position and was able to get the stick up and the roof open without delay, letting Engine 4 get their big line up the front stairway and knock down the fire promptly.

As was not uncommon on the Hill, particularly when the streets were even tighter because of the snow piles from the seven inch accumulation during the previous week, two car owners were trying to tell Billy that a fire engine had grazed their illegally parked cars while traversing the roadway to get into position. Billy considered himself an expert at being able to ignore such complaints, and would constantly hold his hand up to the citizens as he jammed the portable radio remote receiver against his ear, supposedly listening intently to non-existent reports from the fire fighters operating on the upper floors.

The complainers eventually gave up in frustration and went seeking the police, whom Billy knew were much more experienced at handling such irate folks, affixing parking tickets and calling for tow trucks while demanding licenses, registrations and other means of identification. If this wasn't effective, they might cite the law which made it a criminal offense to interfere with a fire fighter in the performance of his duties.

There was also a minor altercation between the wino who passed out while smoking and set the fire and the gay couple who lived directly overhead and claimed he was trying to kill them because he disapproved of their life style. But this also was routine and the cops got out their notebooks once again.

Billy and Joe left the scene and the car moved up Cambridge Street in the heavy traffic. The road became Tremont Street when Cambridge ended at Court Street and as they crossed School Street Box 1451 was struck over the department radio, followed by the building location while they sped past the Old Granary Burial Ground and the Park Street Church.

"That's right up the street, Deputy." said Joe.

"Yeah, I think I can see smoke from Tremont on the Common."

Jeez, that joint again, Billy thought as the number of serious fires he had in the twenty-five story apartment house flashed through his memory. But as they got closer, he could see that the smoke was coming from a five story building wedged between the huge high-rise and an adjoining structure of equal height to the involved building on its right hand side.

An employee was standing in front of the building, which had an office supply store on the street floor and offices overhead. The man shouted to Billy as he alighted from the car, "It's in a store room, down the cellar and it's a big fire."

He told Billy there was a rear entrance to the basement from the back alley, and Billy told Joe, "Drive right down to the end of the block and come in the rear. I'll send you an engine and a truck," he concluded as he depressed the button on his hand mike and repeated the assignment to the incoming companies. Engine 7 and Ladder 17 both acknowledged the message and cut in Mason Street from Tremont to gain access to the alley.

When Engine 4 and Ladder 24 pulled up beside him, he ordered the officer on the pump to start a big line in the front door and could see that Duke was positioning the aerial to get the roof.

Joe reported to him that they could use another line in the rear, so he directed Engine 10 into the alley from the opposite end and ordered Rescue 1 to join them in advancing the hose line.

In a few minutes Joe reported from the cellar that one line was in operation and that two good sized rooms, full of stock, were involved.

Engine 4 got water in their line and reported they couldn't find any fire on the street level but they could feel intense heat through the wooden floor covering the cellar in the middle of the store, which extended back about seventy-five feet.

Billy told them to back out near the front entrance, turned to Duke and said, "Cap, I don't like the way this is going. I'm gonna back them outta the cellar and then I want you to clean out the show windows."

He called the district chief, whom he had sent to the rear, and as he started to speak, he heard a rumbling sound as the smoke became thicker and blacker. "Car 3, get 'em out," he called but he wasn't sure he could be heard as a loud blast sounded from the back of the building.

He ordered a second alarm and tried to call Car 3 again. "Car 3 answering. Yeah, Deputy, we've had a hot air explosion and we have some injuries."

"O.K. Whaddya need? Are they all out?"

"I think so, but I'm making a count. We can use some more lines back here. I can see fire on the first floor now."

Billy could also see fire through the smoke. He nodded to Duke to take out the plate glass windows and told Engine 10 to hit it from the sidewalk. He ordered another alarm and some ambulances and was pleased when Car 3 told him they had accounted for everyone and that Joe, his aide, was coming around to see him.

Billy was directing additional lines to be stretched and heavy stream appliances to be set up when Joe arrived and told him they weren't in too deep and had just opened the first line when they heard the rumble. The lieutenant on Engine 7 ordered everyone out and the blast took place as they were moving up the stairway to the alley. "Honest to God, Deputy, I felt a rush of air and we all got blown out the door. Engine 7, the Rescue crew, and the district chief."

"How are you?"

"I'm o.k. Didn't get hurt. Whaddya want?"

"Get in the first floor of this building on the right. I'll send you an engine and a truck. The fire wall looks o.k. but check it out."

The bricks dividing the two buildings were about a foot thick but it was always prudent to make certain the fire wasn't coming through.

The black smoke came boiling out the openings Duke had created by removing the windows, and the roof men from Ladder 24 in front and Ladder 17 out back reported they had cleaned out four large skylights located in the front and back of the tar and gravel roof. They reported it was venting very well, with heavy smoke but no fire coming up out of the shafts.

Maybe it hasn't gone by the first floor yet, Billy thought. Might be able to catch it with cellar pipes.

He directed the officer from Engine 10 to use a Bresnan nozzle and operate it down through the first floor into the cellar through a hole which he directed Duke to have cut.

This special tool is ball shaped and has nine holes of various sizes. The pressure of the water in the hose rotates the nozzle continually and is ideal for spreading water in all directions into a cellar. But, since there's no way of determining if it's hitting any obstructions to distribution, its effectiveness often depends on luck.

Billy had an additional line with a regular nozzle advanced behind Ten to protect them and Ladder 24; he also had a twenty foot straight ladder pushed flat along the floor towards the group inside. This ladder was a precaution; it would give them something to grab if the floor suddenly collapsed. It had been a successful safety measure in the past.

But, Billy was well aware that this operation had to succeed promptly or forget it. If the fire started getting ahead of the attack, it would be too dangerous to continue.

He had the safety chief inside with them and he knew he was constantly watching the floor for possible collapse.

After a few minutes, the smoke started getting whiter and Billy thought they were making progress, but just as he was feeling optimistic, the safety chief reported a sag in a section of the wood beyond where they were operating, and he knew the attempt had failed. "O.K., back 'em out. Make sure everyone gets the word."

His next message was by radio and he directed Fire Alarm to order everyone out of the original fire building and restrict operations on it to an outside attack.

He could see through the smoke the fire was now bursting through the hole they had cut; it was also visible through the seams of the high metal ceiling overhead. Gone, he thought as he struck another alarm.

Joe called from next door and reported that halfway back along the common fire wall, the brickwork was reduced to one thickness, where someone had removed a large portion of the wall, probably in some long forgotten illegal renovation.

He wasn't certain but he thought the fire was coming through into the ceiling between the first and second floor.

Shit, thought Billy as he ordered a fifth alarm, and sent a chief arriving on a multiple alarm into this exposure to assume command.

Heavy smoke continued to push out of every opening in the original fire building, and a twenty foot wide section of the second and third floors was covered by an advertising sign that was restricting proper ventilation.

Billy felt certain the fire couldn't extend to the high-rise apartment house, but to confirm this, he sent two companies into the structure to investigate up to an area a couple of floors higher than the fire building.

The chief in the building Joe was in reported the fire was now in the ceiling as Billy's aide had suspected; The chief was requesting an additional line on the first floor as well as a couple more on the second, in case it was up there. He also required two more ladder companies to help open the walls and floors.

This information caused Billy to strike a sixth alarm and to change the position of some of the companies he had on Tremont Street; he also placed two ladder trucks at the now involved building as well as the next adjoining one on its right, and instructed them to raise their aerials to the roof.

All of these actions took time, but the strategy was effective in stopping the horizontal spread.

The original fire building eventually showed fire on every floor as it spread upward by way of the flawed fire wall as well as other unprotected vertical openings.

Once he was assured that the high-rise, while it had been invaded by the smoke, had no fire extension into it, he was able to relax somewhat.

Heavy streams were hitting the main fire from both front and rear, although he had them moved back further out front and hit from an angle in the rear because he was concerned that they could have a collapse, particularly because he couldn't hit the fire behind the sign which was obstructing the streams.

He managed to make a survey in the building on the right and was pleased to see the district chief not only ordered all possible areas of extension opened thoroughly, he had also had the wall coverings opened for an additional two floors above the extension. The amount of fire that had gotten into the first floor ceiling was significant and had gone horizontally about half way across towards the next building before they had been able to contain it. Yeah, but they did, smiled Billy as he returned to the front of the building.

The fire in this second building was completely extinguished in about another hour, and Billy was able to reduce the number of companies to just a couple of precautionary crews.

But the main fire continued for several hours with the smoke filling a large part of the downtown area.

He was eventually able to walk out back and was pleased with the positioning of the equipment that Russ, the chief from District 3 had directed, and he was satisfied that they were taking all the action they could. Just gonna be a long night, he thought. The fire building would become a parking lot when they got done, but it couldn't be helped. The inability to get water into some of the floors because of the obstructions would result in the fire continuing to eat away at all of the combustible supports and materials inside.

He was able to reduce the size of the operating force around 0100 hours; he was also able to have the number of companies he had to retain relieved by other units from other sections of the city.

He knew when he came on duty that the boss was out of town and this was his baby for the rest of the night. Jackie Franklin had a multiple alarm in Division Two out in Jamaica Plain, but it sounded as though it was knocked down, so he would be able to handle the rest of the city, as he had been doing since Billy's fire had begun.

Billy got a cup of coffee from the Sparks Canteen, Joe got him a cheeseburger from the all night fast food joint up on Winter Street and he sat in the front seat of Ladder 24, gazing up at the powerful streams flooding the building through whatever openings were accessible. He turned to Duke who was standing on the running board beside him and said, "Lookit the cornerstone on this joint. 1879. Lot older than you and I are gonna be, old pal."

"Yeah, but it lasted a long time, didn't it. Wonder how many businesses opened and closed while it was here."

"Plenty, I bet," said Billy. "But cellars are a bitch, ain't they?"

"Sure are," replied the Duke.

"In these old places," Billy continued, "if you can't find out exactly where it is, early after you arrive, it's probably gonna sneak by you, and get up, just like tonight. When it does, forget it, you'll be looking for the building commissioner to order it torn down, like this one's gonna be."

"Yeah, Deputy. But we did the best we could. What the hell else can you try that you didn't."

"Nothin'."

When Jackie Franklin stopped by about 0400, he grabbed Billy by the shoulder and turned him around so he could see his face. "Hey, Billy," he said, "do you know your eyes are almost closed? You look lousy. How's your vision?"

"To tell ya the truth, Jack, not so hot. This shit has never stopped all night. I'm a little bit blurry."

"Yeah. Well, listen, I'll take this over. You should really go get them looked at." When Billy protested, his friend replied, "O.K. to hell with ya. When you can't see the golf ball in a coupla months, I'll just tell everyone it's your own fault," he finished with a laugh.

"Alright, alright," said Billy, "but let me show you around first." He took Jackie on a tour of the area involved and pointed out why he had everything set up the way he did. Then he notified Fire Alarm that Jackie was assuming command and Joe took him to the MGH.

While he was waiting for the optometrist to arrive, he was sitting in a small room when he heard a commotion outside his door. It was the crew from Rescue 1. They had just completed their duties at an auto accident they had been sent to after returning from the fire and had now stopped by to see Porky, who was one of the three members kept in the hospital.

"Who else is up there, Luft?" Billy asked.

"Lieutenant Toland and Crunch, from Engine 7."

"How they doing?"

"They all got headaches and Crunch has a lot of pain from his shoulder but they'll be o.k." he concluded.

"A dislocation's worse than a break," said Billy. "Jerry McEachern got one at a fire I was at and he was in agony 'till they were able to put it back in place. Bet he was out for three months before it was better."

"Yeah. Say Deputy," the lieutenant said a little hesitantly, "if you hear anything, we really didn't cause any trouble up in the ward, honest to God."

"Whaddya mean?"

"Well, while we were there, Porky told Crunch that him and Nellie saved his life from the cellar and you were gonna get them both a medal, sir. Then Crunch started yelling they were both fulla shit and the nurse came in. Boy, was she pissed. It's four in the morning and all of her patients are awake. She said, my brother's a jake but he ain't an asshole, like all of you are."

He continued, "Then that ball-breaker, Lieutenant Toland, gets in the act and says to the nurse, 'Please miss, these two brave fire fighters,' pointing to Porky and Nellie, 'saved this poor slob when he panicked at the fire.' Well, that was it for Crunch. He tried to jump outta bed to get at Toland and his shoulder almost got torn from the socket. Boy was he screaming. The nurse called security and I figured we'd all get arrested so we screwed down to here."

"Nellie," asked Billy, "what really happened down the cellar?"

"Well, sir, to tell ya the truth, we were a little ahead of Seven's line, tryin' to find the fire. It was hot as a bastard and we couldn't see shit. We heard this kinda rollin' sound start and could feel the air suckin' past us and the lieutenant," he pointed at Dinny, "told us to move out quick. He didn't have to say nothin' 'cause we were already movin' back as fast as we could. Seven's line was open, hittin' towards the fire. We plowed into them so hard that we pushed them right up the stairs and out inta the alley. Crunch was on the nozzle and I think it got jammed between the door and his shoulder as he flew out inta the alley."

"No medal, then, huh, Nellie?" Billy asked with a smile.

"No sir, not unless you wanna give them out to guys for shittin' their pants, 'cause that's what we were all doin".

Billy shook his head as they left. There's some pretty strange characters on this job, he reflected. And I think I got most of them. Gonna keep them, too.

As Billy continued to wait for the eye doctor, he started thinking about the relationship between Lieutenant Toland and Crunch. Toland was one of the brightest guys Billy had met and probably could have become a chief many years before. But after he made the first step, he never opened another book. When Billy became a deputy and assumed command of the division, it didn't take him long to figure out that this guy not only was a terrific jake with outstanding judgement at fires, but his I.Q. had to be up in the super intelligent division.

As time went by he got to know him better; he said to Toland one day, "Luft, how come you never take an exam?"

"Probably because I'm so content, sir," was the answer.

"That's the worst enemy of a good student," said Billy.

"Oh it is, it is," said Toland. "But I'm about as happy as anyone you've got on this job. I love the company, I love the running card, we get all the work I want, and these guys," he waved his hand, to encompass his crew who were watching TV in the nearby recreation room, "keep me laughing all the time. Lookit that Crunch in there. Has to be the world's most gullible person. They're all working on him now and telling him he's better than any of those NFL linemen they got on the football reruns.

"You know, Deputy, I watch guys like yourself, also. Oh, you seem to like the job too, but I don't ever wanna get involved in all those personnel problems you're always running into. I got four guys. We've been together for years and we respect each other very much. This is a team, and I'll be here until I get pensioned."

I guess I couldn't argue with that logic, thought Billy. A happy guy is something worth keeping and I hope he's around as long as I am.

Yeah, but Dinny is right. He's a ball-breaker, particularly with his star, Crunch.

Crunch had been a hockey and football star in high school and continued on the gridiron in the Boston Park League long after graduation. He married the high school cheerleader and had a few kids, settling down in his old neighborhood in the Charlestown district of the city.

"Townies," as they are called, are about as independent a group of people as can be found anywhere, although the people from the Southie district are not especially noted for their compliance with legal or political directives they disagree with. Maybe that's why they get along so well. Both communities fiercely resisted the forced busing system established by the federal courts in the seventies, and they became even more parochial as a result of what they perceived to be interference with their lifestyles.

Yep, they had great pride and didn't mind displaying it, either.

Billy smiled as he distinctly remembered the fire he had last summer over there. It was on the north side of Charlestown on a street that continued on into the city of Somerville.

The fire was in a row of three deckers and it was so intense it jumped across an alley into a similar building in the adjoining city. Of course, Boston had a Mutual Aid arrangement with the town, so Somerville jakes had responded on the initial alarm anyway and the operation was handled without regard for border lines in the usual cooperative manner.

Three deckers, because they are made entirely of wood, burn with great intensity. However, since most of them were built in a time when labor and materials were cheap, they were constructed sturdily by craftsmen who took immense pride in their trade and made certain there was no shortage of nails and screws to lock in the massive timbers that constituted the framework.

Consequently, three deckers hardly ever collapse in a fire, and on the rare occasions when they do, are usually pulled in upon themselves. There's an old fire fighting axiom that is pretty accurate, although nothing is certain in this strange business. It says, "Brick walls fall out, wooden walls fall in," and it comes from the way both styles of buildings are erected.

That fire was one of the rare ones, recalled Billy. Three of the involved buildings had a common fire escape structure attached across the rear, into the supports of the buildings.

The fire, which had entered several rooms in each occupancy, ate into the beams and without warning, the entire back of the three buildings fell out into the vacant lot in the rear.

Billy was directing operations at the front and he was startled by the report. He promptly ordered evacuation of all jakes working inside and was gratified to find out, by sheer luck, nobody had been killed.

He chuckled now, but not then, as he remembered one engine company didn't get the word and when he realized they were still up on the top floor, he sprinted up the front stairs and yelled at them to get out.

The officer, who was a very dedicated jake, was startled when he heard the voice and looked around and said, "Jeez, Deputy, we don't hafta leave, we're doin' great. I think it's startin' to lift."

"Oh, yeah, Bobby? Take another look." The smoke had cleared as a result of the huge opening and now it could be plainly seen there was no back wall. Just the moon, hanging up in the clear night, surrounded by stars.

"Whoa, let's go, boys," said the officer and they all scrambled down the front to the street.

Billy used heavy streams both front and rear, and the lack of walls made penetration from the rear very effective.

He happened to glance to his left and could see one ground ladder still up to a third floor window and for cripessake, there was a jake up on the top rungs, playing directly into the fire.

All of the other companies were pouring water in from safe positions across the street, but here's this clown trying to get inside.

He moved down to the foot of the ladder and saw Lieutenant Toland casually leaning against the line that extended up the rungs.

"Lieutenant, what the hell are you doin'. Get that guy down, right away."

"Deputy, you don't understand," was the cool reply.

"Understand what?" he asked incredulously.

"That's Crunch up there and he wants to get killed. See across the street, there's his wife, the cheerleader, his kids and all his neighbors. He's gonna prove how brave he is by getting burned to death."

"Not at my fire, he ain't. Get him the fuck down, right now."

As Crunch descended, Toland grabbed Billy by the arm because he could see he was in a rage. "Lemme speak to you a minute, Deputy," he pleaded as Billy pulled away.

"I thought you had more brains, Luft."

"Listen, sir. When the back walls fell out, we were up in that front room. I got them all down the ladder right away, even before you gave the word. But, then I snuck back in to take a look around. Honest to God, this section here is really o.k. The back is intact and we probably could have stayed there, but it's not worth it.

"Crunch was really in no danger up on top of that thirty-five but he thought he was and he wanted to be a hero. So, I let him go. But believe me, I was watching him all the time."

Billy shook his head and was raising his finger to deliver another tongue-lashing. Toland said, "Look over there, Deputy. 'Ja ever see such worship." There was Crunch, the cheerleader's arms around his neck, his kids circling his knees and his neighbors staring at him in awe. True rhapsody.

The eye guy gave him a thorough examination, a bottle of drops and a prescription. He told Billy to stay home for a few days and he should be alright. Just irritation from the continuous smoke and the particles that were carried throughout the area. Billy's group was scheduled for seventy-two hours off so he didn't have to go on injured leave.

The department hospital representative took him back to quarters, waited for him to get cleaned up and brought him home. He arranged to have Billy's car delivered to him and gave him the morning papers, which had dramatic pictures of the fire.

Those hospital reps are great, thought Billy. What a bitch it used to be going to the hospital before the department established the position. He could remember sitting in the waiting room of City Hospital on a Saturday night, waiting his turn to get stitched while a lineup of guys with gunshot and knife wounds would be whipped past into the emergency rooms, with the cops who were arresting them carrying them in for treatment.

But a few commissioners ago, an on duty guy was assigned the duty of going to the hospital whenever a jake went for services of any kind and making certain he was admitted promptly. The theory is that a guy working for the citizens who is hurt while serving them shouldn't have to get in line behind anyone else.

When the hospital rep position was formalized, the assignments were given to jakes who were in their sixties and had at least twenty-five years of continuous fire fighting assignments. This rule was established to prevent the job from becoming a soft tit for someone politically connected.

Yeah, and it worked swell, thought Billy. The Relief Fund made certain the reps were well supplied with enough dough to provide newspapers and any other articles hospitalized jakes needed. It also saw to it that all the emergency room nurses, doctors and attendants in all of the area hospitals received nice little presents at Christmas time.

The hospital reps were provided with a list of all of the best specialists in the city for any type of injury or illness and would willingly produce the names whenever wives or kids of jakes needed help.

With all its faults, the job sure takes care of its own, thought Billy, as he groped his way up his front stairs and into his house.

15

Boy, I feel much better today, Billy thought as he pulled his car up onto the apron of the firehouse. The three days off had done the trick. By yesterday afternoon, his headache was gone and the eye drops had taken away the bluriness from his vision.

Good thing, because he had heard on the radio news that there was a fire in progress downtown on West Street, the short street that runs from Tremont to Washington.

Yeah, the temperature had dropped again, and the weatherman reported it was six degrees at 0630. He had been hoping as he traveled along Summer Street, heading in the direction of downtown, that maybe his pal, Jerry, had knocked down the fire and was back in quarters. But, as he crossed the Summer Street Bridge, he could see that clouds of grayish smoke were visible rising from ahead, beyond and just to the left of the Jordan Marsh and Filene's department stores. These two retail giants face each other on Summer Street as it ends and becomes Winter Street. Washington Street slices between both arteries and the intersection constitutes the heart of the city's major shopping district, called Downtown Crossing.

Only foot traffic is permitted in the area during business hours, but that doesn't mean the fire won't fuck up the rush hour, Billy thought, because the cars would be diverted from surrounding streets as a result of the fire.

Think I'll let the cops worry about that, he thought, as he backed his car into the garage of the empty firehouse.

He called Fire Alarm from his office, asked what they had, and told them to notify the deputy at the fire that his relief was in quarters.

The operator replied, "Yes, Deputy, we'll let him know, right away. We've got a third alarm at Box 1451. The chief reported an overlapping fire on two floors when he arrived and struck a second before he got out of the car. He kept everyone out of the building and the Communications Unit reports it's strictly an outside job."

"What's burning?" Billy asked.

"The Brattle Book Store," was the reply. Oh, yeah, Billy remembered, that's a famous joint. Lotta irreplaceable stuff in there. The literary intelligentsia will be pissed. I'll have to tell the press it's Jerry's fault.

He carefully dressed for what he suspected would be an outside job in the bitter cold. Thermal underwear and socks, black Navy CPO shirt, which he bought from the Ships' Stores down at the Coast Guard Base on Commercial Street, and a knitted woolen watch cap he got from the same place.

He also grabbed an extra pair of woolen mittens from the top shelf of his locker. Every year, as soon as the first ice showed up on the ground ladders raised at fires in December, a salesman automatically arrived at each firehouse in the city and did a land-office business selling this vital winter hand protection, which fire fighters forgot were necessary once April arrived.

Of course, the wool cap made him look a little goofy, with his leather helmet squeezed on top of it, but who gives a shit—long as your ears don't freeze. Besides, the low temperatures that made such cumbersome gear necessary reduced the observers at the scene to only the junior members of the media, the volunteer manned canteen trucks, and a small contingent of the most dedicated sparks and buffs. The undedicated curiosity seekers would glance down the street, towards the fire, and speed rapidly past to their destinations, figuring, fuck that, I'll see it on TV tonight.

When he went downstairs, the car had arrived, and "Sugar" Kane, Jerry's aide, was climbing out of the ice-encased Crown Vic. Joe was waiting to start exchanging radios and gear and he helped his frozen partner out of his frozen clothing.

"How is it, Sugar?" asked Billy.

"Deck gun job, Deputy. We never got in. Too much fire. Place looks like an ice ball now but the car's warm. Kept the heater on high since we got there."

Joe handed Billy a container of coffee and they drove out of the house towards the scene. High Street to Pearl to Franklin and as they turned left on Wash, the visibility was dramatically reduced by the combination of smoke and steam choking the streets. Funny, thought Billy, when the temperatures're in the single numbers, smoke doesn't rise as well as when it's warmer.

There's probably a great theoretical explanation for that, he thought. But since most of the recognized fire experts who cranked out articles in the national trade journals never made it to the scene of cold weather fires, the mystery would remain intact. Come to think of it, he reflected cruelly, as he alighted from the car, the views some of them express make it clear they don't make it to many warm weather fires, either.

Jerry was standing on the sidewalk across from the fire building and he greeted Billy, "Hi pal. Lookit what I left ya."

"You're wonderful, Jer. What's the story?"

Jerry then gave him a detailed explanation of the fire. The upper floors had been completely consumed by the intensity of the fire. The roof was gone and there were some cracks in the front and back walls. These dangerous flaws were now concealed by the ice which was several inches thick from the tons of water that were still pouring in from the heavy stream appliances.

"There's no extension out back or to either side," he continued. "I've got lines in both adjoining buildings, but nothin's gotten inside them. I also got lines up on both of those roofs, playing down into the fire.

"I called the building inspector and he's called his boss to get a crane. He said o.k. but he doesn't know if they got a contractor nearby. I told them, sure there is. There's one working right around the corner on Tremont, where my pal, Billy ruined that perfectly good building the other night."

"Thank you, Jer," replied Billy, as he gazed at the ice-encrusted street lights, hydrants, fire engines and buildings that the water spray had reached along the length of West Street.

"This scene you've created reminds me of a Currier and Ives print, Jer. You oughta be proud of yourself."

"Reminds me more of the Avery Hotel that you saved a coupla weeks ago. Bet they got another crane over there," he said as he waved goodbye and walked down towards the car.

It took most of the morning to get enough apparatus moved and the crane brought in and erected into position. Once it started to chew away at the upper floors, however, the water streams were able to hit the parts of the fire that had been inaccessible and conditions rapidly improved.

Billy had been gradually reducing the operating force to just enough companies to provide the streams needed and could remove the companies and equipment from the adjoining buildings, which had remained unaffected by the fire.

He did the noon news shows but his participation was brief, being overshadowed by the literary authorities who bemoaned the loss of the venerated bookstore in their interviews.

Billy estimated the loss at over a million dollars, and when the interviewer moved away, a distinguished looking, bearded elderly man grasped his arm.

"Young man," he said, in a stern voice, with his Beacon Hill Yankee accent clearly evident, "how can you so casually snap out a dollar figure off the top of your head? Most of the books lost here are irreplaceable, and no price can really be placed on them, but your estimate is ridiculously low. What is your name, sir?" Billy, just as casually, gave him Jerry's full name and title, and walked away.

In the car, returning to quarters, he laughed as he thought of the various estimates he had made over the years. Wonder if I've ever been even close. When he first came on the job he heard an old chief telling someone that in a three decker, in those days, if you burned out a room, you'd give a thousand dollar loss. The whole building, about twenty-five grand.

Nowadays they sold for about $300,000, and when you got used to it, you could try to look wise and give any number that came to mind, while the reporters scribbled away their lead to the story. Yeah, the old geezer's right, but since no legitimate insurance company would depend on a fire chief's figures, what the hell's the difference?

Billy responded to a difficult job at the waterfront in Charlestown soon after he got back from the West Street fire; the rest of the afternoon was required to complete the gruesome task.

He was notified that the chief at the scene had requested a Navy crane to assist in removing an accident victim from a ship, and he wanted the deputy notified that the companies would be tied up for quite a while.

When Billy responded to the incident on the Mystic Docks, the district chief met him at the bottom of the gangway of an ancient, rust spotted freighter.

"Deputy," he explained, "this ship has a load of sugar for the American Sugar Refinery," which was located adjacent to the piers. "One of the cranes on the ship was picking up a load and the supports its mounted on broke away. It fell into the hold and, unfortunately, the operator went out the door and the crane landed on him and crushed him."

"He dead?"

"Oh, yeah. Poor guy's head is mashed flat. But, we can't get any purchase underneath the crane to get him out. The bags of sugar won't hold the jacks the Rescue's trying to use. The crane is enormous."

The district chief, whom Billy knew was a commander in the Navy Reserve, went on to explain that he knew the Navy had this monstrous crane available, permanently fixed to a barge because they had been practicing with it last weekend at the reserve meeting.

The two chiefs had mounted to the main deck and were starting to go to the access ladder into the hold. "How long will it take to get here, George," Billy asked.

"Take a look," was the reply and Billy stared out towards the main harbor where he could see this huge superstructure, about a half a mile away, the barge creating whitecaps as it breasted the waves against the frigid northeast wind.

Billy could see when he descended to the scene how impossible the task was. The crane was certainly huge; it had to be to unload the cargoes it hoisted to the docks. The ship was specially designed for this type of materials so there were no regular cargo booms such as are common on other carriers.

The fire companies had dug as much sugar away from under the victim as they could and had tried to use a steel plate as a base for the lift jacks without success. Part of the victim's head was exposed but its flesh had turned deep blue and it was obvious the man had died instantly.

Billy returned to the deck and was fascinated, not only by the size of the crane, but also by the skill the sailors exhibited moving it alongside the waterside of the freighter.

A chief boatswain's mate scrambled up a rope ladder and George explained the problem to him. He yelled down to his crew and in a very short period of time they rotated the crane over the cargo hold and lowered the thick wire cables expertly down to the bottom.

The jakes assisted the sailors in securing the hoist and when everything was ready, the boatswain, using a portable radio, directed his own crane operator to commence taking a strain and then making a lift. The jakes only needed about a foot's elevation to grab the victim's body, and the crane was then lowered back onto the piles of sugar.

Billy was delighted and he told George and the navy people how grateful he was. The only way he could have accomplished the recovery that he could think of was to send for a civilian crane to respond by land, and that would have surely taken hours to arrange along with the usual query, who pays?

At least when the building commissioner ordered a crane to a fire, such as this morning, the city usually won the legal battle with the building owner, whose insurance company got stuck for the tab. That commissioner was empowered to take such actions in the interest of public safety. But no fire chief was granted such authority in this town, so thank God for George and the U.S. Navy.

Of course, if Uncle Sam sent a bill six months from now, the boss up the street would refuse to pay it from his Fire Department budget and George would end up the oldest seaman second class in the entire navy reserve.

Funny business, reflected Billy. Sometimes you go for years without ever requiring a crane and I've used three this month.

He glanced through the paper as Joe was driving them back to quarters and when he got to the weather page, he glanced down the list of temperature projections. Boston tonight, 2 degrees, Chicago -5 degrees, Minneapolis -10 degrees. He glanced over at the list of foreign countries. Acapulco 84 degrees, great. Bermuda 68 degrees, nice. Shudda stayed there, he remembered fondly.

16

Well, stupid, how you gonna handle tonight's activities? This will certainly require some of your sorely lacking ingenuity.

It was 0230 and Billy was at his desk once again, just returned from a third alarm on Columbia Road in the Dorchester section of the other division.

The tour had begun kind of funny anyway, he recalled. When he arrived at work, the commissioner called and asked him if he'd conduct a class at Fire College on high-rise operations during the next few days. He wanted him to tell the students about the most recent incident with the blind elevator shafts. "I plan to have the district chiefs there, too," he said.

Billy replied, "Sure, boss. I think that's a great idea. Should I tell them we were scratching our heads quite a bit? Oh, not you, sir, of course. Just us subordinates."

"Billy, you're getting as bad as the Redhead. How's your vision? I understand you tried to blow out an eyeball on Tremont Street while I was away."

"All better. If you wanna see a Winter Wonderland, get a look at the Ice Palace on West Street that Jerry created."

"I tried to, but the crane had destroyed all of the artistry the *both* of you designed. Wish we could have caught the earlier classes for this high-rise stuff, but this will have to do. See you the day after tomorrow at 0830."

The Fire College is a very short and intense course that each company officer is required to attend once a year. It had been going on for as long as Billy had been on the job and the current boss was determined to make it worthwhile. He required the deputies to recommend the curricula at their fall meeting and he would then have the training deputy chase around for the best department instructors, while the personnel deputy arranged the attendance schedule.

The course is given so that each officer attends for two full day tours, about thirty captains and lieutenants at a time.

The reason the course is so short is because of the vacation calendar. Fire departments cannot shut their doors during July and August so that everyone will get a chance to take their kiddies away while they're out of school. Nor can they reduce the operating force to a token response hoping there'll be no fires. Fires don't give a shit what the date is.

Consequently, vacations begin in the middle of February and end on December 31st and they are equalized so that company strength is maintained.

Oh, it's rotated over a period of nine years so that every member gets a prime summer time assignment every third year, but it's a complicated system that requires one officer to be devoted all year long to making certain there's always enough help to put out the fires everyone was hired to fight. He also has to make sure no one gets screwed.

Since the whole program is part of the union contract, any complaint would become a grievance, but the computerization of Headquarters has eliminated most of the glitches, and the system operates efficiently.

Because of the numbers game, there are only six weeks all year when there are no vacations scheduled. This is the period commencing January 2nd and ending in mid-February. It's the one time all year when companies have extra help, and thus the only time a portion of the officers can be pulled out of their units for classroom training without jeopardizing the capabilities of the suppression forces.

The fact that they'll be back on their companies for night tours makes for a stronger response to fires during the six weeks, but with the number of fires, the snow and cold weather that show up each year, the extra help is welcome.

The deputies' input, into the subject matter is much better than in the past, thought Billy. The company officers at least got instructions that help them do their jobs better in everything ranging from fire fighting and haz-mat operations to personnel problems and infectious diseases.

Billy chuckled as he thought about the courses when he was a junior officer many years ago. After being promoted to lieutenant, he conscientiously reported to Memorial Hall to attend his first Fire College. He sat next to Philo, a guy who had been an officer longer than Billy had been alive and who was startled to see the new kid equipped with a yellow block of legal paper and a couple of pens.

"You won't need that stuff, Billy. This ain't Harvard Law here, ya know."

The instructor, who was even older than Philo, announced they were going to concentrate that year on the brand new Boston Fire Code and a test would be held on the last afternoon, so pay attention.

Billy did his best to keep his mind from drifting but it was the most boring shit he had ever heard. It required a supreme effort for him to stay awake, particularly after lunch, but he tried as hard as he could. At one point, during the monotonous drone, he noticed the instructor lost track of what he was saying. I think the son of a bitch fell asleep from the sound of his own voice, Billy reflected.

They called him Mother Beecham because he was a very prim and prissy guy who retreated to Headquarters soon after making lieutenant. He found the jakes on the companies far too crude to handle.

He was usually very enthusiastic, no matter what nonsensical subject they had him deliver, because, after all, he didn't want to go back to a fire company on the line. But the Fire Code was so dull, it even got to him.

Billy glanced around the room and realized he was the only one who noticed that Mother had dozed off for awhile. Sure. All the rest of class was sleeping anyway. Philo had a gentle snore going, prompted by the two beers he had consumed during lunch hour.

How the hell are these guys gonna pass the test? The whole fuckin' class will flunk. Jeez, I hope they don't make us come back.

He should have known better. After Mother passed out the test questions on the last day, he left the room and did not return for at least thirty minutes. Immediately, most of the jakes grabbed their previously unopened Code books and scribbled away furiously, copying the answers verbatim.

All except Philo, who scrawled for a couple of minutes and said, "Hey Billy. Turn this in for me will ya?"

"Sure, Philo. Where ya goin'?"

"Home. Good to see ya, old pal. Ja learn anything?"

"Yeah. I think I did, Philo. This ain't for real is it?"

"Naw, but it keeps Mother outta the cold. See ya at the big one," he concluded with the standard departure phrase used by jakes everywhere.

When Billy finished, he glanced at Philo's one page answer to the test. It was pretty concise and said, "Up yours, Mother," among a few other niceties.

Billy figured, well, at least I should get a good mark. I answered every question without cheatin'.

When the marks were released in March, Billy received a gentleman's B along with most of the class.

Philo got an A plus and was designated as Most Attentive Student. Good system. Fear is a wonderful weapon.

Early during the night tour, Billy responded to a second alarm in a four story brick and wood dwelling in South Boston. The first company at the scene ordered the extra alarm because there was a woman with two kids at a top floor window, cut off by the fire which was extending up the only stairway from a fully involved room on the first floor.

Fortunately, everything worked out well. The first truck got the stick up to the occupants without difficulty and the first engine company got water immediately so that by the time Billy arrived at the scene, the people were out of the building and the fire was almost knocked down.

Nice, Billy remembered. Those are bonus jobs. Sometimes it goes good and some times not so hot. If the water does not arrive promptly, or the ladder is blocked by wires or some other obstructions, the eleven P.M. news will have a different lead story.

While Billy was talking to the district chief, Joe notified him that an engine company had just ordered a second alarm sounded from the opposite end of the same district. Billy notified Fire Alarm he was available and was responding. Joe managed to get the car out of the congestion around the first fire without too much difficulty.

While they were enroute, the address was announced and Billy realized the location was on the opposite side of Columbia Road.

This meant the fire was in the next district and also in the other division since the dividing line runs down the middle of this main artery. But he kept going because it was an actual fire; boundaries can be sorted out later.

As they passed over the MBTA tracks at JFK Station and under the Southeast Expressway, the visibility was sharply impeded from the heavy smoke and the street lights' usual brightness was reduced to a dull, yellow glow.

When they crossed Dorchester Avenue and passed St. Margaret's Church on the right, Billy could see the fire on the opposite side of the street. It involved one side of a duplex three decker, and his first impression was that people were coming down everywhere. Each of the thirty-five foot ladders within his view were crowded with occupants scrambling down and the fire was still extending upward.

He ordered a third alarm as he looked directly ahead of him at a short roof, one story high, that connected the two separate three story occupancies.

The other two floors were set back from this lower protrusion and a short ladder was leaning against this roof. Another ladder extended from this surface up to a top floor window and black smoke was swirling around the top of the rungs.

At the bottom of the ladder, an unmoving figure was visible, stretched out on the top of the short roof.

Billy called for ambulances and ordered a ladder company to "Get that body off there."

When Fire Alarm received the correct address, they notified Jackie Franklin and the chief of the Dorchester district that the fire was on their side and they soon arrived as Billy was having hose lines moved into both buildings.

He told Jackie when he relieved him that at least one person appeared to be dead and several others, mostly elderly, had been taken over ladders and transported to hospitals.

He decided to remain at the scene and entered the original fire building to make an evaluation for Jackie. Engine companies were effectively knocking down the fire on the first two floors, but the third floor was much more difficult. There was a three foot cockloft separating the ceilings from the roof and the fire had gained tremendous headway throughout the area while the fire fighters were rescuing the occupants.

He requested more ladder companies from Jackie to get all of the ceilings opened and told him the fire was extending into the adjoining building through the same concealed spaces.

He managed to cross over to the other side via the rear porches and was not surprised to see the fire had already entered the loft above three rooms.

More assistance was sent up to his location and he could hear power saws cutting holes in the roof, over his head. The job proved to be extremely difficult, primarily due to this unavoidable delay in providing effective overhead ventilation, but the ladder companies were committed to the task as they became available.

When it was over, Billy returned to the street and said to Jackie, "Everything's all set. How many killed?"

"Far as I know, Billy, none. We got them all," Jackie replied.

"What about the one lying on the roof?"

"Tell him, Frank," Jackie said to the officer from the first arriving ladder truck, who was standing beside him.

"Yeah, Deputy. When we came in, they were hangin' out everywhere. We got up two thirty-fives to some people in the alley." He continued, "Engine 21 threw that short ladder from there up to the third floor window. They couldn't run a line, 'cause there was no other truck here yet. Tony," he named the lieutenant on the engine company, "went up the top floor, and honest to God, he found two old women and an old guy stumbling around in the smoke." He paused and said, "I have no idea how he did it, but he got all three over to the window and his crew pulled them onto the ladder. By the time the last one got out the window, Tony was collapsing and he fell head first down the ladder and onto the roof. His guys were lugging the victims down to the street and didn't know he was hurt."

Jackie told Billy the lieutenant was unconscious when he was transported from the scene and they had no report on him yet.

Billy agreed to stop at the hospital and relay word back to the fire. When he arrived, the department hospital representative told him the injured officer was going to be alright. He had inhaled a substantial amount of carbon monoxide while getting the people out and he had a concussion from landing on the roof, but his helmet had saved him from more serious injuries.

Billy managed to speak to him in the emergency room, and while he had a severe headache from the CO and the blow to his head, he was lucid. Tony confirmed what had happened and expressed regret that he couldn't run a line first, but he really had no choice.

"Tony," Billy said, "you did terrific. Your judgement saved a lot of lives. Sometimes the SOPs have to go out the window and this was one of them." Tony was pleased to hear no one had died, and he was dozing off to sleep from the medication when Billy departed.

He stopped back at the fire and saw Jackie dismissing many of the companies.

When he reported Tony's condition, Jackie said, "That's great. Do you think we should write him up for this job?"

"Absolutely. I'll be a witness. He was tremendous."

"O.K. old pal. Glad you think so. But you'd better vote for him next year."

"Oh, I will, I will."

"Swell," said Jackie, "what about Spider?"

Oh shit, Billy said to himself. You dummy. Let me see you get outta this one, he thought as he leaned back in his desk chair.

Let's see, you're gonna propose Spider's name and then be a witness for a guy from the other division.

Hey, he thought, as he wiped the complications from his mind, you haven't even got by this year's meeting yet and you're worried about next year. Forget it. Something'll happen. It always does.

17

Billy stood at the podium in Memorial Hall and looked around the room. Boy the place looks good, he thought. The Hall is on the top floor of the Headquarters building and it is named in honor of the Boston jakes who have been killed in the line of duty. Just below the ceiling, at the top of the wall, is a moulding that travels around the room; resting on the moulding are the official photographs of the members who have been killed. Since some men died before the advent of cameras, those plaques have Maltese Crosses and list the members' biographical data.

The count is up to 166, mused Billy. Be nice if it never went any higher, but unfortunately it will.

He was so pleased the current boss had gotten the place cleaned up. The last administration, which survived for far too long, had let the place go to hell. Never painted, never cleaned, a lot of junk stored in corners. What a shithouse it had become.

The guy we got now had made it priority to make the Hall a fitting tribute to all those who had been lost.

At the first deputies' meeting the new commissioner conducted, he said that all of these fellows who died are our true heroes and they must never be neglected. New windows, new lights, new paint job, wall to wall carpet, new students' desks and chairs. He even had all the picture frames restored to their original splendor. Place looks classy, thought Billy.

He liked the new system on promotions, too. Billy remembered each of his four advancements in rank. His name came out in orders and that was the end of it. Now they had an official ceremony in this hall, with wife, kids and friends present to congratulate those who had made the grade. A small buffet, plenty of photos, the whole thing lasting only about an hour. But the newly promoted members really felt important.

Billy glanced down at the group he was to teach and saw that it was the usual mixture of young, old and mid-career guys. A sprinkle of minority officers in the class indicated how the job continued to evolve.

He talked to them at great length about the high-rise fire and what they had learned from the incident. First of all to consider that there may be victims in elevators in blind shafts, which no one had even thought about at the recent incident. They would from now on, you can bet, he told them. He also emphasized how valuable the members' personal lights were in the totally black stairways; how they not only assisted in lighting the way for the evacuation, but how they had a calming effect on the badly frightened occupants.

When he was finished, he asked for questions and was quite pleased when many members of his audience raised their hands. It was great that they were so interested in the subject, and he answered the best he could. He chuckled when he remembered that Mother Beecher never got any questions except from Philo who always asked, "What time do we go to lunch?"

Billy even told them about his first experience with high-rise buildings when he was a company officer on a ladder company a couple of decades ago.

When he arrived at the scene he was notified there was a fire on the eighth floor of a twelve story apartment house. Because he didn't know any better, he and his crew took the passenger elevator right to the fire floor. No masks, no hose, no brains, no nuthin'. It was just shear luck that any of them survived.

When the door opened, he could see to his left that the kitchen of the apartment was heavily involved in fire. The heat and smoke immediately enveloped all of them and drove them out of the elevator onto the fire floor. They were forced to crawl to their right away from the kitchen and, fortunately, there was an exit stairway on the side that they fell into in their scramble to escape.

"If the stairway had been beyond the fire, we all would have had our pictures up on the wall," Billy told the class.

"Stupid? Probably. But you see, we just never ran into that situation before. This business is learned by experience more than anything else I can think of—but a little common sense wouldn't hurt either. That's why the boss wanted me to come here today and pass on what we learned."

In answering several other queries, he revealed many of the tactics for operating in these big buildings that he had learned over the years.

"Always use a big line on the initial attack," he said. He was constantly amazed when he read in the trade journals about fire departments starting the attack with smaller lines. "Remember, you're going up several stories high. It's not like a three decker where you can dash down to the street and get what you need quickly. Bring your best weapon with your from the beginning. It will work much better on the fire, but its primary purpose is to protect you and your company. You can always make a big line smaller, but you can never make a small line bigger. Those smaller lines also require a hell of a lot more pressure than is available from the building fire pumps in order to produce the streams they're designed for."

He went on to relate how the elevators always seemed to get screwed up in high-rises, so it's imperative to take as much gear as you can up initially, otherwise everything may have to be carried up the stairways later on. Extra air cylinders, power saws, open up tools, resuscitators, ropes and anything else you think you might need.

If you're coming to the fire as a response to a multiple alarm, use one hour cylinders on your masks and bring as many thirty minute ones as you have for spares.

Keep in mind that the electrical power is usually on until the individual floors can be killed because the juice is necessary for the elevator, lights and possible use of exhaust systems. Always use your fire fighter's key to control the elevators, and, if possible, use the freight or service cars. They're bigger, can handle more people and equipment, and also stop at every floor, which is not always the case with passenger elevators.

On the way up, push a button four or five floors below your destination, to make sure you have proper control of the car. The SOPs tell you to get off two floors below the fire, but if you're first to arrive, keep in mind that you may have been given the wrong floor number.

He discussed a number of other safe operating practices and particularly emphasized they should never go above the fire floor unless there were endangered occupants who had to be saved.

He kept answering questions until the designated time for class ended and was delighted that some members even stayed to ask more before he left the room. He was pleased with their thirst for knowledge and was convinced the new breed was going to do fine.

It didn't mean the guys in my early years weren't as smart. The leadership of the department in those days simply wasn't very skilled at knowing what the members were looking for or how to get the message across.

You have to keep the information job related and interesting. At least I didn't catch anyone nodding off this morning. Hm, maybe they wont' do any better than we did after lunch.

18

Billy chuckled as he hung up the phone. I like that guy, he thought. Shudda sent him up the street to see the boss.

The caller had been a young research scientist from the Boston University School of Public Health. He said he had been alarmed when he read about the number of fire fighters who had been injured at the recent cellar fire on Tremont Street.

The article had expanded into a review of how dangerous the job of fire fighters is and how many are killed and incapacitated each year, nationwide.

The researcher had come up with what he thought was a brilliant concept and he wanted an official opinion on its value. The School of Public Health, where he did his research, had just completed a number of long term experiments using Rhesus monkeys who came from India and were noted for their intelligence. As a matter of fact, some of the scientists thought they were much more astute than some of the employees, although they would never state this publicly. He went on to explain that these cute little fellows could be taught just about anything.

He was quite certain they could be taught some of the more hazardous jobs fire fighters are called upon to do, such as crawling into tight spaces or working in cellars or tunnels. He had just read about that darling little girl in Texas who had been successfully rescued from a hole in the ground. But it took so long! Why, a Rhesus monkey would have crawled down and got her out in no time.

Billy correctly figured this call had been transferred to him by that wise-ass Fire Alarm operator Don Quade. He had a warped sense of humor—similar to Billy's own somewhat caustic wit.

The operators are very adept at fending off strange calls and requests, or if the citizen proved too insistent, they'd transfer them to Public Relations at Headquarters.

Lieutenant Michael Simmons was even better than the operators in disposing of the complainants. He was so polite and charming and spoke so rapidly, using a lot of ten dollar words, that the customer would finally hang up satisfied, or in many cases more puzzled than before he dialed the number.

The reason Don gave Billy the call was because Headquarters closed at five p.m. and it was now after six. Besides, he wanted to see how clever his friend was at salving the citizens for a change, particularly since one of Billy's fires had prompted the call.

Billy and Don's relationship went back many years to when they were both brand new officers. Billy was dispatched on an engine company to what turned out to be a fire in a street sweeper, one of those weird looking vehicles with the rotating brooms underneath that scoop up all the debris from the gutters.

Billy got a bit tongue-tied in describing what they had, first reporting a fire in a "sweet streeper" and when Don asked for clarification he said a "see sreeter" and then a "sweep sister." He finally got pissed off and unwisely reported "We got a fire in a fuckin' broom truck." Don smoothly replied, "Alright Lieutenant, you're reporting you have a fire in a motor vehicle."

Billy was worried all the way back to quarters. They say the Federal Communications Commission monitors all radio frequencies, but nobody knows that for sure. What is certain is that all the stool pigeons at Headquarters, plus every firehouse and all of the sparks and buffs, hear every goddamned thing and the civilian fire commissioner at that time seemed to hate all jakes with a passion. It's the reason the particular mayor had appointed him because he hated us, too, Billy recalled.

As it turned out, the transmission was somewhat garbled by outside interference and when the commissioner's assistant called Fire Alarm to see if what they thought they heard was true, Don Quade denied it had happened. He was instructed to play back the tape of the call and he reported politely that it had been accidently erased.

He made a friend for life with Billy, although every now and then he would bring it up, just to keep the act going. He'd also occasionally give Billy a call such as this one and then listen in to see how brilliant the upper echelon is.

Billy was just smart enough to know that B.U. had been under substantial heat lately from the animal activists. These folks were much more concerned with the lives of rats and monkeys than they were with human beings. They had recently zeroed in on the protection of the Rhesus strain as their focal point of attack.

While Billy was sure the caller was very sincere, he concluded he was probably the most junior graduate student at the school. His superiors had given him the chore of trying to unload the cute little, almost humans, on those dummies over at the fire department. What a public relations score it would be if they could pull it off! Monkeys saving people, including those brave fire fighters.

Yeah, thought Billy. Wait 'till the first one gets killed or injured. The picket lines would wind around Headquarters for weeks.

"Well, doctor," Billy replied, after pondering the proposal dramatically, "I want to thank you so much for your kindly offer. But I can foresee a number of problems that would have to be resolved before we could accept your most generous proposal."

"Oh. Like what sir?" came the query. Billy answered as though he was quoting a recruiting poster: "First they'd have to attend the Department Drill School for ten weeks, 'cause the commissioner permits no exceptions to that rule. Then they must learn our Standard Operating Procedures in order to form part of a team with the regular personnel. Would we have to install separate toilet facilities for them? Are they male or female, or some of each? Are they promiscuous or monogamous? Do they use condoms?" The kid tried to interrupt him but he continued.

"They will no doubt climb ladders better than our rookies. Will our human personnel become despondent when they watch these little folks scramble past them? What if they score better than the other recruits on the written exam each Friday?"

"But chief—" Billy cut him off. "What kind of shoulder patches should we design for their uniforms? What if they take the exam and become lieutenants?" he paused, and the student finally managed to speak. "Thank you for your time, Chief. You've certainly given me a lot to think about."

"Yes," Billy said. "In this day and age with everyone enjoying equal rights, a lot of thought has to go in to each and every decision."

"Yes sir, I agree. Now in the meantime, while I'm thinking about the answers to your very incisive questions, I don't know if you personally are either promiscuous or monogamous and I don't even know if you use condoms, but why don't you go fuck yourself, sir?" He slammed the phone down.

Billy's line rang immediately. "Yes, Don," Billy answered, no doubt about who the caller was.

"Deputy, sir, what a marvelous public relations coup that was. Would you like a copy of the voice tape, sir, perhaps to share with your peers, or even with your wonderful wife and family?"

Billy's less than thoughtful reply recommended that Don perform a number of anatomical exercises on himself, most of which, the young scientist could have told him, were impossible.

Soon after this exchange, the companies and Billy were dispatched to a report of a fire on the twelfth floor of the forty story office building at 100 Summer Street, downtown. That's the Blue Cross-Blue Shield building, Billy grinned as he got into the car. Maybe I should ask them if they'd cover Rhesus monkeys' medical problems if they come on the job. Alright, enough's enough. Let's see, twelfth floor, this place is fully sprinklered, he recalled. Yeah, but they have a big night shift working. Cleaning people up there, too. Good security force, though.

The uniformed head of security met them out front as they approached the entrance, passing by the famous lollipop art work. This rather strange looking mobile entity, with its many black arms sticking out at all angles and topped by orange disks, rotated constantly from the strong breeze that swept down the street as a result of the wind tunnels created by the numerous high buildings that led into Downtown Crossing.

"A guard reports smoke on twelve, sir," the leader reported, "he thinks he can hear the sprinklers operating and we have a water flow alarm registering at the command post."

Russ, who was the district chief, Joe, the first engine and truck crews, as well as Rescue 1, captured the elevators with the fire fighters' key and soon were ascending to the tenth floor as Billy continued questioning the head guard.

"What floors are occupied? Are the cleaners working yet? Any electrical problems?"

The district chief reported he was establishing the upper command post on ten and yes, there is smoke on twelve with at least one sprinkler head operating.

Billy was able to inform him that people were working on floors fifteen to twenty and they had not been evacuated. The cleaning staff hadn't arrived yet so those were the only floors occupied.

Russ dispatched Rescue 1 to those floors via the stairway with instructions not to evacuate anyone yet.

The ladder company members entered the fire floor and promptly reported that a desk was burning inside one of the office enclave partitions, as the engine company crew was stretching their 2-1/2" attack line into position. The truck officer further reported that a waste basket was also burning and had apparently ignited the desk. One sprinkler head was operating and dousing the fire.

Billy approved the request to shut down the sprinkler sectional valve which supplied that floor, but gave instructions to keep a jake at the control valve, just in case.

The Rescue Company reported no smoke on the occupied floors and Billy told them to hold their position there until he called them again.

The district chief had a small first aid house line stretched and filled to complete the extinguishment. He requested the air exhaust system, which had automatically shut down when the sprinkler head fused, be turned back on to get rid of the smoke.

Billy directed the head security guard to comply with the request. He had the remaining first alarm response company members standing by in the lobby with him as he waited for confirmation that the fire was confined to the enclosure.

A few minutes went by and the district chief called again, "Deputy, the smoke isn't lifting at all. I think we may have another fire. I'm turning the sprinklers back on."

Billy alerted the Rescue Company to prepare to evacuate the occupants of the upper floors and ordered the remaining fire companies in the lobby to take the freight elevator and bring all of their gear up to the tenth floor. He had the exhaust system shut down again and notified Fire Alarm that the fire wasn't under control. He also requested the Arson Squad be sent to the scene.

The floor area that had to be investigated was about 15,000 square feet; Billy ordered another big line to be stretched from the opposite stairway in order to cover the entire floor.

When light smoke started drifting up the stairway, Billy directed the Rescue Company to lead the group of employees, totaling about fifty people, down the stairway below the fire to the upper command post where they'd be safe.

Other sprinkler heads had fused on the fire floor and the force of the water drove the smoke downward, thus slowing the complete investigation of the area. But, eventually it was accomplished and Russ reported that a total of four desks were involved, widely separated across the various office spaces. He had determined there was no extension of fire to either the floor above or into the ventilation system and he requested permission to shut the sprinkler system down once again. This time it turned out o.k. The exhaust system was reactivated and the smoke was rapidly dispersed.

Billy directed the fire companies to initiate a floor by floor search of the entire building to determine if there had been any other arson attempts. When nothing was found, he gave the manager permission to allow the employees to return to their floors.

The workers all wanted to go home, some of them complaining that the arsonist might still be in the building. Billy diplomatically left that decision to the manager after explaining that the maintenance people were restoring the sprinkler system on the fire floor, the security forces were being doubled with the recall of the day crew, and fire fighters and the Arson Squad would be on the scene for a couple of more hours.

When he arrived back in quarters, he recorded some notes on the incident that he felt he could use at the next session he had to teach in Fire College. Even though the fires were minor, the incident confirmed for him, once again, that even with a fully sprinklered occupancy, you can have problems, particularly in the high-rises.

Don't shut down the system until you're sure the fire is under control; if you do, be prepared to reactivate it immediately in case a problem develops.

Also, in a large tight building such as this one, the operating sprinklers keep smoke and the carbon monoxide near the floor; it's essential, therefore, that everyone operating in the area keep their masks on until the area is well ventilated.

Didn't have to remove any windows tonight, but it's always an option to consider, provided the spectators in the street can be moved out of danger by the police.

Funny job, he mused, particularly in these big buildings. An old chief told him once when he was a rookie, "Kid, you'll keep learning this business 'till the day you retire, and believe me, even then you still won't know everything."

Yeah, he recalled, that wise old geezer told me that when there were only a few high-rises in the whole city. He sure as hell didn't know anything about fires in them back in those days. Nope, but he fully understood what every fire fighter should. The dangers and hazards of the profession keep changing and expanding and you better pay attention to them.

Oakie and Bob Pine, the on duty Arson Squad investigators, stopped by to tell Billy they had grabbed a suspect for the four fires. He was locked up at Police Division One and, unlike the solution to most arson cases, this one was a piece of cake.

A guy from the maintenance staff had been fired tonight. He was a drunk who had received numerous warnings and counseling about his problem and this evening was his last chance.

Instead of leaving the building when he was dismissed, he went up the stairway to the twelfth floor and used his passkey to gain access. He set all four fires. When Oakie and Bob received the information, they took the superintendent of maintenance with them to canvass the several bars in the immediate downtown area.

The suspect was in the first joint they entered; the super knew it was his favorite hangout.

"The guy smelled of smoke, just like a jake after a fire," said Oakie, "and he offered no resistance. My clever partner," he nodded towards Bob Pine, "sat down beside him, bought him a drink, and pretty soon the guy blubbered out his life story. He waived his rights at Police Division One and will be arraigned tomorrow."

"Yeah, I wish they were all that easy," said Bob.

"Naw, ya don't," said Billy. "You love that challenge and all that investigating shit. The pair of you shouldda been cops."

This team had been together now for well over a decade and both men were close friends of Billy. Oakie and Billy had been stationed together long before he went on the Arson Squad, and Bob had broken into investigative work with Oakie as his lieutenant. Bob eventually made lieutenant himself, but by then the team had recorded so many successful cases that they were kept together even though that was not the usual procedure.

They had gained nationwide prominence as a result of the major cases they had solved, and while they worked a regular work shift, they were frequently put in charge of difficult operations that would require long term investigation.

Their most notable case involved a serial killer back in the seventies, but they had many less newsworthy arrests and successful prosecutions since then.

Billy asked the pair if they were having any luck with the most recent fires. January was always busy, but the last few weeks seemed like a crime wave to Billy.

"Well, Deputy," said Oakie with a grin, "the number of buildings you personally have destroyed this month should keep us in business for the rest of the year. Thank God you went away for a week or we'd never get finished."

Bob Pine explained that the fire in East Boston was definitely set. In spite of the bitter cold, some nut had ignited a pile of rubbish under a rear porch and the fire spread to a five gallon can of gasoline that was kept outside, illegally of course, for an outboard motor that the owner kept down the cellar during the winter. When the can let go, the fire was everywhere. For once, those people who reported an explosion were right.

Witnesses were always saying something "blew up" and, in most cases, they were wrong. It's just an impression they get when they first notice a fire, and it's an impression they'll continue to believe no matter what the real evidence turns out to be.

The three men spent an hour or so reminiscing, then the team had to return to the police division, giving Billy the same admonition every jake uses: "Hope we don't see you again tonight."

Billy thought about how they kidded him for all of his recent fires. Yeah, they're right, but it just confirmed how strange the business is. He believed that if you took a ten year look at the records of the deputies in the two divisions, they would come out almost identical in the number of major fires they had commanded. But, each individual year there was one guy who did more than all of his counterparts combined. Then it would die out for him and someone else would become the leader.

Looks like it's my turn again. No sense in complaining "why me?" 'cause it will move along in time. It better, he thought, or the boss will have me up the street cutting out paper dolls.

At 0221 hours Box 7527 was struck for the report of a ship fire in the old South Boston Navy Yard.

Boston used to have two navy yards back in the days when the world kept trying to destroy itself. But following the Vietnam conflict, both yards were phased out in the mid-seventies.

The one in the Charlestown district, which was the older of the two, had many of its buildings renovated and converted into condos, and new structures were also built. It's presently the location of hundreds of upscale occupancies with docking berths for their power and sail boats as well as a few real yachts. None of the expensive residences are owned or occupied by any of the former Navy Yard employees.

The site is also the home of the *U.S.S. Constitution*, the oldest and most famous commissioned ship in the U.S. Navy. Along with "Old Ironsides" is a decommissioned World War II destroyer.

Both vessels attract tens of thousands of visitors annually, none of whom, like the ex-workers, ever get near the condos or their current residents.

The South Boston Yard was closed first and was used to store a large number of ships in the Navy's mothball fleet following the second world war. But these craft were sold for junk as the years slipped by and the cold war dragged on without any need to reactivate these units. A couple of shipyards came and went through the decades, and eventually the entire complex was taken over by the city during the eighties.

The buildings are rented by hundreds of private businesses today and it is, once again, a thriving area. Its many piers and docks remain intact and it handles about thirty cruise ships that visit the port during the year. There are also frequent stops by warships from the U.S., Canada and other nations.

The size of both yards was more than sufficient to handle all of the Tall Ships that visited during the bicentennial in 1976 and their repeat stop in 1992. The South Boston drydock is intact and accommodated the *Q.E. II* without difficulty when she required temporary repairs following her grounding in New England waters the same year.

But the fire tonight was not in any famous or newsworthy craft. It was on a 150 foot long motor vessel at an old dock that is also the final resting place of a number of retired and decrepit old harbor ferries, tugboats and former members of the Boston fishing fleet which works the Grand Banks out in the Atlantic.

The first fire company at the scene reported fire showing from the main deck and pilot house. When Billy reported off at the location, he could see it was a much newer vessel than all of the other hulks; the lights glowing at the tops of the masts indicated it was an active ship.

The fire boat was able to maneuver into position on the water side, but Billy didn't want to utilize its heavy stream appliances because he felt an interior attack was feasible.

When it was over, he thought maybe he should have swept it with the major streams because the attack proved so difficult.

The companies made good progress in the pilot house but there was much more fire than first anticipated along the inside passageways of the main deck, the fire having extended throughout the overhead. Even when this attack was proving successful, it was discovered some staterooms were located below deck and the mattresses and other contents were involved in fire.

Four 2-1/2" lines were necessary to knock down the flames; with the use of so much water, Billy had the crew of the fire boat constantly monitoring the stability of the ship and watching the waterline in case she started settling rapidly.

The Coast Guard was also at the scene and Billy had them arrange to have the ship towed to the outer harbor if it became necessary.

Jeez, I hate any kind of ship fires, Billy reflected when it was over. The dangers to the operating force are always present because there are so many unknown factors involved. Besides all the other hazards associated with them, you must constantly consider the danger to the port itself, in the event of an explosion or rapid extension to the docks.

Every chief officer who ever works in seaports is familiar with the Texas City disaster back in the forties which killed so many fire fighters and citizens and wiped out part of the community.

In this case, none of those things happened, but it was pretty hairy, just the same.

Since it became obvious to Billy soon after his arrival that there was more than one fire, he requested the Arson Squad to respond, and Oakie and Bob were promptly at the scene. They donned their fire fighting gear and went aboard while the attack was in progress, attempting to preserve any evidence of accelerants.

As the jakes were succeeding in controlling the main body of the fire and the several smaller ones, Billy directed the fire boat personnel to set up portable pumps and get rid of the excess water which had filled the bilges and was knee deep above the deck plates in the engine room.

Oakie and Bob reported they were able to recover plenty of samples that appeared to be saturated with gasoline and they'd deliver them to the department laboratory for analysis by the chemist in the morning.

They also learned from a security guard that the ship had been impounded because it had been loaded with marijuana; the Coast Guard had boarded it once it got inside territorial waters. It had lain at the dock for over a year, awaiting the trial of those who had been apprehended, and watchmen had been assigned to guard her constantly.

But, as time passed and the usual trial postponements multiplied, reductions in the federal budget had terminated this protection and a cursory glance by patrolling guards was the outcome. If the fire had succeeded in destroying the ship, the expensive team of defense attorneys would have had a ball citing lack of evidence and other factors. The alleged perpetrators would probably die of old age or overdoses before they ever saw the inside of the courthouse at Post Office Square.

The Arson Squad was joined by members of the FBI the ATF, the U.S. Marshall's Office as well as folks from the Massachusetts State Police, so by the time Billy had most of the fire companies made up and dismissed, quite a crowd was gathered on the dock. It appeared to Billy that each group had its own agenda.

Billy bowed to Oakie and Bob as he was departing: "I'm gonna leave all of you scientists to your deliberations. Hope I don't see you again tonight. Where the hell'd I hear that before?"

19

Billy opened the thick manilla envelope and shuffled through the sheaf of papers. It was 1700 hours and his tour had just begun. His final, high-rise class yesterday had once again prevented any review of the commendations, but tonight is the night.

This is the last chance I'll get to review this stuff because the day after tomorrow is the Board meeting and then it's all over.

He was able to separate the two dozen high commendations into two groups without difficulty. The Board had established a policy a few years back that seemed to be appropriate, although as the age of the deputies increased, sometimes they weren't sure what procedure they had developed the year before and any new deputies were always challenging the Board regulations anyway.

The rule book does not recognize seniority in the deputy fire chief rank as it does for all lesser positions. Hey, once you make it up that high, the only one who is above you is the commissioner/chief of department and no one is more aware of that than a guy who just made the grade.

Thank God for Pat, the commissioner's secretary, and JJD, the district chief/executive assistant to the boss.

Pat has seen just about everything, Billy thought. Not only a parade of deputies during her two decades in the front office, but a mixed bag of commissioners as well. The bosses ranged from the civilians that used to hold the exalted post, through the uniformed guys who currently run the show.

If she ever decides to write her memoirs, it could be a best seller, he figured. She possesses a wry sense of humor that would delight most critics of public service employees if it could be captured in print. Hope it never happens, reflected Billy. If it does, we'd all end up in a "Barney Miller" type sit-com that would certainly qualify for nominations in the annual Emmy Awards.

Naw, she'd never do it. She's too kind for that. Plus she loves the department too much. Her superior intellect has kept most of her bosses from making fools of themselves from time to time, or of being indicted either. She's responsible for not only the professional reputation the office enjoys, but also the friendly atmosphere which relaxes the most frightened jake who has an appointment with the boss.

JJD, or the Commissioner's Stoolie, as he is called by the chiefs, is another matter. He really gets pissed off when someone calls him by his nickname, and his map of Ireland features twist into a scowl as his face turns beet red.

He actually is about as effective an assistant as anyone could want, and his duties include protecting the boss from all trivial matters as well as most serious complaints. He drew the assignment because of his loyalty and his knowledge of the inner workings of the bureaucracy. His fire fighting career began as a jake in the Roxbury district, where he also served as a company officer on the most active companies in the tenement ghetto areas. He moved to the downtown and South End districts as a captain and chief and was one of the most respected fire officers in the department. His organized and low key approach to fires and their control resulted in a calm atmosphere when he was in command. Not much yelling and screaming when he was directing an operation because he wouldn't permit it.

He had been transferred to Fire Prevention, following a couple of serious medical problems, and served as the assistant fire marshal for a few years at the request of the head of that division. This truly thankless job gave him the task of ruling on everything in the fire codes and state laws ranging from lighted candles on tables to erecting sixty story buildings.

He used the same approach in that assignment as he had in the field, and soon became the recognized expert, not only on legal matters, but also on how the system works, which is a rare gift.

Anyone who can figure out how city hall and the cast of weirdos who run that show downtown, as well as the state fire marshal's office and all of the other agencies and businesses who need approvals, licenses, permits and information from the department, should get a medal of their own, Billy thought.

JJD was also called by every chief and company officer. Most of them only knew fire codes and laws on the Saturdays that they took promotional exams; he answered each request patiently and seriously.

No wonder the present boss scooped him when the executive position became available. Who wouldn't? He became just as expert in that slot and the same number of guys still called him.

His friends liked to test his temper by making asinine requests, and while he knew what they were doing, he couldn't hold back when they asked more stupid questions than his usual clientele.

Billy had worked with him for several years in the field and knew a couple of things that most guys didn't. First of all, he had a much less serious view of life and the job than his demeanor indicated. A couple of Dewars and water brought out a really funny personality that made a good party better.

He also liked to gamble a bit and his daily number plays with the department bookie as well as the state lottery commission were essential components of his work day.

Billy and a select few other friends of JJD made an annual trek with their wives to Vegas. From the time they arrived until they left five days later, JJD would use all of his secret systems at the blackjack, roulette and dice tables before departing for McCarran Airport, just as broke as his companions.

He'd have to be dragged from the slots in the terminal onto the plane before the door was closed, determined to recoup his losses while refusing to admit that his pockets were empty.

The Board's current procedure established that if the request for a high commendation, submitted by the deputy in charge of the incident or division where the act occurred, concluded after his investigation that the personal risk involved in the action was "extreme", the report would be relegated to consideration in the Medal category. If the investigation resulted in a finding of "great" or "unusual" personal risk, the act would be considered for the Roll of Merit or one of the lesser awards.

Of course, the Board reserved the right to upgrade the degree of risk if the full body reached that verdict, but it seldom happened.

So Billy skimmed through the pile and quickly ended up with one thick stack for less than "extreme" risk acts and a very thin sheaf of reports for jakes qualified for Medal consideration.

He read each report thoroughly, starting with the lesser awards and was pleased by the number of really good jobs that had been performed. He felt the same way each year during his review and it always increased his pride in the job and the type of people he worked with.

The percentage of reports that didn't involve fires in these categories grew each year and he thought it was a legitimate reflection of the changes in society. Nowadays there was always a member or members being cited for capturing or pursuing a criminal who mugged someone, snatched a car, sold dope or even committed an armed robbery.

Jakes even got caught up in a couple of hostage situations and occasionally talked potential suicides out of killing themselves. Years ago, street crime was pretty rare, especially in the daytime when most of the current incidents occurred.

Yeah, the world keeps changing and jakes see it happening just as quickly as cops do.

There were two incidents involving apprehension of felons by minority fire prevention inspectors who worked the ghetto districts; in both cases Billy would be certain to vote for a Roll of Merit because of the risk each member took.

One guy chased a drug dealer he saw selling crack to some school kids and tackled him in an alleyway, and sat on him until the police arrived. The other jake was making a routine inspection of an oil burner in the basement of an apartment house and heard a woman screaming from an upper floor. He raced up the stairs and burst into a room where a huge man was beating the shit out of a young girl, a classic pimp-hooker confrontation. He flashed his badge, said he was a cop, let the girl get by him and then ran like hell as the giant figured out the patch on his shoulder said Boston Fire Department.

Billy laughed as he recalled reading about this particular incident in the paper. The jake had held the city record for the 220 yard run when he was an All Scholastic track star at English High School. He stated that he easily eclipsed every mark he had ever set while dashing up Warren Street until the cops finally caught up with the culprit.

There were a couple of requests for Distinguished Service Awards that didn't involve bravery, just quick action and common sense. Both incidents required the use of the Heimlich maneuver to save people who were choking and they would certainly be approved in that category.

Jeez, one of these jakes was his old pal, Willie, who was finishing out his career as a Hospital Rep. Must be getting close to the maximum age by now. Son of a gun had half a dozen kids already when we were in drill school together back in the fifties.

The drillmaster for their class was Fire Captain Augustus Beaupre and the school was located on Bristol Street in the South End. It's now the location of the Pine Street Inn which is the haven for hundreds of the homeless who roam the city streets. Yeah, another lousy change in society, thought Billy.

The drill school featured an eight story tower and every jake had to reach the top window opening several times, using the sixteen foot, single beam pompier scaling ladder to climb up the face of the structure. The pomps as they are called, are used primarily to instill confidence in jakes working at heights, although they were originally carried on every ladder truck to be used for rescue attempts when all other resources had failed.

The last time one of these devices was used at a fire in Boston was in 1917 when a jake ascended to the tenth floor of the Hotel Lennox and picked off an occupant who was trapped by a fire. By the 1970's the design of ladder trucks had changed and there was no longer room to carry these tools so they disappeared from actual fire fighting while being retained at the school.

The modern tower height is now only five stories, a much less intimidating task than the old training facility had.

Classes were and are required to do a rope slide from the top window, but while it is frightening for most jakes, it isn't as physically demanding as the pomps, plus it only requires seconds to accomplish the descent.

The pomps went on for hours and days and everyone was glad when the evolutions were completed, especially the drillmaster who had to sweat out the moves of every frightened candidate.

Willie wished the fuck they had never started. He was scared shitless of heights and bitterly complained whenever Captain Gus laid out the plans for the tasks to be accomplished each day. Gus was a kindly old fella who wanted every rookie to succeed and had a wealth of patience to coax all of the young jakes through the difficult procedures.

But even he faced a challenge with Willie who was determined to keep both feet firmly on the ground at all times.

The funny thing was, though he had a very slight build, he would eventually complete whatever the evolution was while bitching all the time. His most frequent comment after Gus explained what was to be done next was, "Not me, Cap. No way. Don't you realize I'm assigned to an engine company. I don't have to do all that climbing shit."

Gus, who had retired as a Colonel in the Army Reserve would say, "Willie, the department is kind of like the Marine Corps whose policy is, 'everyone's a rifleman,' and that applies here too. Every jake has to learn to do every task and that's the only way you're gonna graduate. What about all those kids if you flunk? Who's gonna feed them?"

Gus must have heard Willie talking about his love life on one of the work breaks. Height wasn't the only thing Willie complained about. He would freely give advice on marriage to single jakes who would listen.

His own marital status was strictly the result of his own thrill of the hunt, he claimed. He had been drafted into the army during the war, over his strong objections, and spent a couple of years in Europe bitching about all of those people trying to kill him, including his own platoon sergeant, as well as the whole German army.

When he was discharged, he got a job with a tool supply company and spent his time distributing the products city-wide in a small delivery truck. One time when he stopped by the warehouse to pick up more orders, he noticed a cute, new blond secretary busily typing in the office. Willie took great pride in his success with the ladies, although most of his romantic conquests occurred overseas from a grateful female populace who were delighted to be freed from the Nazi hordes. The particular ladies with whom he had liaisons did require an exchange of francs, lire or marks for their favors, but Willie believed that was incidental. He firmly believed that his charms were such that they would have performed for nothing.

The intriguing element about this new girl in the office was that she was displaying a beautiful diamond engagement ring on her left hand. What a challenge, thought Willie. Here's a lady already spoken for. What if I could get her to go out with me?

He initiated a campaign of charm and wit that eventually, after weeks of persistence and resistance, resulted in her agreeing to one date, probably in an effort to get rid of him.

But, she demanded that he pick her up at her home, rather than meeting somewhere else.

O.K., thought Willie. I only need one date to score anyway. When her old man gets a look at me, what the hell, he'll make sure it's just a one time deal. He's already got her engaged and will be unloading her soon, so he doesn't want to stop that progress. Poor guy's got a flock of other daughters to get rid of before he gets any peace, so he'll cut me short for sure.

As it turned out, Willie's conclusions were totally incorrect. He was greeted with open arms by both parents of the girl. The reason would be difficult to comprehend in today's society, but it was a different world back in the forties, Billy recalled. The guy she was engaged to was a Protestant and in her totally Irish-Catholic neighborhood, the thought of such a marriage was tantamount to being condemned to the fires of hell for all eternity.

The parents loved Willie and before he knew it, the engagement ring disappeared and he was married. The happy couple moved into one of the housing projects that sprang up in the post war period and the babies appeared methodically year after year.

One day, the over-used washing machine broke down and when the repairman arrived, Willie's wife was dressed in a housecoat, her hair was in curlers and her stomach was protruding due to her third trimester condition.

The guy who entered the apartment was her former fiance.

He promptly located the source of the problem and accomplished the proper repairs. He explained that he now had his own business and actually had three other trucks on the road doing similar work in this babyboom period where washers, dryers and other household appliances needed constant attention.

He was married, with only one child, had a new home in the newly suburban community of Braintree and a summer place on Cape Cod. He and his wife had matching automobiles, and all in all life is just great, he commented as he snapped shut his sparkling tool kit and departed.

From then on, Willie would occasionally catch his wife staring at him with a somewhat bewildered and speculative gaze, and once he thought he heard her mutter, "Why me?" Why her, indeed he mused, what about me?

Billy remembered the last day of the drill class when Gus was wishing them all luck in their assignments as he handed them their graduation certificates. When he got to Willie he said, "Well, Willie, of all the evolutions you preferred, what did you like best?"

"Remember the day it rained, Cap?" he said. "You had us all tying knots and doing all that other shit inside in the classroom. That was my best day. I didn't have to climb a fuckin' thing. Bless you for that, sir," he concluded with a snappy salute he had perfected whenever he had taken leave of those precious mamselles, signorinas and frauleins in the European Theatre of Operations.

Yeah, Billy thought, gotta make sure my classmate gets an award. I know he'll be squawking at the Ball that he should get the top medal, but his wife will shut him up. Still with him after all these years. She raised that gang of kids and now they got a dozen grandchildren. Whenever he brags about all he's done for them, she gets that same look she got back in the project.

Most non-fire fighting acts didn't result in medals, although Billy could quickly think of a few that did.

Bob Mackey going out on a fifth floor ledge on Essex Street in Chinatown one day. He grabbed a distraught, elderly Asian woman who couldn't speak any English so he couldn't communicate with her. She was going to, so he had to move quickly once she spotted him creeping toward her. The TV cameras and still news photographers recorded the whole daytime incident and it was pure luck that he didn't plunge to the street as he swung in front of her and pushed her inside to safety from her suicide attempt.

Billy Boyle was another matter; equally hairy but no pictures. He managed to talk his way into a room where an escaped mental patient sat with an enormous knife threatening to kill himself as well as Billy, once he got inside. The confrontation went on for over two hours, with the deranged man occasionally waving the knife and then plunging it into his thighs and slashing his arms. Each time Billy tried to get close to him, the guy would sweep the knife towards him; it was only when the loss of blood finally distracted the man that Billy was able to overpower and disarm him.

Eddie Loder's rescue was more recent and he had received a medal at last year's Ball.

A young woman stood on a ledge at the sixteenth floor of the Ritz-Carlton Hotel on Arlington Street one night and refused to come inside despite every effort of a police Suicide Negotiation Team. The scene had a carnival atmosphere because of its location opposite the Public

Gardens. A huge crowd gathered opposite the prestigious hotel, while spotlights and TV cameras zeroed in on the hapless girl.

Up on the roof, three floors above her, the members of Rescue One laid out their rappeling gear and Eddie Loder donned the harness with its snaps and hooks. The company officer was in communication with the negotiators down in the jumper's room, and as time dragged on it became clear they weren't having any luck in persuading her to come in.

The team leader finally reported that she appeared to be going to jump momentarily and Eddie slipped quietly over the edge of the roof.

It was obvious he was only going to get one chance, so they lowered him as quickly as possible. The protrusion of the roof kept him away from the building, so just as he reached a point directly opposite her, the crew swung him in towards the wall, according to their plan, and he kicked her with both feet into the room where the cops grabbed her.

Eddie told Billy afterward it was over that the force of his kick turned him upside down and everyone was so excited about the successful rescue that he was left dangling there, gazing down into the crowd and the spotlights until he started calling all of those inside the room some rather uncomplimentary names.

Billy finished reading all of the non-medal category reports and was reaching for the small stack of extreme risk commendations when he was notified by the man on patrol that he had "visitors on the way up."

It was Oakie and Bob accompanied by a sergeant from the Massachusetts State Police. Billy thought the guy looked familiar and when Oakie introduced him, he was certain he recognized him.

Bob Pine explained that they were working jointly along with the feds on the marijuana ship fire and they had an excellent description of a suspect. He was spotted coming off the boat by a young couple who had been parked in the lot opposite the dock. In spite of the cold weather, their devotion to each other resulted in an amorous engagement that left them both breathless.

While they were recuperating, the young man wiped the condensation from the windshield, which had been formed by a combination of their gymnastic activities in the confined space and the car heater. The street lights gave them a very clear view of the guy as he stumbled to the pier and moved out of sight.

The lovers saw smoke curling out of a couple of portholes and sped to a pay phone to report the fire. At first they weren't going to mention to anyone else what they had seen because they weren't supposed to be there themselves. But after reading the papers the next day, they came forward with the information and the investigation gained momentum.

Billy said to the state trooper, "Donald Cashman. Let me get a look at you. Yep, you were right. You look terrific."

Years ago, when Billy was a lieutenant, this guy had been appointed to the same ladder company in the South End district. He had really taken the job at his wife's insistence. He loved being a trooper, but she was a Boston girl and the "Staties", as they are called, could be stationed anywhere in the entire Commonwealth. She got sick of being out in the Berkshire hills in the extreme western part of the state and talked him into taking the fire exam.

Billy recalled he was a very muscular guy who was just as strong as he looked. But, he had a couple of drawbacks that stopped him from being an outstanding jake. First of all, he hated getting dirty; secondly, he was scared shitless, every time they went to a fire. In the firehouse kitchen he was constantly talking about the state police and how meticulous they are. When they're first appointed, a tailor measures every part of their bodies, and even their leather puttees are custom fitted to the calves of their legs.

Because of the work hours in effect in those years, Billy only worked with the new guy half the time, or one day tour and one night tour per week. One night when Billy came into work, Donald was at his favorite spot in the kitchen, talking about a third alarm he had worked the night before on Compton Street. Billy shook his head as he listened to him complain about what a tough job it had been. He bitched about everything but mostly about how filthy he had gotten.

Naturally, jakes being what they are, they soon had him bragging about the troopers and appeared to listen attentively and respectfully to his dramatic descriptions of that elite organization. One guy stood behind him mimicking his theatrical hand gestures while indicating how full of shit he was.

The company responded to a few incidents before midnight but none of them were significant. Around 0100 hours they were dispatched to Box 221 which was struck for a fire in the Hi-Hat Club at the corner of Columbus and Mass Avenues. This once famous nightspot had been closed for over a year and had been the site of a couple of working fires since it was boarded up.

The location was an entirely black neighborhood, and in a more innocent era, when Billy had been in high school, it was on the list of places that high school seniors would visit on prom night, the year they graduated. The jazz artists and other performers at the club were world renowned. It was a great adventure for the kids, the boys in tuxes and the girls decked out in ball gowns, visiting the Roxbury district, so different than their own equally poor but culturally dissimilar South Boston neighborhood.

The place had declined in the early post war years and it was a sad day when the doors closed permanently.

Billy could see dirty brown smoke seeping out from around the plywood covering the windows and drifting past the streetlights. He had his ladder truck positioned on the Columbus Ave side as he could see Ladder 12 swinging into position at the front of the building on Mass Ave.

The aerial was raised to the roof and he sent two of his five man unit up to open the wood covered skylights. No roof radios back in those days, Billy remembered, so he advised them to get on and off quickly as the rest of the crew were forcing open the rear entrance and starting to strip off the plywood on the lower floors.

Billy entered through the rear door and had Donald and another jake with him. They were followed by Engine 22's crew who were stretching a big line for an interior attack.

The smoke wasn't too bad and Billy was able to get into the auditorium which was surrounded on four sides by a mezzanine.

The upper level had a guard railing which patrons used to lean on while seated at tables, watching the show on the main floor. He worked his way up the stairway and as he reached the second level, he caught a glimpse of fire through several small holes in the high metal ceiling. It was visible on both sides of the auditorium and it was obvious it was burning intensely. It was also well out of reach of any of his tools.

He realized it was going to be impossible to get at from inside. He yelled down to Engine 22, "Back the line out. Tell the chief it's gone and we're coming down." He motioned to his two men to precede him on the stairway. When they were about half way down, a loud crash sounded as a portion of the ceiling collapsed.

Billy shouted, "Don't panic. Just turn right and follow Twenty-two out the door." They all made it to the rear alley safely and Billy was pleased to see his roof men were nearing the bottom of the aerial on their way down to the street.

They told him they had removed the plywood from one skylight and the fire blew right by them. They could feel the roof was pretty spongy in the middle so they came right down, as did the roof men from Ladder 12.

Billy had ground ladders raised to all five floors and commenced the task of uncovering as many openings as possible for the outside attack which had become inevitable. The fire grew to a fifth alarm and they remained at the scene until relieved by the day crew at 0800 hours.

Back in quarters, Billy showered and was in his room, preparing to go home when there was a knock on his door. It was Cashman. "How ya doin', Donald old pal? Long night, huh?"

"Lieutenant, I just want to tell you, I'm quitting." Billy was startled. He thought the kid was coming in to report an injury, or something. Donald continued, "Last night was it for me. You know, the night before, I went to that three bagger on Compton Street and that was bad enough. But this fire was my last one."

Billy started to speak but Cashman held up his hand, "You know when you yelled 'don't panic' at the fire? Well I did panic, but I don't think I was the only one. My feet never hit the ground and I was swept out into the alley by everyone else who was running like hell."

"Well, yeah, it was pretty hairy, Donald, but lissen, that only happens once in a while," said Billy.

"Maybe," was the reply. "But it's not gonna happen to me again. I'm going back to the State Police."

He continued, "Lieutenant, did you ever see a state trooper when he has to retire at age fifty?"

"I don't know, whaddya mean?"

"Well, he looks like he's about thirty years old and he always manages to knock off a soft security job somewhere."

"So what?" asked Billy.

"Well, sir, most of you guys are in your thirties now, and you all look like you're fifty already. By the time you guys retire, if any of you make it that far without getting killed, you'll look a hundred and I'm not gonna be one of you. Goodbye sir, it's been nice knowing you," he saluted, left the room and Billy never saw him again.

"Donald," Billy chuckled as he shook hands with his old recruit, "you look good enough to be drafted."

"Well, sir, you don't look as bad as I thought you would by now," was the reply.

They spent a pleasant hour reviewing their lives since they had last seen each other and then the three men departed, continuing to follow the leads on the ship fire.

Back to the papers, thought Billy, but he never got a chance. At 1907 hours a box was struck for a fire on Mill Street in East Boston. The location was on the waterfront and Billy thought, If it's a pier, I can forget these papers 'cause it's gonna be a long night.

The first company at the scene, Engine 9, reported heavy smoke showing from a one story brick and wood building on a pier and Billy reached into his locker and put on his heavy woolen shirt. Temperature's still below freezing. Better grab another pair of mittens, too.

The district chief reported a "working fire" and Billy slid the pole to the main floor as the house alarm sounded and the man on patrol announced, "Working Fire, Box 6151. Fire's on Mill Street. Rescue 1, Tower Unit, Division 1 to the fire, Engine 10 cover at Engine 9."

The trip over the expressway and through the Callahan Tunnel was accomplished without the usual delays and Joe turned the car right on Chelsea Street, sped down through Maverick Square to Border Street and down onto the docks.

The district chief told him it was a vacant building that formerly housed a lobster company. Billy could see the fire was extending rapidly throughout the long structure and he ordered a second alarm to be struck.

As far as could be determined, the fire was not under the pier, although Billy told the Fire Alarm Office to continue the response of the SCUBA team to the scene, which is the normal procedure for a confirmed waterfront fire. No way he would put them in the water in this weather, but there's always a great danger of a jake falling into the harbor whenever companies are operating on a wharf and the team had managed to save a few guys over the years.

Billy was not convinced of the team's effectiveness operating underneath in spite of their eagerness. They were a highly motivated group of people who served on regular fire companies but were activated by pagers whenever there was a fire or waterfront incident where they might be utilized. Billy had some misgivings whenever he tried to measure their successes against the dangers they faced during operations.

He had seen them perform very effectively under old, rotted piers where there was a lot of dried and decaying wood as well as plenty of openings overhead, but even then he was concerned for their safety.

But an intact pier was much more difficult because you could hit the fire from underneath all day long and it would keep reigniting from the creosote soaked wood. The best way to get that type of fire is to isolate the involved area by cutting trenches across the wooden deck, using hose streams to prevent the fire from jumping across the wide openings you've made.

Then you have to practically dismantle the parts that are burning, using power saws, crow bars and many large and small hose streams.

If the fire is buried underneath a building on a pier and you can't get at it rapidly, forget it. You're going to have an all night stand and use all of those heavy stream deck guns on the fire boats. You'll also get spectacular pictures for the TV people.

The facts that the structure at this fire was still sound and the fire wasn't underneath the floors allowed Billy to properly place hand lines from the waterside along with those from the landside and knock down the fire without too much difficulty. The ladder trucks were able to cut large openings in the roof and the building vented pretty well in spite of the cold weather.

Yeah, Billy thought, the winter brings all kinds of extras, but the one he never saw written up in the trade magazines was how bitter cold temperatures kept the smoke from rising naturally and sometimes even drove it down onto the operating forces. Perhaps all those authors stayed home when the weather reports were unfavorable and missed out on the joys of witnessing such phenomena.

Shit, the most prolific ones are inland and out in the more temperate climates where they wouldn't know the difference between a stalagmite and an icicle, let alone ever see a three day pier fire.

The fire was brought under control within an hour and Billy was grateful there were no serious injuries in spite of several jakes slipping and falling on the ice coated surfaces.

Oakie and Bob showed up at the scene but they said Donald Cashman had declined their invitation to come along with them. "He said he had enough of fires and you, Deputy, years ago. He promised to watch it on the eleven o'clock news though—from his living room."

They told Billy they had a description of a character named Lloyd Murdoch who had been released from Cedar Junction in November after doing seven years for a series of fires he had set in the city of Worcester, about forty miles west of Boston.

Oakie said, "We've had three minor fires in a boatyard over here in the last few weeks and you know Group 1 had that fourth alarm in the Jefferies Point Yacht Club on Sumner Street, back on January 7th. This guy could turn out to become the prime suspect. We're gonna pass his picture around up on Brooks and Morris Street where you had that sixth alarm, too. You never know."

Bob picked up the conversation. "If it is him, he seems to be on a waterfront kick right now, but we're never really sure because they're so weird. There are no piers in Worcester that I know of, but he sure destroyed a lot of stuff out there. Of course, if we could think like the arsonists do, we'd solve every case."

Billy returned to quarters and by the time he had driven the cold from his body under the hot shower and then managed to eat one of those thoroughly tasteless meals consisting of salad, low-fat dressing plus a frozen low sodium, low calorie, shit, low everything, chicken delight, it was well after midnight.

A response to a mattress fire in the North End, followed by a one room fire in Chinatown, both locations within his first alarm assignment response area, brought him back to the desk at around 0300.

He grinned as he thought about the last run. The fire had been in a third floor, rear room of a five story apartment house.

The building was only about thirty-five feet wide and sixty feet deep and it was wedged in between two structures of identical size and occupancy.

The Spider had gone to the roof of the original fire building over the aerial. He had opened the penthouse door and removed a scuttle so the heavy smoke pulled up and out of the building while the engine company crew ascended to the fire floor. He then leaned over the edge of the roof and cleaned out three top floor windows, striking them with his axe. This relieved much of the pressure inside and the jakes with the line of hose moved without difficulty into the apartment involved in fire. The rescue company got past the hose and up the stairway, rescuing two badly frightened Asian men who were chattering away in Chinese.

The Spider crossed over the fire wall to the adjoining apartment house on the right, opened the penthouse and descended through the light smoke, looking for occupants to assist from the building.

Just as the rescue company crew reached the street with the two guys they had assisted, Spider stumbled out of the exit next door, an elderly Chinese man slung over his shoulders in the classic fireman's carry. While Billy watched, the old guy, who was jabbering away, held out both arms with palms upraised and shrugged his shoulders in a gesture of frustration.

A representative of the mayor's office was at the scene and he spoke to the evacuee in his native tongue while the poor guy lay prone on a hospital stretcher, unsuccessfully attempting to push away the oxygen mask the EMTs were clamping on his face.

The city hall representative talked to Billy a few minutes later. "Chief," he said, "the old man was perfectly content to stay in his room. He's got all of his worldly possessions in that apartment. Your guy scared the shit out of him. He tried to explain he was o.k. but since he doesn't know English, the fireman scooped him up and dragged him out. He says he kept hitting him on his helmet but he just kept on coming."

Billy thanked him and as he turned away he saw Nellie and Porky watching and listening intently.

Back in the kitchen, when all of the companies had returned to quarters, Billy sat in the rear of the room, sipping coffee and watching the exchange.

"Say, Spider, old pal," said Porky, "nice job. You're getting pretty good at luggin' people outta buildings." Eddie started to reply modestly that he was just following orders but Nellie broke in before he could finish: "You're fulla shit, Spider. You loved seein' your name in the paper for that phony job on Arch Street." Eddie tried to protest but he didn't have a chance.

"That Chinaman told me he tried to fight you off but you said you were goin' for another commendation. He didn't know what the hell you were talkin' about."

Spider screamed that he couldn't understand him and besides, the deputy said to get everyone out. "Naw he didn't. Ja see the guy shrug his shoulders when you wrestled him out on the street? The deputy shrugged his shoulders, too, 'cause he didn't know what the fuck you were doin'."

Billy thought, why the hell do I even come in this kitchen? I'm always getting sucked into their arguments. He admitted he didn't order the evacuation but as he could see the crestfallen look on Spider's face he said, "But listen. Eddie was right. I should have gotten everyone out on both sides. Nice job, pal."

He drained his coffee cup, rinsed it out, and as he was leaving the room he could hear Nellie's voice, "He's just covering up for you, Spider. He knows you fucked up but he feels sorry for you. He was in China during the war and I seen him and the old geezer laughing and talking in Chinese. I could hear one of them say somethin' that sounded like 'asshole' but I don't know which one." Billy shook his head and kept on walking.

20

At 0326 hours, Box 12-1437 was struck for a fire at the Hotel Essex on Atlantic Avenue opposite the South Station Train Terminal. This is a building every jake in the district knows pretty well because of the number of responses to fires in the joint. It's an eleven story, first class building over a hundred feet wide and 150 feet deep. But it is a pre-code building, erected before 1920 and doesn't' have either a fire department standpipe or an automatic sprinkler system.

There is a 2 inch riser that has 1-1/2 inch outlets, but there is no fire pump in the building nor any siamese connection to increase the supply or pressure.

The first two ladder companies that normally respond are assigned to raise their aerials to specific windows on each side of the building, near the front and whatever floor the fire is located on, if they can reach it. The reason for this placement is those locations will gain access into the long corridor that travels horizontally from one side of the building to the other, and subdivides the front rooms from the identical ones that look out into an inner court. These entry points also give direct entry into the stairways leading up and down as well as to the corridors which extend to the rear of the building.

There is no access for ladder trucks in the rear of the building because of other adjoining structures; apparatus placement is, therefore, restricted to three sides.

The ceilings above the dropped panel blocks are terra cotta brick so there is little or no chance of a fire extending upward from floor to floor, but the radiant heat created by a room fire can produce superheated air that funnels along the tightly enclosed passageways. However, the metal stairways have doors with wire glass windows that are frequently broken or the doors themselves are warped so smoke can be sucked upward rapidly to other floors.

In the past, Billy and the other deputies would often strike a second alarm for a one room fire, depending on its location, just to get enough help to assist in evacuation activities.

When the Essex was originally opened, around the turn of the century, it had been a high class hotel because of its location adjacent to one of the two major train terminals in Boston; visitors from around the world would keep it occupied to capacity.

It's only a few blocks from the Boston Common, the state house, city hall and many historical sites as well as the heart of the downtown shopping district. Its convenience certainly contributed to its popularity.

But in later years, the increase in the use of automobiles and then air travel reduced train passenger use to primarily commuters from the suburbs; the hotel had been in decline for decades. The clientele frequently occupied rooms by the hour, so to speak, and no in-depth interviews were required for registration by the desk clerks.

More recently, in addition to the entrepreneurial ladies, many of its rooms were occupied by welfare families who were burned out in fires in other parts of the city. They were waiting for placement in the oversubscribed public housing projects sprinkled throughout several residential districts.

When Billy arrived with the first fire companies, fire was blowing out of a sixth floor, front window and heavy smoke was pushing out of many windows along that floor as well as lesser amounts from the floors above.

People were waving and screaming at many locations, so the preplanned ladder placement was abandoned. It was essential that ladders be elevated to rescue occupants immediately and Billy ordered the Aerial Tower and both ladder trucks to take positions at the three accessible sides of the building and get anyone they could reach at the fire floor and above.

The sixth floor is about seventy-five feet above the street and out of the reach of hand raised ground ladders. The evacuation possibilities were down over the 110 foot aerials or the ninety-five foot Aerial Tower platform. The stairways might be useful, but more than likely were presently choked with smoke.

Billy struck second and third alarms and ordered the dispatch of four additional ladder companies which would bring him a total of ten aerial devices.

He directed Engine 10 and the other two first alarm engine companies to join as a team and get one 2-1/2 inch hand line stretched to the fire on the sixth floor via the left front stairway which exited onto Atlantic Avenue.

Other stairways terminated at East Street on the left rear side and Essex Street at the right rear side, with the remaining front stairway emptying into the main lobby inside.

The crew of Rescue One ascended up the front stairway in advance of the first attack line, rushing past the people who were stumbling downward, trying to get out. The members carried two 1-1/2 inch donut rolls of hose, as they usually did in this building, because of the lack of a large standpipe with its customary 2-1/2 inch connections. The assistant manager told Billy the elevators were in the lobby and he wasn't sure if they were working. Billy chose to ignore them as part of the operation because they had been so unreliable during his previous experiences at this location.

He was startled when one of the extra ladder companies reported fire was showing from a ninth floor rear room with people visible at windows higher up. This location made it clear to Billy that there had to be more than one fire; there was no possibility of fire communication between the two involved areas. He ordered fourth and fifth alarms to be struck and directed that 2-1/2 inch lines be stretched up both rear stairways.

He realized that the high-rise standard operating procedure would provide him with extra chief officers on the sounding of the multiple alarms but he requested a couple of additional ones to be assigned because of the enormous number of rooms in the huge structure.

He also directed that the responding Arson Squad duty force send members up into the building because of the two fires and the preservation of evidence would become essential.

A report of fire showing from a seventh floor window on the left hand side convinced Billy that the arsonist might still be inside the building, touching off rooms, and he had that information relayed to all of the operating forces.

He struck sixth and seventh alarms and called for a much larger police detail than was normally dispatched as well as more ambulances, paramedics and the department's other heavy duty rescue company.

Although he had lines now being stretched up each of the four stairways, he was able to place one ladder truck opposite the side window which provided access to the interior stairways, and he sent an additional line upward, over this aerial.

The safety chief notified him the water supplies were adequate and so far, no frozen hydrants were reported, in spite of the twenty degree temperatures.

The newly established assignment of a network chief had been activated with the striking of the third alarm, and when he reported to Billy, he saw it was Rico Civiterise from the Mattapan district. Good, he thought. This young guy was one of the smartest new chiefs on the job.

The new position's duties entailed determining where every unit at the scene was located; the "net chief" was assisted in this awesome task by his aide, the Communication Unit's fire alarm operator at the scene and the fire alarm operators at the Central Station.

While the officer in command of a fire had a pretty fair idea of where each company was located at most fires, it was usually just a general perception.

When OSHA, the federal Occupational Safety and Health Administration, fined a chief on the west coast $100,000 following the death of a fire officer a couple of years ago, all of the rules changed nationwide. They found the chief guilty of not knowing where every member is at all times during operations.

Although the chief won a reversal on appeal, this impossible task made chiefs everywhere start establishing systems to try to comply. The network chief had been initiated in Boston by the boss. It seemed to be evolving o.k., thought Billy, but it still had a long way to go.

"Civie, old pal," he said as he slid his arm around his shoulders, "you got your work cut out for ya. I got no idea where they all are and I'm still placing companies everywhere."

The new chief smiled and replied, "I'll take care of it, Deputy. I'll report back to you when I find everyone."

The commissioner arrived a few minutes later and assumed command. Billy gave him a full report of everything that was transpiring and was assigned to direct operations from the left hand side on East Street while the extra duty Headquarters deputy was placed on Essex Street.

The design of the building and the small size of the lobby precluded the normal establishment of a command post on the first floor or even an upper command post, two floors below the fire, but the chief of the district was already on the fire floor directing traffic. The commissioner assigned district chiefs to a number of locations on the upper floors to take command of the units working inside.

When the crew of Rescue One reached the fifth floor, two members commenced connecting and stretching the small 1-1/2 inch hose to the outlet in the stairway as the lieutenant, Nellie and Porky climbed up to the fire floor, donned their mask facepieces and entered the corridor. The intense heat drove them to the floor immediately and smoke made visibility impossible. Porky was carrying the hydraulic Rabbit tool door opener while Nellie had the manually operated Halligan Bar. They crawled to the first two doorways, popped the doors opposite each other and crept inside looking for victims.

These rooms and the next two were already empty, so they broke out the upper and lower window panes and sashes to try to vent the area and reduce the heat.

As they moved from room to room, penetrating deeper into the corridor, they managed to find three elderly men who were cowering under beds, confused and frightened about what to do. They herded them back towards the stairway, shielding them with their bodies until the other members managed to grab them.

When Porky and Nellie attempted to get to the room involved in fire, the extreme heat prevented them from going any further. The 1-1/2 inch line was pushed along the floor to them and the lieutenant instructed them to direct the stream upward, knocking out the ceiling tiles and striking the red hot brick surfaces up above. The pressure was pretty good at first but they knew it would drop soon as the weight of the water coming from the height of the standpipe would decrease as it drained through the nozzle.

Both jakes were just attempting to maintain their position until a larger line arrived from the street via the stairway.

Suddenly, they could hear a faint scream from somewhere ahead, beyond the fire that was now in the corridor from the involved room. Without hesitation, Nellie and Porky flattened themselves prone on the floor and moved forward. The officer pointed the hose stream directly at them both and they kept going.

They never actually saw the fire because of the black smoke that enveloped them, but the heat beat down on them as they passed under the flames. They could feel their ears blistering and even their bodies seemed to be scorching through their turnout coats and boots.

When they got through, the screaming was louder and Porky forced open a door on the left. Inside, over next to the window, a young, black woman was leaning out into the inner court. She was the one doing the yelling. When they reached her, they could see she had two little kids huddled in front of her while her body protected them from the heat.

Porky pulled her and the children back as Nellie cleaned out the window panes. They carried the children and dragged the woman out of the room and across the corridor into a front room that faced Atlantic Avenue. The kids kept pressing the jakes' facepieces against their cheeks, sucking in the cool air.

As the rescuers cleaned out these windows, they were spotted by two members of the Aerial Tower crew, who had just picked off a couple of occupants from a window further along on the same floor. The Tower jakes used the upper control levers in the bucket to maneuver to the location where they grabbed the victims and pulled them to safety. Porky and Nellie clambered into the bucket and the device was rotated away from the heat and smoke. One of the Tower jakes communicated by radio to the rescue company officer that his men and the victims were out.

Engine 10's big line stretch of hose reached the sixth floor and was filled with water as soon as it was in position. The high pressure, high volume stream proved to be very effective and the jakes crawled down the corridor slowly, passing the remaining rescue company jakes with their pitiful stream. While it had succeeded in permitting Nellie and Porky to reach the trapped family, the 1-1/2 inch line was much too small to effectively control the fire or reduce the intense heat.

While this part of the operation was continuing, laddermen from the several trucks at the scene were bringing some occupants down from the upper floors over the extended aerial ladders. Others fanned out throughout the areas above the fire, some opening the penthouse doors to vent the stairways and others assisting victims down the stairways as conditions improved.

Hose lines were snaked up the inside routes and eventually reached the fires on the seventh and ninth floors. The extension in these rooms was not as severe as the fire on the sixth floor and they were soon under control and knocked down. It could have been accomplished more rapidly if the lines could have been stretched over the aerial ladders, but they were all engaged in rescue operations so the more time consuming method was employed.

Quite a few of the occupants were kept on the upper floors and some even on the roof by the jakes who managed to reach them. They were kept in safe areas until the word was spread that it was o.k. to bring them down and they filed down the stairways to the street.

All of the evacuees who didn't require hospitalization were guided across Atlantic Avenue and into the huge, warm train terminal. About a dozen guests were transported to area hospitals but the remainder were given first aid by the EMTs and paramedics in the train waiting rooms and the concourse.

Several jakes from the operating force were hospitalized for exhaustion and minor burns received while operating in the oven-like corridors and rooms of the three floors involved in the fire.

Nellie and Porky had more extensive injuries and Billy was notified they were both at the Shriners Burn Center next to the Mass General Hospital, along with the mother and kids from the sixth floor.

The commissioner ordered a final room by room search of the hotel be conducted, and once it was completed, he directed all of the chief officers to commence dismissing fire companies that were no longer needed.

The boss was delighted with the way the operation had gone and he kept emphasizing to the press that no one had died in spite of the number of people who were trapped above the fire. He also harped on his favorite theme that the building had no automatic sprinklers or other fire protection equipment. His final point was that these types of fires would be eliminated under the recently enacted legislation that required the retro-fitting of all unsprinklered high-rises throughout the city and across the state.

Lieutenant Simmons from public relations tugged at Billy's arm and whispered, "Oakie wants to see ya, Deputy." He led him through the press people into the hotel lobby where his friend was standing, looking very un-detective like, in his turnout gear and with his face blackened from the smoke on the upper floors.

"What say, Oak, old pal? You look like one of the regular guys," said Billy.

"Yeah, no wonder Donald Cashman got out of the business. You have a lot of unkempt jakes under your command, sir. Thank God my superior intellect has allowed me to rise above such duties most of the time."

He became more serious as he described how his partner, Bob Pine, had spotted Lloyd Murdoch in South Station while he was interviewing some of the people from the hotel staff. One of them indicated Lloyd was a registered guest, although his name didn't sound familiar to the staff member. Oakie concluded the conversation by saying he'd keep Billy informed but it looked like a real good lead.

The commissioner returned overall command to Billy following the interviews and he then left the scene. Before departing, however, he congratulated Billy on the operation and told him he was going to commend the entire response force for their outstanding performance of duty.

Boy, thought Billy, he must have been impressed. The commissioner seldom recognized a specific incident in orders because, after all, he knew there'd be another good job by someone else tomorrow, next week or next month and it would lessen the importance of general commendations if they were routinely issued.

Billy continued the tasks of directing the overhauling operations and releasing the units no longer needed until he was relieved at the scene by his partner, John, at 0800 hours. He requested John's aide to take him to the Burn Center before returning him to quarters. He arrived shortly after the boss had departed from a brief visit to the injured jakes. He was pleased to find that most of them had already been released following their treatment for first degree burns and exhaustion.

The hospital rep took him to see Nellie and Porky and he thanked them for the job they had done. They both had thick bandages wrapped around their necks and ears but their spirits were just as high as ever.

The nurse told Billy they'd be released shortly, adding "I'll be glad to get rid of the pair of them. They were raising hell with all of your other men we were treating and the place was in an uproar. Good thing I got a brother on the job or I'd file a complaint."

Billy could see she wasn't really as mad as she made out, but in the interest of maintaining good relations with the staff, he offered to take them back to quarters with him.

In quarters, after Billy finished showering and changing into his civilian clothes, he descended the stairway and crossed the main floor towards the kitchen to grab a cup of coffee before going home. He saw Nellie, standing outside the entrance, peeking inside. He looked pretty goofy with his bandages topped by another stupid hat, price tag dangling down. This one was red, white and blue and bore the CH logo of the Montreal Canadians, the Bruins' arch rivals whom the Spider hated passionately, as did all Bruins fanatics.

"Wait a minute, will ya, Deputy? Porky's setting up the Spider." Billy looked into the room and could see Porky entering from the other doorway. Boy, does he look down in the dumps, thought Billy.

Spider was sitting with a few other jakes who had just come back from the fire and he yelled to Porky, "You look like an asshole with those phony bandages. Where's that other nitwit?"

"Eddie, please," came the solemn reply, "Nellie didn't make it"

"Whaddya mean he didn't make it?"

"I was with him in the hospital when he turned in his rifle."

Thoroughly alarmed now, Eddie rose from his seat, "You mean, you mean, ah, he died? Holy Jeesus." Eddie and all of the others at the table were stunned.

"Yeah, and I even heard his last words. He told me to tell the Spider that he was sorry he kidded him about that rescue on Arch Street, it was a great job."

Eddie looked like he was going to cry. "But the very last thing he said with his final breath was that the rescue in Chinatown was a lotta shit. He said that old geezer was safer in his house on Tyler Street than he'd have been in Shanghai."

With that, Nellie pushed open the door, shouted "Sucker" as loud as he could and Eddie collapsed on the bench.

Billy walked away thinking, I can get coffee somewhere else. I don't want to be a witness to what's gonna happen now.

21

Billy was awakened from a deep sleep by the sound of his doorbell ringing. He glanced at his bedside digital clock and saw that it read 1:25 P.M. God, I'm beat. Wonder who that is. He could see the sun had broken through the clouds and hoped it would start warming up for a change.

When he had arrived home from the night tour, he told his wife, Phyllis, he was beat and was going to flop for awhile. She said she was going in town shopping and would be back in mid-afternoon. As soon as his head hit the pillow, Billy was gone and he was still pretty drowsy as he pushed the buzzer, releasing the front door lock at the entrance to the apartment complex, three floors below.

"Deputy, it's me and Bob," shouted Oakie. "O.K. if we come up for a few minutes?"

"Yeah," Billy answered unenthusiastically. Must be important for them to see me off duty.

They both looked worse than he did—they hadn't been to bed since the fire—but he could see they were pretty excited. He put on water for coffee and seated them in the living room.

"We've got some great news for you. We got a confession out of Lloyd Murdoch."

"No shit. Howdja pull that off?"

"We got a picture of him from the Worcester Fire Department and showed it to the assistant manager of the hotel. He positively identified him as occupying a room on the fourth floor under the name of Leonard Masters. Bob," he nodded towards Pine, "had been questioning other guests who were assembled in South Station." Bob picked up the story, "I found out from a group of ladies that one of their co-workers, so to speak, a woman named Wanda Blake, had been threatened a couple of nights prior to the fire, by a John who said he'd kill her."

Oakie and Bob visited her at Boston City Hospital and she also identified the picture. She said he was drunk and had followed her up to her ninth floor room, demanding that she let him in.

"I been in this business a long time and I seen all kinds of weirdos. Been with most of them, too. But this John scared the hell outta me. Somethin' in his eyes. Smelled funny, too. Like smoke or sumthin'. I didn't want no part of him."

Wanda managed to get inside her room and snapped the security lock, but he kept pounding on the door. She continued to refuse him admittance and he finally drifted away, shouting he'd "get her". She said that really didn't bother her because she'd heard it all before, but it was a creepy feeling.

The night of the fire, however, Wanda was entertaining a client about 0230 and there was a knock on the door. She kept the chain on and opened it a crack. It was Lloyd again and she told him to go away, slamming the door shut and turning the double lock. This time, she recalled, he didn't look drunk but had those same wild eyes. He didn't yell or scream or say anything after she turned him away.

She returned to her John who had been hiding under the bed covers, figuring it was the hotel's non-existent house detective. When her date was leaving, she warily opened the door but there was no one there. She thought she could smell smoke though, and she could see a light blue haze drifting past the corridor lights. Wanda and the John walked down to the next room and the door was slightly open. They pushed it wider and could see the mattress smoldering. The pair ran back to her room and filled two glasses with water, dumped them on the burning patch and went back for a refill. The second time the smoke and visibility were much worse and the detectors in the room and corridor started to operate.

The noise scared the John and he disappeared immediately, running like hell towards the stairway. Wanda made another unsuccessful attempt to douse the flames. This time she saw that the blanket and sheet had been rolled up into a ball and were burning briskly underneath the bed. They must have ignited the mattress from the bottom and she realized there was no way she could stop the fire.

Oakie said, "She grabbed her purse from her room and pulled the local fire alarm box as she passed it on her way to the stairway. In her rush to get out, she tripped and fell down the stairs, breaking her left leg. The poor woman tried to crawl down towards the street, but the smoke pushing up from the fires on the lower floors gagged and choked her, forcing her into the eighth floor corridor. A couple of jakes who were looking for victims found her.

"Yeah, Wanda is really a heroine but she sure as hell don't want any publicity."

Bob Pine related that the Murdoch photo was also identified by a room occupant on the sixth floor, whom he rushed past just before the fire alarm bells commenced sounding.

"We picked Murdoch up in South Station without any difficulty and told him we were gonna have a hearing to revoke his probation this morning and he'd be tucked away forever. But, guess what. Now he's lookin' for a deal and the feds might put him into their witness protection program."

"For what?" asked Billy. "What the hell do they care about a local arson job?"

"Remember how Wanda said he smelled of smoke the first time she saw him?" asked Oakie.

"Yeah, I remember."

"Well, it got us thinking, maybe he did the ship job that night. We showed the same picture to the young couple in the car at the navy yard and they both said he's the one they saw leaving the ship. He weaved past them right under a streetlight; the girl even described the pants and jacket he was wearing."

He went on to tell Billy that when they confronted Lloyd with what they knew, he decided to talk. He said he set the fire in the room next to the hooker because she pissed him off when she turned him down again. After he touched off the bedclothes under the bed, he waited out in the stairway for several minutes, but nothing seemed to be happening.

He didn't want to go back along the hallway so he dropped down to the seventh floor. He found a big burlap bag full of rubbish on the stairway landing. He dragged it down the left side corridor and touched it off outside a room.

He found another bag on the sixth floor and pulled it along the corridor and found a room with the door ajar. He pushed it open and found it unoccupied. When he lit this bag it really started burning intensely and he ran out, passing a guy who was startled by the running figure and flattened himself against the wall.

This fire moved much more quickly than the other two and was the one the fire companies and Billy first spotted when they arrived at the scene.

Oakie broke in, "Yeah, but then Bob hit him with the ship fire and right away he said he wanted to see the feds. We said sure, but we told him it would be awhile before we could get them, so Bob kept him talkin'."

"It seems he had a cellmate down at Cedar Junction in Walpole named Joe Risema. Joe's a pill freak who's doing big time for shooting a clerk named Frank Masonotti during a robbery attempt in a drug store in Central Square, East Boston.

"The thing is, though, Joe didn't kill the clerk, he only hit him in the arm and the kid whacked him with a baseball bat he kept behind the counter. He fractured Joe's skull so he still gets these massive headaches. You'll never guess where the kid lives, or lived until a few weeks ago."

"Don't tell me Morris Street," said Billy.

"Bingo," replied Oakie. "Risema knows how much Lloyd likes fires. Hell, that's all he ever talked about in the can."

Bob Pine said, "Yeah, Lloyd did that fire as a favor, and he did the old lobster place on Mill Street, too."

"How come?"

"Well, this kid Frankie's old man owns the building and used to have the lobster business too before it went Chapter Eleven. Those guys up in Maine and Canada are making it tough for the shell fishermen down here." He continued, "You know those small fires we had in the lobster boats recently? Those were the old man's too. Not much damage to them but Lloyd was sure trying. Risema wanted to wipe out everything the family has. Those headaches must be brutal but I guess he thinks revenge will ease the pain."

"Hey, how about the Jeffries Point Yacht Club? You guys get him for that, too?"

"Naw, we don't think so. They had a big party there that night and we think it's coincidental and accidental."

"Well," Billy said, "it's hard to believe a guy would do all this stuff for nothin'. What the hell, are he and Risema lovers or what?"

"Nope, we're pretty sure Lloyd's straight. He gets his kicks from fires and the ladies. He's no switch hitter, either," said Oakie.

"Risema promised to put him in touch with a guy who needed a real big job done and a couple of weeks ago he was contacted. Murdoch refuses to identify who it was 'till he talks to the Feds but we're certain it's Risema's man. The job was to torch the boat and it paid five hundred up front and another fifteen if it did the job.

"Poor Lloyd still had most of the five hundred on him when we scooped him. The night he got the dough, he was half bombed when he did the boat. He has a couple of more drinks after and decides he'll score a chick to help him celebrate. She turns him down and boy, was he bullshit. I mean, jeez, he's got the dough, and is on a roll from the fire and this dame won't let him in. He figured no one could save the ship after all the fires he set. He's gonna get fifteen hundred more and she has to ruin his night.

"The other night he was even more pissed because the ship didn't sink and he finds out he ain't getting the rest of the dough. He's afraid of the contact guy but he's gotta take it out on someone so he heads for what he calls, 'that uppity whore.' You know the rest."

"Hey, Deputy, now that I think of it, maybe Lloyd does like guys, certain ones anyway."

"Whaddya mean?"

"Well, when we went through the stuff in his room, we found newspaper clippings of the fire on Morris Street, the lobster place and even the ship. Each one of them had your name underlined. He even had a nice picture of you covered with ice in Eastie. So, either he likes you or he figures if you're workin', there's a good chance the fire won't be stopped."

Billy's response will not be reproduced because it could seriously affect the reader's view of the quality, not only of the superior officers in the department, but the fire service as a whole.

22

Billy got to the conference room shortly before the Board meeting was scheduled to begin. He had tried to read through the reports that he'd never gotten to, but had to give it up when he received a couple of routine radio messages from Fire Alarm while traveling the expressway towards the Headquarters complex in Roxbury.

He joined the twelve deputies already in the room having coffee and donuts, and it didn't sound a hell of a lot different to him than the kitchen bullshit in any firehouse.

Everyone was talking at once and the Redhead was yapping away at Jackie Franklin. Billy could hear he was chastising him for letting Billy beat him in to the fire on Columbia Road; the other guys were involved in similar banter with each other. The only times the whole group got together during the year were at these meetings, the Ball, Memorial Sunday and at funerals, so they made the most of it.

When the Redhead spotted Billy he shouted, "Here he is now, Beano Junior. I thought when that little shrimp retired these meetings would be a lot shorter. But Billy Boy screwed up so many fires lately, half of his troops are in for commendations."

Billy made an appropriate gesture and reply as he poured a cup of coffee from the pot. JJD and Pat entered the room and were followed by the commissioner.

The procedure requires all of the commendations be read by the deputies who submitted them, in the order they had occurred during the previous calendar year. As each individual report is finished, the group asks questions of the deputy who read it until everyone is satisfied that a full understanding of the incident has been presented.

When all of the reports are completed, Pat and JJD distribute ballots beginning with the Most Meritorious Medal Award and working downward.

The ballots are counted for each award before moving on to the next one. The task of tallying the scores falls to Pat and Billy's partner, Jerry, unless he has a commendation of his own to be considered. Jerry was elected to this post by acclamation following the retirement of John O'Mara a few years previously. There was never any question that John was by far the most honest of the group, and he was also the senior deputy by several years.

When he left, Jerry got the job. Oh, he was honest enough to handle the chore, particularly with Pat helping him to count, but the Redhead said he really got it because his mother was the cook at the rectory in St. Francis de Sales Church in Charlestown, and everyone knew she was a saint.

Billy's turn to read his report on Lieutenant Canney and Fire Fighter Geiger of Ladder 15 for the job on Commonwealth Avenue was rapidly approaching when a knock came at the door.

It was Billy's aide, Joe. "Excuse me, Commissioner, District Eleven just reported a working fire in Brighton, sir." Billy rose to his feet and the commissioner nodded to him to respond. The policy is that fires come first and everything else is secondary, so he moved towards the door.

"There he goes again," shouted the Redhead. "Hey Boss," he said to the commissioner, "you'd better start suiting up. He'll be calling you soon." Jackie Franklin told Billy he'd read his report for him and he and Joe rushed to the division car in the garage.

While he was pulling on his fire fighting gear, he could hear Car Eleven reporting a fire on the first floor of a large 2-1/2 story wood frame lodging house on Washington Street. The high number of the address indicated the location was at the furthest end of the district, near the city line separating Boston from Newton.

"Better use the Mass. Pike, Joe, that's a long way from here," said Billy as the car sped up Mass. Ave., weaving its way through the heavy weekday traffic. Joe turned into the turnpike entrance at Newbury Street, jamming his foot on the gas pedal as they reached the flat surface of the toll road.

Billy concentrated on listening to the radio fire ground frequency; when he heard a company report the fire had extended into the second floor, he was quite certain the district chief would order a second alarm.

The Allston-Brighton district has many of these massive structures, in addition to numerous three deckers, multi-storied brick and wood apartment houses, hospitals, nursing homes, factories, railroad yards and a business district that travels for miles through the center of town. The population is listed as 70,000 but no one really knows how many people live there because of the number of students who flock in from September to June to attend the several colleges and universities in the city. Thousands of them occupy just the type of building they were responding to, and the upper floors were sub-divided into cubicles housing as many occupants as could fit for the significant rents that were collected.

The district is also a long way from downtown and most serious fires rapidly become multiple alarms because the chiefs in command want additional companies to be enroute to the scene in case they are needed. It's a far more prudent course than to wait until the fire extends beyond the capabilities of the first alarm response and then have to wait for extended periods for more assistance.

While Billy was reflecting on this procedure, the radio crackled, "Car Eleven to Fire Alarm. Strike second alarm, orders of Chief Erland." Billy grinned as his reflections proved accurate. Yeah, Wayne Erland just read my mind. Shit, hope we don't need a third or the Redhead will never get off my back if the boss has to leave the meeting.

The speedometer was hovering around seventy as they were waved through the Allston toll booths and Joe told him he could see red lights in the rear view mirror which confirmed that the multiple alarm companies from downtown were not far behind them.

Billy could see heavy smoke off to the left of the highway as they approached the Newton city line. The car left the Pike at the next exit, swung around a group of buildings on the left and headed back into Boston, along Washington Street.

After Wayne reported that the fire had made its way into the attic, Billy directed the next arriving ladder truck to get its aerial up to the long pitched roof. He could see laddermen from the Brighton truck companies attempting to make large openings, but they were hampered by the severe slope as well as the number of dormers and peaks extending in all directions. The jakes were working off roof ladders which they had fastened over the peak with retractable hooks but they had difficulty making their cuts.

Billy also kept a spot open for the placement of the Aerial Tower which was enroute to the extra alarm; its bucket would provide an ideal work platform to ventilate the overhead.

The battle proved to be a long one as the fire had not only crept into five rooms on the second floor, but into four more in the huge attic area under the roof. Additional lines of hose had to be advanced over hand-raised ladders to the upper floors because the narrow stairways could only accommodate one line each.

But as time went on, the holes became large enough and the black smoke turned to white and finally to steam. The building was indeed a dormitory for students but since classes were in session, no rescues had to be made. Thank God, reflected Billy. The Redhead's got enough on me now. One more dramatic job and he'll never let up on me.

He returned command to Chief Erland and glanced at his watch. Jeez, it's after eleven. He was once again amazed at how rapidly time passed at fires; it always seemed to be a much shorter period. He realized the events at the scene required continuous decision making on the part of the officer in command, but while everything seemed to be happening in split seconds, the clock just kept moving along.

At Headquarters, he got off the elevator at the second floor and dashed down to the conference room. Shit. The side entrance door was open and all he could see was a bunch of empty cups, plates and donut crumbs lying around the table.

The only occupants were the leather fire buckets on the shelves along the wall, each of which had a hand painted portrait of a guy who had served as chief of department, going back into the 1850's. They started at one end with bearded faces, then mutton chops, then just mustaches, then the long sideburns that were popular back in the sixties and finally the current "boys regular" cuts of the early nineties. Billy figured, pretty soon they'll have earrings, although the current boss is too old to get a pierce job done.

But, where the hell is everyone, he wondered as he stepped into the commissioner's outer office. Jeez, even Pat ain't here.

"Hey, Deputy," he heard a voice call from the inner sanctum. He stepped inside and there was JJD, feet up on the desk, leaning back in the oversized leather executive chair.

"Where's the boss?" asked Billy, "and what about the meeting?"

"It's all over, pal. The commissioner had to go downtown to city hall. Got a call from the mayor's office."

"Well, what about the vote and the medals? Is it postponed or what?"

"Naw. They finished up early and they all went over to the Victoria Diner for lunch."

"You mean they voted without me? Hey, that ain't right. You tell the boss I wanna see him as soon as he gets back. I never heard of such a thing."

"O.K. Deputy. I'll make an appointment if you want. By the way, you wanna see how the votes went?" JJD smirked as he slid a computer printout across the top of the desk.

Billy snatched up the paper and grabbed JJD's glasses, staring down at the one page document. It read:

1. John E. Fitzgerald Medal for Most Meritorious Act-

Fire Lieutenant Thomas M. Canney, Ladder Company 15.

2. Walter Scott Medal-Fire Fighter Gary R. Geiger, Ladder Company 15.

3. Patrick J. Kennedy Medal- Fire Fighter Christopher Marr, Engine Company 24.

When he finished reading, JJD said, "Deputy, you still want that appointment?"

"Er, never mind," Billy replied, "but what the heck happened?"

"Well after Chief Franklin read your report, he told everyone he had watched the operation that night and like everyone else who saw it, he couldn't believe anyone could save those two women. He felt so helpless and he figured if anyone did get to them, they'd never make it back alive."

JJD continued, "When he got done talking, the only further discussion was which guy should get the top medal. The boss said if it was a tie vote, they'd wait for you to get back but it wasn't necessary. They finally settled on Lieutenant Canney for the Fitzgerald because his injuries were the most extensive and he was hospitalized longer than Fire Fighter Geiger. It was a good decision, although it would be nice if they could have both gotten it."

He went on to explain the third medal went to a jake from Engine 24 who had done a terrific job getting a baby out of a room on Intervale Street in North Dorchester. The Redhead had that fire, but since his jake made it out without injuries, even he voted for Billy's guys. It was unanimous.

Billy was thrilled at the outcome. He laughed when he remembered how conscientiously he had tried to read all of the reports; he not only never got to them all, it didn't make any difference.

He stopped by the Victoria Diner and went into the back room where all of the Board members were eating lunch.

"Hey, Billy," the Redhead shouted, "we been waiting for you to pick up the tab. I convinced all of these stiffs to vote for those Back Bay jakes of yours and you really owe us all big time."

Billy could see Jackie Franklin sitting in the corner; he waved his thanks to Jackie and received a wink and a nod in return.

"You got it, Red, but lookit, go easy on the dessert, will ya? I only got a coupla bucks."

He slid along the booth beside Franklin and said, "Thanks a lot, Jackie. That's why we got the best work group on the job. We stick together in spite of division lines. Right, old pal?"

"Sure, and I'm glad you feel that way, Billy, 'cause next year, I expect your support for my lieutenant on Columbia Road. I know you'll be with me, right, my friend?"

"Uh, uh—" Shit, what about Spider, Nellie and Porky?

Gonna be a long year.